THE
GIRL HE KNEW

ENDORSEMENTS

In her novel, *Party of One*, Clarice G. James explored the grief that comes from losing a longtime partner. In *The Girl He Knew*, she turns her focus to a young widower and a marriage cut short. She mines human experience and emotions to show God's healing hand in Charlie's life. She uses a contemporary issue to expose Juliette Dawson's weaknesses, but points Charlie and the reader to God's redemptive love. A good read.

—**Kathleen D. Bailey**, journalist and award-wining author of *Westward Hope* (Western Dreams Series)

Take a dash of romance, a spoonful of humor, and a hearty portion of mystery, and you've stirred up a sure-fire Clarice G. James hit. I'm enthralled with this author's ability to weave wit into a plot as serious as death. *The Girl He Knew* will claim you from the start.

—**Linda Brooks Davis**, award-winning author of *The Calling of Ella McFarland*, *The Mending of Lillian Cathleen*, and *The Awakening of Miss Adelaide* (Women of Rock Creek Series)

Nothing is more difficult than losing the person you love most in the world ... unless it's finding out that person had been hiding a web of painful secrets. When Charlie Dawson finds himself in this agonizing situation, it takes all of his faith and the love of family and friends to help him heal and learn the truth. *The Girl He Knew* delves into the realities of grief, which is well-traveled territory for novels, particularly in the Christian Fiction genre, but never resorts to platitudes or moralizations. Instead, the narrative follows Charlie through brokenness and doubt, allowing the reader to identify with him and consequently discover hope as well. The characters, especially Charlie, are genuine and familiar; and the plot addresses many real-world issues with sympathy and grace. Best of all, themes of family, faith, and forgiveness pervade each chapter. I definitely recommend this uplifting read!

—**Chloe Flanagan**, author of *Forward to What Lies Ahead, A Time for Every Matter, and No Longer a Stranger* (An Offer of Grace Series)

Wonderful dialogue and nice pacing draw the reader through the difficult subjects of opiate addiction and grief as they delve into the mystery of *The Girl He Knew*. Faith and hope grow with each turned page. Another great story by Blue Ridge Mountains Christian Writers Selah Award Finalist, Clarice G. James.

—**Sherri S. Gallagher**, best-selling author of *Sophie's Search, Out of the Storm,* and *Pine Cone Motel* (Search the North Country Series)

The Girl He Knew is a well-crafted story that immediately captures and holds the reader's interest. The hero journeys through the loss of a spouse, and all the stages of healing, while also searching for the mystery behind her passing. Clarice James has a way of weaving loss, mystery, joy, and humor with authenticity, all while addressing contemporary issues.

—**Janet Grunst**, award-winning author of *A Heart Set Free* and *A Heart for Freedom*

The Girl He Knew—An engrossing tale of bereavement, laced with mystery and intertwined relationships. The iconic backdrop of Plymouth Rock gives substance to the novel's authentic approach to crime and dysfunction. Written with spiritual insight, attention to detail, and a sprinkling of the author's signature humor, *The Girl He Knew* both entertains and pulls the reader into the depths and heights of grief and love.

—**Eleanor K. Gustafson**, author of *An Unpresentable Glory and Dynamo*

Take a group of likeable characters who are by turns sympathetic and maddening; make them suffer through an excruciating dilemma ripped from today's headlines; add a healthy dollop of plot twists and some real belly laughs in the most unexpected places; and you have *The Girl He Knew* by Clarice G James. It's both sobering and fun, and it kept me guessing right through to the satisfying conclusion.

—**John F. Harrison**, author of *Fighting Back*

I was immediately grabbed with desperate concern for Clarice James' character [protagonist] from the very first chapter and was compelled to continue. I consumed the following pages with great enthusiasm and satisfaction. True to her skill set, her characters were genuine and believable, and I half expected to run into them in real life. *The Girl He Knew* has many amazing features—one of which I'll share as a spoiler: God is a character in the story! James expertly weaves an important story into a tapestry you won't soon forget.

—**Travis W. Inman**, playwright and author of *When Love Called* (Glenfield Series)

The Girl He Knew tells a story of an unexpected loss and the mystery surrounding it through the lens of faith with plenty of humor and intelligence. Rich characters, a suspenseful plot, and honest writing make this book a page-turner. You'll be rooting for Charlie from the first page.

—**Christa MacDonald**, author of *The Broken Trail, At the Crossroads*, and *The Redemption Road* (Sweet River Redemption Series)

Buckle your seatbelt. Clarice James's latest will take you on the roller coaster ride of losing a spouse who, it turns out, you never really knew. Riddles, relationships, and restoration make *The Girl He Knew* a must-read.

—**Linda Shenton Matchett**, author of War Time Brides Series and Women of Courage Series

In *The Girl He Knew*, Clarice G. James courageously tackles a difficult issue with knowledge, compassion, and dignity. While still sprinkled with plenty of the author's signature humor, this well researched story opened my eyes to prescription drug addiction and trafficking. Bravo!

—**Terrie Todd**, award-winning author of *The Silver Suitcase, Maggie's War, and Bleak Landing*

THE
GIRL HE KNEW

CLARICE G. JAMES

PUBLISHING THE POSITIVE
ELK LAKE PUBLISHING INC
Plymouth, Massachusetts

Cover and Interior Design: Derinda Babcock

Editor(s): Judy Hagey, Deb Haggerty

PUBLISHED BY: Elk Lake Publishing, Inc., 35 Dogwood Drive, Plymouth, MA 02360, 2019

Library Cataloging Data

Names: James, Clarice G. (Clarice G. James)

The Girl He Knew / Clarice G. James

332 p. 23cm × 15cm (9in × 6 in.)

Description: Shocked by the facts surrounding his wife's sudden death, Charlie Dawson fears losing the girl he knew, the one he'd fell for in tenth grade French class, married right out of college, and planned to have babies with soon.

Identifiers: ISBN-13: 978-1-951080-44-0 (trade) | 978-1-951080-45-7 (POD) | 978-1-951080-46-4 (e-book)

Key Words: Plymouth Massachusetts 400th birthday, women's inspirational books, women's struggles fiction, husband's grief after wife dies fiction, women struggling with addiction fiction, women's adventure fiction, moving beyond grief fiction

LCCN: 2019951203Fiction

DEDICATION

To the choicest of friends: Kellie Parham, Susan Loud, and Brenda Loud, whom God used as a source of comfort as well as a hedge of protection for me as I stumbled on the road of grief and navigated the potholes of loneliness after the death of my husband, Terry Tully, in 1998. I have not forgotten your kindnesses—nor will I ever.

ACKNOWLEDGMENTS

In 1998, I personally experienced the loss of a spouse when my husband Terry Tully lost his battle with cancer. Writing this book twenty years later wouldn't have been possible without the love and support of my present husband (Ralph) David James. A widower himself when we met, he understood like no one else in my circle of writers and friends. Over and over, I have been blessed by this man.

Once again, I am grateful for my gifted and picky critique partners: Mike Anderson, Cricket Lomicka, Jeremiah Peters, Kathleen Bailey, and David James. Much thanks to my superstar beta reader and fellow author, Terrie Todd, whose input helped me submit a polished manuscript to my publisher.

Thanks also to my fellow writers who took time out of their own busy schedules to read and endorse this book: Kathleen D. Bailey, Linda Brooks Davis, Chloe Flanagan, Sherri S. Gallagher, Janet Grunst, Eleanor K. Gustafson, John F. Harrison, Travis W. Inman, Christa MacDonald, Linda Shenton Matchett, and Terrie Todd.

This book wouldn't be in your hands without the talent and professionalism of the team at Elk Lake Publishing, Inc.: publisher and editor, Deb Haggerty; editor, Judy Hagey; and cover and interior designer, Derinda Babcock.

May God get all the glory!

CHAPTER ONE

May felt more like March as Charlie Dawson fought the wind, lugging three full canvas totes into the house. Silkscreened with the works of modern architects Frank Gehry, I.M. Pei, and Frank Lloyd Wright, his wife Juliette had bought them for him from PBS … or maybe the Museum of Fine Arts … he wasn't sure which.

Though he was an architect himself, carrying these tributes to the industry icons seemed rather presumptuous—like maybe he thought he was in the same league. Besides, he lived in Plymouth, Massachusetts—not exactly known for its modern architecture. The town's largest tourist attraction was Plimoth Plantation, a living museum of life in the seventeenth century. The four hundred-year-old town's most famous monument was a not-so-big rock in a hole in the ground surrounded by a wrought iron fence.

No, he used these totes simply because doing so made his wife smile.

Today, Juliette needed much more to cheer her up. This morning, she'd discovered another month had passed without her getting pregnant, when just last night she'd added Cooper and Liam to their list of boys' names in their "Before Our Baby Is Born" journal. He'd suggested Cosimia and Kapono for a girl. She hadn't bothered to write them down. He grinned at the memory.

They both wanted a baby, sure, but the burden to get pregnant seemed to fall more on Juliette than him. Her mood swings over the past many months had reflected that—no matter how much he reassured her. Keeping up with the whole baby journaling thing might be more stress than either of them needed.

Charlie sighed. He hoped her training session today with her father would lift her spirits. This would be her third time competing in the New England Season Opener Triathlon on Memorial Day weekend in Hopkinton. Though a serious ankle injury had sidelined her last year, she'd placed first in her age division the previous two races.

He rushed to put the groceries away before she got home. After church the next day, he planned to surprise her with an organic, vegetarian, and gluten-free meal. All he had to do now was make the food taste good.

As he had time for a quick shower, he took the stairs two at a time to the master suite. When his phone rang, he hurdled the overflowing laundry basket near the bed and raced back down the steps. He reached his phone before the message went to voice mail.

Hey, not bad for a thirty-year-old.

The caller ID read "Colonel Annandale," as if Colonel was his father-in-law's first name. Which it wasn't. His name was Wickford.

Out of habit, Charlie pulled his shoulders back. "Good afternoon, Colonel. May I ask why you're keeping my wife so late? Didn't Juliette tell you we have plans with Kyle and Sarah this evening?"

Silence. He took a second look at the phone. "Colonel? You there?"

"Yes, Son, I'm here."

Son? The only time the colonel referred to him that way was when he wanted something or was trying to be nice … because he wanted something. Most recently when he sought

Charlie's approval to train Juliette for her first triathlon since her ankle surgery.

The colonel cleared his throat. "Charlie, it's Juliette."

"What about her?" Charlie's skin prickled. "Is she okay?"

"No, she's not. We need you at the hospital. Now."

We? Her father wouldn't have called unless Juliette had asked him to. Charlie massaged his neck. "What happened?"

"I don't know. We'll talk when you get here." *Click.*

The six-mile drive to the hospital seemed like sixty. Had she fallen? No, she had quick reflexes. Twisted an ankle? Isn't that what those new high-performance and outrageously-priced shoes were for? Torn her Achilles or meniscus? Or worse, another stress fracture? When that happened last year, she'd been sidelined and miserable for eight months. So had Coach Colonel.

Smirking at his wife's private nickname for her father, he ignored the worry that rose inside him. "Please, Lord. Don't let it be her ankle again."

He entered through the ER doors. At the welcome desk, a kind-faced volunteer greeted him, then led him to a small sitting room off the main hallway. Beyond the closed door, the colonel sat hunched over. A man in a white lab coat sat nearby. They stood when he entered.

His father-in-law staggered toward him, his face pale. "Juliette's gone, Son."

Charlie's mind stumbled over the word *son* before it twisted around the word *gone,* trying to make sense of it. "Gone? She left? Or did they take her to Boston?"

The colonel looked lost. "No, Charlie, the doctors think the cause may be cardiac related."

Hands up, palms facing out, Charlie tried to stop him from speaking. "Wait! Cause? What are you saying?"

The doctor extended his hand and spoke in a soothing tone. "Mr. Dawson, I'm Dr. Ivan, the attending physician. The EMTs did everything possible to treat Mrs. Dawson at the scene. We took over here. I'm sorry, sir. Your wife did not survive."

The room spun. Charlie's stomach spasmed. He slumped to a seat and covered his face with his hands. "Oh God, oh God, no …" He tried to compose his thoughts. "Why? I mean, how did this happen? She was in top shape. Colonel?"

"I don't know." His father-in-law looked dazed. "She left me back at base camp while she took to the course again." His voice cracked, he looked away. "A few minutes later, a woman ran toward me, yelling, 'Call 911! My phone's dead.' I called, then took off in the direction she pointed. I had no idea I'd be performing CPR on my own daughter."

Charlie bowed his head. *Let this be a nightmare, please, Lord, please.*

Dr. Ivan cleared his throat. "Learning more about your wife's lifestyle could help us determine the cause. Was she on any medication? Did she have special dietary concerns or allergies?"

"No medications or allergies that I know of." Charlie was distracted by the sound of his own voice. "She ate healthy, exercised daily, and was religious about taking supplements."

Dr. Ivan jotted a few notes. "Did your wife ever have a bad reaction to something she'd taken?"

"No … I don't think so … not that I recall."

The colonel barked, "Why are you asking all these questions?"

"The more we know, the more it will help the medical examiner when he performs the autopsy."

"Autopsy?" the colonel growled. "That won't be necessary."

Charlie steeled himself. He would not back down. "I disagree."

His father-in-law reacted like he'd been struck. "Why? It won't bring her back."

"Because I want to know what happened to my wife." Broken, he turned to the doctor. "When will you have the results?"

"The cause of death, maybe in three or four days," Dr. Ivan said. "The tox screen may take several weeks. A list of those health supplements you mentioned might help." He handed Charlie a card. "Email or text would be fine."

Charlie stared at the business card. "Sure."

The colonel dropped to the chair behind him and scrubbed his face with both hands. "I was too late to save her." He stared straight ahead then pushed himself up. "I need to get home to her mother. She doesn't know yet."

"Go ahead, Colonel. I'll head over to your place when I leave here."

Why didn't I insist Jules take a longer hiatus between races? Would she have listened? Maybe, if I'd stood up to her father …

Before he fell apart, Charlie needed to say goodbye to his wife. "May I see her?"

"Of course," Dr. Ivan said. "Follow me."

The colorless room was quiet. Like death. No monitors beeping, no alarms sounding. Juliette looked like she'd wake up any minute. He held her hand. Questions flew at him. Did she know? Was it quick? Did she suffer? Was she cold? Juliette hated the cold. He placed her hand between his, trying to warm it.

She's in heaven now—no better place.

I'm supposed to let go, right? Why can't I?

Because if you let go now, Juliette might be gone forever.

Charlie pushed the alarm key to find his Jeep Cherokee in the parking lot. Eight rows over, he climbed inside, slammed the door, and slumped over the steering wheel. He couldn't breathe. A primal groan escaped him. "Jules, oh Jules …"

Once this round of tears was depleted, he called his sister Edy.

"No, Charlie, no-o-o … Are you home? I'll be right over."

"I'm headed to the Annandales' now. I'll call you later, okay?"

"Sure. Should I call Grams and Pop?"

Charlie's eyes filled again, just thinking about his grandparents. "Maybe we can do that together later?"

"Right. They'll want to hear your voice."

He called his best friend, Kyle Yates. They'd known each other since second grade. While Charlie had studied to become an architect, Kyle had joined the Marines and done two tours in Afghanistan. After his stint, he'd joined the Plymouth Police Department.

Kyle answered. "You better not be bailing on me, Dawson. We promised the girls a chick flick and a frou-frou restaurant tonight. Don't make me go without you."

"Kyle—" He tried to swallow. "Ky-le." The lump in Charlie's throat grew. He remembered how huge a deal it'd been when Juliette and Kyle's wife, Sarah, became best friends. The guys liked to joke, "We get to hang out more than we did when we were single."

"What's the matter? You all right?"

"No, I'm not." He lost it when he told Kyle about Juliette.

"Aw, Charlie, I don't know what to say." He paused. "Where are you now?"

"Hospital parking lot. I'm on my way to see Juliette's parents."

"Anyone I can contact for you? How 'bout Pastor Ted?"

"Right. Ted. Thanks."

Charlie had been a kid when Ted Westfall became pastor. He and his wife, Binnie, had two sons six or seven years older than him. One was a pastor himself now, the other a science teacher. He and Juliette had shared many a Sunday dinner at the Westfall table before and after Ted married them.

Now he'd be officiating Juliette's funeral.

Dark clouds appeared along the route to his in-laws'. The temperature dropped with each passing mile, both inside his Jeep and out. Raw wind and hard rain greeted him in their driveway. It was almost a relief when numbness set in.

But one look at Juliette's mother brought a new wave of grief.

She hugged him and wept. "Oh, Charlie, what will we do without our girl?"

The colonel led her to the sofa. "Natalie, we need to hold ourselves together now. Charlie needs us. How can we help, Son?"

"I'm not sure. Haven't had a chance to think."

She wiped her swollen eyes. "Forgive me, Charlie. I didn't mean—"

"Natalie, you don't need to apologize. Juliette's worth our tears, don't you think?"

She hugged herself. "Yes, but I need to be strong."

"You don't need to be any such thing. Not for me."

She smiled a sad, kind smile. "How about I make some tea, then we can talk about the arrangements. That's if you want to. We don't want to interfere."

How had a sweet woman like her put up with an overbearing man like Wickford Annandale for over thirty-five years? He could stand his ground with his father-in-law, but never with Natalie. "Sure. Tea. Let's talk."

They discussed Juliette's wishes—or what they might have been if she'd lived long enough to express them. How many twenty-nine-year-olds have planned their funerals? Charlie made an appointment to meet with the funeral director on Wednesday. The director would make arrangements with the medical examiner once the autopsy was complete.

"They couldn't give you a day?" Natalie tore at the tissues in her hand.

"No. The funeral director has to wait on the ME." Charlie refrained from looking at his father-in-law.

The colonel stood. "Are you saying we'll have to wait a week to bury our daughter?"

My wife. "Colonel, I'm afraid it'll be even longer with Memorial Day weekend complicating things. And, our wishes aside, Dr. Ivan told me an autopsy is required by *law* when death is sudden, and the person is in apparent good health."

Natalie patted Charlie's hand. "We can only do what we can do." She looked up at her husband. "Isn't that right, Wick?"

His father-in-law grunted.

Charlie rose to leave. "Edy and Kyle and Sarah are coming over later. Probably Pastor Ted and Binnie too. If you're up to it, why don't you join us?"

The colonel shook his hand. "Thanks, we'll call if we decide to stop by."

Using the military *we* was his father-in-law's polite way of declining the invitation.

CHAPTER TWO

After three nights of hot tears and jagged sobs, Charlie awoke to cold reality again. He raked his hands through his hair as he leaned against the closet door. Was he really choosing an outfit for his wife to be buried in? His beautiful, vivacious, loving wife? The girl he'd fallen in love with that first day in sophomore French class? The one he was ready to have babies with?

He brushed his fingers over the rows of her clothes in the large walk-in closet, one of Juliette's favorite parts about renovating the house. Hugging an armful, he put his face into the sorted-by-color bunch and breathed in her scent: lavender, salt air, and vanilla—pure unadulterated Juliette.

Stepping back, he studied his choices. In their eight years of marriage, the job of picking out clothes for special occasions had been Juliette's, never the other way around. How could he decide for her now? He left the closet and went to the kitchen, hoping a dose of caffeine would clear his head.

He turned the coffeemaker on and opened the cabinet door. The wide shelf above the collection of mismatched mugs was filled with bottles of Juliette's supplements—vitamins, minerals, and what not. She always ignored him when he referred to her health food and supplements as *quackology*.

He needed to make that list for Dr. Ivan, but not now. He grabbed a plain mug and shut the door.

Leaning against the counter, he surveyed the kitchen. He was the cook in their family, but with both his and his sister Edy's approval, Juliette had taken charge of interior design for the four-bedroom Cape-style house which had been in the Dawson family for years. She'd done an especially good job with the kitchen. The light gray Shaker cabinets with the matte black cup handles, the marbled quartz countertop, the subway tile backsplash, and the oversized farmhouse sink—all added to the look they wanted.

They'd argued over the appliances. He wanted stainless steel, she wanted black. He thought black would make the space too dark, but once they opened a wall to the living room, she'd won. Now with all the light streaming in from the French doors and kitchen windows, the room was always bright.

What does all this matter now?

After his second cup, he called Natalie. "I hope I'm not imposing, but I could use your help. I'm meeting with the funeral director tomorrow, and I don't know what Juliette should wear." He managed to hold it together.

Natalie agreed to come over. He hoped she'd come alone.

He bowed his head. "Please, Lord, forgive me. The man just lost his only child." Charlie knew his feelings didn't make sense, but right now he resented his father-in-law for being the last person to see Juliette alive. The privilege or pain or whatever should have been *his*. That's what husbands and wives did for each other.

Till death us do part.

Natalie lifted a black and white botanical print dress from the closet rod. "This was one of her favorites. I was with her when she got it half-off at Bloomingdale's. Remember, she wore it with her apple-green bolero jacket at the Best Foot Forward fundraiser?"

"Yeah, I liked that one on her."

She caught his eye. "Who are you kidding? You liked everything on her."

He shrugged. "I did, didn't I?" His throat tightened at his first use of past tense.

Her blue-green eyes filled. "Okay, let's make a decision before we fall apart again. Juliette would not be pleased if we chose poorly."

He handed her a tissue and kept one for himself. "Or if we got nasal mucus on her outfit." He glanced sidelong at Natalie. "According to Juliette, that's the polite way to say *snot*."

She shook her head, but he caught her upturned mouth.

Good. He'd made her smile.

"Your first choice was a fine one, Natalie, don't you think?"

"Yes, and Juliette would agree." She ran her hand over the fabric before putting the dress in the garment bag with the jacket. "Do you want me to get her undergarments?"

"I would have, but I wasn't sure." He pointed to a wide dresser. "That one's hers."

She found what she needed in the top drawer.

He handed her a J. Crew shopping bag. "One of the many designer bags from your daughter's extensive collection."

Natalie chuckled. "I'm afraid she developed that habit from watching her mother." She added a necklace and bracelet to the bag then went back to the closet. "These flats will do nicely."

Do nicely for what? Why did wearing shoes seem less necessary than wearing a dress? Was there a burial norm? If so, was this it? This whole discussion seemed unreal.

"Charlie?"

"I'm sorry. Did you say something?"

"I asked if you were going to the funeral home alone."

"No, Edy's coming with me. She wouldn't take no for an answer."

"And Lana and Rollie? They're still in Greenville, right? When will they arrive?"

"Grams and Pop are flying back Friday. They'll be staying with me since they won't be able to move back into their house for another week or so."

"My daughter was blessed to marry into your family. Edy always treated Juliette like a sister, and your grandparents, like one of their own grandchildren. I never worried if she'd be cared for, not once. You were an excellent husband."

"Thanks." He swallowed hard. "Juliette felt everything was complete the day you and the colonel moved back to Plymouth after he retired."

"I wanted him to retire sooner, but once he got the teaching position at West Point, he insisted on serving a full ten years." Her shoulders began to shake. "I only wish we'd had more time with her."

He put his arm around her. "Her being gone is so hard to believe, Natalie." Would his throat ever stop aching?

"I know." She eased herself down to the tufted bench at the foot of the bed and fell apart.

Charlie peeked through the sidelight before answering the door. "So, the famous Dr. Edy Dawson does make house calls."

"Only for you, little brother." She tossed her handbag on the chair then hugged him tight. "How're you doing? Don't answer that dumb question." She tried unsuccessfully to tuck her too-short, dark blonde hair behind her ears. "Did Grams email you their itinerary?"

"Yes. But is she right? *You're* meeting their flight in Boston on Friday?"

Edy drummed her fingers on her crossed arms "I know what you're thinking, but I can find my way to Logan Airport."

"If you say so."

She swatted him. "I know I can be a bit directionally-challenged at times—"

"A bit? At times?"

"Anyway, I might ask my friend Matt to accompany me."

"MIT Matt? The guy you've been dating for over a year, the one none of us have ever met? I was beginning to think he didn't exist."

She gave him her best attempt at an evil eye. "We haven't been dating, per se. We're more like reciprocal plus-ones."

"That's the story you're going with, huh? I wanna see you run that one by Grams."

Edy's shoulders sagged. "Why does everyone have to make such a big deal over me not being married? Why can't the enjoyment of my work and my single life be enough for them?"

Will the single life be enough for me?

He put an arm around her shoulders. "Sorry, Sis. Personally, I think you're amazing."

She cut a sharp glance at him. "Sure, you do."

Charlie turned her around and held her shoulders. "Edy, you are one of the most intelligent, caring people I know. And don't forget that—because it'll be a while before I tell you again."

She shook her head and smiled. "Love you too."

"Now that we've settled that matter, what were we talking about?"

"Is there anyone else I can contact for you? By the time the weekly newspaper comes out with the obituary, it might be too late."

It's already too late.

Charlie redirected his thoughts. "Sarah offered to get a hold of Juliette's boss, and Pastor Ted said he'd send an email out to the church members. I left it to my partner, Hank, to tell our employees." He looked at his watch. "Edy, did I use up all your lunch hour? Don't you have patients to see?"

She took him by the arm. "I got coverage for my office hours, remember?"

"Right. What was I thinking?"

"Under the circumstances, thinking clearly isn't easy." She sighed. "I only wish I could write you a prescription for grief."

"With God, I'll get through it." He saw the doubt in her eyes. A scientist by nature and profession, she fought faith every quarter step. "My life's in his hands, so was Juliette's."

Those words just rolled off your tongue without a thought, didn't they? Do you believe them now?

Edy took her public-speaking stance. "According to the Kübler-Ross model, there are five stages of grief: denial, anger, bargaining, depression, and acceptance."

"So I've heard. Can't wait. Do I need a ticket for every ride?" His hurt had morphed into sarcasm.

She blinked. "Please forgive me. People blather when they don't know what to say."

"No, I'm sorry." He winked at her. "You may be a doctor, but you're still people."

"Thanks ... I think."

"Changing the subject, I have a question. As I mentioned yesterday, Dr. Ivan suspects a cardiac-related cause. But, with no family history of heart problems, they can't be sure. Tell me, what exactly is a tox screen, and why would they need one?"

"If the problem was with her heart, they want to know why. A toxicology screen is a set of blood tests for common poisons and pharmaceutical and recreational drugs."

"Poisons and drugs?" He shook his head. "They're wasting their time. Juliette was in training and always careful about what she ate." He hugged his arms, trying to hold himself

14

together. "Besides, she was being extra careful about her diet. We've been trying to get pregnant."

"I didn't know." She cleared her throat. "To ease your mind, doing a tox screen is standard hospital procedure. All part of the process of elimination."

"How long before I get the results back?"

"Depends on the lab, but the test can take three to five weeks." She gestured to Juliette's clothes. "Did you find everything you needed?"

"Yes, Natalie came by yesterday to help."

"How're her parents holding up? Losing a child is never easy."

"Her mother's a wreck, but the colonel is his usual stiff-upper-lipped self."

"Don't be too hard on him, Charlie. People handle grief in different ways. When Mom and Dad died, I took twice as long as you did to accept it."

"Probably because you were afraid you'd have to give up college and be stuck raising me."

"I didn't feel stuck, I was nervous. You were ten, I was seventeen. But you did okay with Grams and Pop, didn't you? We'll get through this too."

By 'this' do you mean my wife's death? What if I don't want to get through this? He didn't answer her.

Edy checked the garment and shopping bags. "Looks like we're ready."

"As I'll ever be."

Next time I see my wife she'll be in a coffin, wearing a dress she got half-off at Bloomingdale's.

He wanted to take back the dress and run, like that would somehow change the outcome.

The appointment at the funeral home was as surreal as everything else felt like in his life. And since the ME had not completed the autopsy, they weren't able to schedule the services and fill in the blanks.

Once Edy dropped him off at home, another barrage of gut-wrenching what-if questions attacked him. *What if Juliette had stayed home that morning? What if the colonel had clocked her on his bike like he often did? What if Charlie had said yes when Juliette had invited him to come along?* Entertaining these thoughts made him hurt more, so why did he continue?

There was the haunting question he dared not verbalize: *What if the colonel had stopped CPR one compression too soon?*

CHAPTER THREE

Edy gave a throw pillow on the sofa one last chop. "There. All set for guests."

"*Guests*? Grams and Pop? They'd be insulted if they heard you, especially since they raised me in this house."

"*Raised?* That's debatable," she teased. "But you're right."

Rollie and Lana Somers had moved in with their grandchildren the week their daughter and son-in-law had been killed in a car crash. The transition had been as smooth as anyone could expect from grieving parents, a hormonal teenage girl planning for college, and the sad ten-year-old boy that he'd been.

After he and Juliette married, Grams and Pop had relocated to a modest ranch across town, giving Charlie and his bride a chance to grow as a couple in the only home he'd ever known.

Over the past few days, with Edy and Sarah's unbidden help, bed linens had been changed, dust banished, laundry done, and cupboards and refrigerator stocked in preparation for his grandparents' arrival.

Sarah sprayed polish on the coffee table. "Are you sure we can't prepare a meal or two in advance … uh, I mean, other than the mystery casseroles the church ladies brought over?"

Charlie and Edy echoed each other's laugh.

"That would be the ultimate insult," Edy said. "Even Charlie's advanced culinary skills never swayed Grams from the job."

"I should've remembered," Sarah said. "Kyle's told me how many nights he spent around your supper table as a kid."

"Speaking of supper," Charlie said, "I'd offer to make you ladies something, but I don't want to mess up my nice, clean house."

Edy elbowed Sarah. "Grateful chap, isn't he?"

Sarah folded her arms. "I know, right?"

"That's okay. Edy yawned. "I promised to see a few patients in the morning before I leave for Boston."

"I almost forgot." Charlie smirked like only a young brother could. "Grams and Pop will finally get to meet your Matt."

His sister put a hand on her hip. "Will you stop? He's not *my* Matt. Anyway, I decided not to ask him."

Charlie flapped his arms like chicken wings. "Bwahk, bwahk!"

She threw him a warning glance then poked him in the ribs. "And you, little brother, better get some rest. You'll need it to keep up with Grams."

The next afternoon, Charlie was watering Juliette's plants near the front steps when Edy pulled into the driveway. His five-foot-nothing, white-haired grandmother hopped out of the car and bustled toward him, her arms wide open. The memory of the day his parents died came rushing back. He almost cried at the sight of her. Somewhere deep inside, he wished he were that little boy again.

He leaned down for her embrace. "So glad you're here."

She hugged him then cupped his face with her hands. "Wouldn't think of being anywhere else, sweetie."

His grandfather took his turn at a hug. "Only wish the circumstances were different."

"Yeah, me too." Charlie helped unload the car. "How was your flight?"

"Very little turbulence," Pop said. "And even with a slight delay at Greenville-Spartanburg, we made pretty good time."

"And the traffic out of Logan?"

"Your sister planned the trip perfectly," Pop said. "I think we missed the rain and rush hour by a minute."

In the midst of Charlie's grief, how could these snippets of mundane conversation seem callous and comforting at the same time?

Early last fall, his grandparents had rented out their home in Plymouth, then flown off to South Carolina to provide long-term care for Pop's youngest sister recuperating from heart surgery.

Charlie surveyed their two bags and three small carry-ons. "Is this all you have? You've been away for almost a year."

"We brought what we needed for now," Grams said. "Once we're settled back in our house, Uncle Fern agreed to drive our car back up, along with the rest of our belongings."

Charlie asked, "Is Aunt Silvia still doing well?"

"Perkier than ever," Pop said. "You'd never know she'd had a triple by-pass."

Great Aunt Sylvia, more than twice Juliette's age, had smoked a pack and a half a day for over fifty years, and now she's 'perkier than ever.' *How's that right?*

His grandparents' extended stay in Greenville meant they hadn't seen the renovations he and Juliette had made to his parents' forty-year-old house. He opened the front door and stepped aside to let them enter first.

Grams stopped in the foyer. "Oh, my! I feel like I'm in one of those before and after TV shows!"

"Is that good or bad?" Charlie put the suitcases down and waited.

"Even better than the pictures you sent us. Juliette has … had excellent taste."

Pop managed to smooth over the bump in the tense. "Yup. Must've been Juliette—'cause Charlie doesn't know one color from another."

He smirked at his grandfather. "You're not going to let me forget, are you?"

"How could I?" Pop said. "Your grandmother had to set your clothes out all through high school!"

Edy laughed as she hung their coats in the front closet. "Then Juliette inherited that task. I suppose it'll be my turn now."

Charlie rocked on his heels. "So this is how it's gonna be, huh?"

"Rememberin' is what family does best together." Grams patted his arm. "The good times, the bad, the happy, the sad—even the embarrassing." She took a tissue from her sweater sleeve to wipe her eyes.

"Your grandmother's right." Pop's eyes glistened. "Our Juliette's worth holding in our hearts"—he tapped his chest then his temple—"and in our minds."

"*Not* talking about her almost seems harder," Edy said. "Is reminiscing okay with you, Charlie?"

"I'd like that."

Grams unzipped her carry-on. "Great. 'Cause look what I brought." She held up a thick, leatherette photo album. "I've got two of 'em, packed with a lot of memories."

Charlie snickered. "You mean like Edy's bandanas and mini butterfly hair clips?"

His sister shot back, "And your tacky trucker hats and holey jeans?"

Grams slipped the album back into her bag. "Before we look at pictures, Rollie, why don't you let Charlie show you to our room while Edy and I fix us some supper?"

Pop saluted. "Whatever you say, Boss. Lead the way, Bud."

Edy grimaced at Charlie.

He felt for his sister. She hated to cook. But Grams refused to accept that fact.

Charlie grabbed the luggage. "Actually, you and Grams are in your old room, which is the guest suite now. We moved the master bedroom upstairs when we added the dormer last year." *To be closer to our future kids' rooms.*

Pop raised his eyebrows. "Guest suite? Sounds a bit fancy for us old fogeys."

Grams called after them, "There's only one old fogey in this couple, and it's not me!"

"As you see, your grandmother hasn't changed."

Charlie started down the hall. "And aren't you glad?"

Pop winked. "You bet I am."

Charlie laid the suitcases on the wide bench at the foot of the bed, while his grandfather took a seat in their old hickory rocker—the one they'd planned to rock their babies in.

Pop fingered the nail head trim on the leather upholstery. "Tell me, Bud, how're you holding up?"

Charlie sank to the edge of the bed. "Sometimes the past six days seem like a thousand, other times like they never happened at all. Juliette was healthy one day and gone the next. Wrapping my head around that is impossible."

"I understand."

"Of course, you do." Charlie tried to remember his mother's face and his father's laugh. "Does the grief get any easier?"

His grandfather stopped rocking. "The pain fades, but the memories sharpen. I've learned to cherish every one of them."

"I've forgotten so much about Mom and Dad."

"You were a little boy, but I believe you remember more than you think."

The olfactory flash of his mother's scent whisked by Charlie. "One memory stands out. The Christmas after the accident,

Edy dragged me into one of those Bath & Body Works stores in the mall. I was not a happy camper … until I passed a display of products that smelled just like Mom. I stood there crying and refused to leave until Edy sprayed Juniper Breeze on my mittens." He smiled at his sister's kindness.

Pop chuckled. "Yes, you wore those mittens to bed every night for months."

"And I think about shaving with Dad. He'd soap up his brush, lather both our faces, then give me a bladeless razor." Charlie's eyes misted. "After he died, Pop, you gave me his mug and brush, and we 'shaved' together."

"For a few years, I remember." His grandfather cleared his throat. "Grief shakes a person like an earthquake. But if your foundation is firm and true—and God's a pretty good structural engineer—your faith will stand."

"I sure hope so." Was it worrisome that Charlie hadn't considered the state of his faith?

"Gentlemen!" Grams called down the hallway. "Supper's ready. Rollie, wait until you see this kitchen!"

After a meal of minestrone soup and ham salad sandwiches, they pored over old photos: Juliette, as a teen, with his family on their annual apple-picking trip to Brooksby Farm. Edy's graduation from Harvard Medical School. He and Juliette dressed in Plymouth North's school colors—blue, white, and silver—for the homecoming dance. Edy cutting the ribbon the day she opened her pediatric practice. Junior Prom snapshots of him in a gray tux and Juliette in her pale lavender gown.

His grandfather shook his head. "I never could figure out how my goofy grandson ended up with the prom queen."

Edy jumped in. "I think Juliette felt sorry for him."

"What are you talking about?" Charlie pulled the album toward him. "I was a stud—and quite smooth for a sixteen-year-old."

The corner of Edy's eyes crinkled. "More like pitiful and persistent."

"All that matters is I got the girl." He touched the photo. "Biggest blessing ever."

"And Juliette knew how you felt." Grams pointed an arthritic finger at him. "You've got no regrets there."

Charlie smiled. "Worked out well for both of us, I think."

Pop nodded. "Sure did."

"Though, not nearly as long as I'd hoped it would." Charlie's voice cracked.

The next few album pages were turned without comment until Grams broke the silence.

"Charlie, we'd like to visit Wick and Natalie soon. My heart goes out to them. We're their only family now."

Would his heart ever be as big as his grandmother's? "I'll give them a call."

Grams put her hand on his arm. "Don't be offended, son, but Pop and I would like some alone time with them. With their daughter's husband in the room, they might be tempted to ignore their own loss."

Charlie hadn't thought of that. "Sure, I understand." Besides, not spending more alone time with the colonel was fine with him.

With one final poke at each other's hairstyles and eyeglasses, they finished up the first album, leaving the second one for another night. Soon after Edy left for home, his grandparents hobbled off to bed.

When had they gotten old? Why, they'd been three-legged race champs at the church picnic five years in a row. Was it so long ago that Pop had wrestled with him on the living room floor? That Grams had played Twister with Edy and him until they all fell out laughing? That he had brought Juliette home to meet them?

Charlie cut the lights and sat in silence. Reliving the old days with Grams and Pop and Edy this evening would have been sweeter if Juliette had been here to share them.

CHAPTER FOUR

Charlie woke the next day to Grams clattering in the kitchen. A familiar aroma greeted him when he came downstairs. "Mm-mm. I haven't smelled baked goods like that in the morning for years. How long have you been up anyway?"

"A few hours. The older I get, the less sleep I need. And since Natalie and Wick always liked my cranberry walnut bread, I thought I'd bring a few loaves over to them."

"I had cranberries? … And walnuts?"

"No, but the supermarket did."

"How'd you get to the store?"

"I didn't. Edy picked up what I needed and dropped them off on her way to the office." His grandmother shook a loaf out of a pan. "How 'bout a warm slice to go with your coffee?"

"Sounds good." Agreeing with her was easier than telling her he seldom ate breakfast. He opened the cabinet for a mug and spied Juliette's supplements. He muttered under his breath.

"What's the matter?"

He motioned to the shelf. "I was supposed to get a list of these to the medical examiner." He sighed. "I guess I've been putting it off."

"Let me help. I'll read the names on the bottles while you record them. If this information helps the doctors determine what happened to Juliette, then it might help someone else too."

Was it bad that he didn't care about "someone else" just yet?

"Thanks." He opened his laptop then took a few eye-opening sips of caffeine. "Ready when you are."

With her glasses balanced on the end of her nose, his grandmother read out loud, spelling when she had to, "Glucosamine … Fish oil … Tumeric … Vitamin B6 … St. John's Wort … Fenugreek." When she finished reading all the labels, she returned each bottle to its former place on the shelf. Not once did she ask if he needed to keep them.

Was she being sensitive? More likely, she didn't want to throw out "perfectly good" vitamins.

He shot the email off to the ME with a brief apology for the delay. "Done."

"Done?" Pop wandered into the kitchen in his old plaid bathrobe. "Hope you two left some for me."

"Oh, sit yourself down, Rollie. In the fifty-two years we've been married, have I ever neglected you?"

"No." Pop kissed his wife's cheek. "But a person mustn't take things for granted."

Lord, you know I would have done my best to make sure Juliette and I were still kissing after fifty-two years.

He filled a mug for his grandfather. "I can make myself scarce if you'd prefer to meet the Annandales here."

Grams took two more loaves out of the oven. "In this case, I think going to them to pay our respects is proper."

Pop joined him at the counter. "Of course, that depends on whether we can borrow your car."

"Sure." He slid his car keys to his grandfather but kept his hand over them. "Unless they've taken your license away?"

"What are you talkin' about? I drive as well as I did when I was a teenager."

"Rollie, you're not helping your case any since Charlie's heard all your old stories."

Charlie raised an eyebrow. "On second thought—" He pulled the keys back.

His grandfather laughed. "Why, half those stories aren't even true."

"The other half is what has me worried!" Charlie grinned. "I suppose I can trust Grams to keep you to the speed limit."

After a good bit of fussing and fretting over him, the house, and each other, his grandparents didn't leave until noon for his in-laws' place. Although he was glad to have them around, he coveted his private time with thoughts of Juliette.

He threw on a light fleece and stepped into the backyard through the French doors off the dining room. The clouds were sparse, the sun warm, the breeze nippy. He settled into one of their twin Adirondack chairs set side by side on the slate patio.

While fat squirrels played, chipmunks scavenged, and sparrows sang, Charlie tuned in to the love of his life. Memories of her floated by with each soothing breeze. Juliette brushing her sun-streaked hair nightly. Snuggling up to him under the covers. Waking him with a kiss on the back of his neck. She'd been gone a week, yet her presence lingered. Not sound theology but the feeling was real nonetheless.

He whispered, "I miss you, Jules."

Snap!

His eyes shot open. *What was that?* He eyed the gardening spade leaning against the side of the garage not more than five feet away.

A skinny guy, maybe late teens, early twenties, peered over his shoulder as he rounded the back corner of the garage, about ten feet away from Charlie. He wore a ratty green hoodie and a Pittsburgh Steelers knit hat. Matching black and gold gloves stuck out of the back pocket of his jeans.

Charlie stood and reached for the spade. "May I help you?"

"Agh!" The kid's hand flew to his chest. "Sheesh. You scared me half to death!"

"What are you doing in my backyard?"

"Uh, um, I was, uh, taking a shortcut." He motioned to the end of Charlie's lot. "Through the woods over there."

"Is that so?" Charlie eyed the tree line. "Go on, but make this your last time cutting through my yard, okay?"

"Yes, sir. Sorry." The intruder jaunted to the edge of Charlie's back lawn then stepped gingerly into the thick growth.

Charlie could almost hear Juliette scolding him. *Now was that a nice thing to do? You know those woods are so thick with thorny briars even the animals stay away.*

"Yup, I know." He chuckled at the kid's fading yelps. "But that's what he gets for trespassing."

He returned to his chair. An uneasy feeling rose up, causing him to walk around to the front of the house. Pop had left the garage door up. With no car inside and none in the driveway, someone prone to snooping could be tempted.

"Shortcut, my eye. What was he up to?"

That evening, Charlie answered a knock at the front door to find Kyle and Sarah standing there. "Unbelievable. Did you two smell my grandmother's pot roast all the way from across town?"

"Maybe." A smile played around Sarah's upturned eyes. "But we were invited."

Grams quick-stepped into the room. "You don't mind, do you, Charlie?"

He shrugged. "Well, too late now, they're here."

Grams gave him a playful slap. "Come in, you two, come in."

Kyle picked her up in a bear hug. "Missed you, Grams."

She gave him the once-over after he set her down, "My, my, Sarah, your husband's impressive in that police uniform. I wouldn't want to tangle with him."

"Tangle with *me*?" Kyle scoffed. "What the force needs are people like you to put the fear of God in these criminals." He looked around. "Speaking of criminals, where's Pop?"

"Probably rocked himself to sleep again. I'll wake him in a few minutes." She led them into the living room and sat on the sofa, patting the cushion beside her. "So, Sarah, are you still working at the Plymouth Philharmonic?"

"I am," she said. "Part-time."

Grams eyes sparked. "Is the conductor still that handsome Greek man with the dark, curly hair?"

Sarah laughed. "Nothing wrong with your memory. Except now his curls are gray."

"I always liked him." Grams repositioned herself. "So, Charlie tells me you'll be speaking at Juliette's service."

"Yes." Sarah's voice thickened. "Eulogizing your friend is one of those hard things you want to do even though you wish you never had to. Does that make sense?"

Grams took her hand. "Your words will be a blessing, dear."

Charlie nodded. "Juliette always said you were the most authentic friend she'd ever had. Just be yourself, Sarah."

"That's what I've been telling her," Kyle said.

Pop boomed from the hallway. "Is that the Yates boy I hear? The one who married up?"

Kyle shook his head then walked toward the older man. "Hey, Pop, good to see you."

Their hug was a series of loud, manly slaps on their backs.

Pop looked him up and down. "They're still letting you carry a weapon? Goodness! I knew you when you ate paste. Who's in charge over there anyway?"

Charlie enjoyed hearing him razz Kyle like he had since the first day he'd brought him home after school. Weird how the little things stayed the same even when the big things didn't.

Grams stood once she finished her initial round of questions for Kyle and Sarah. Of course, everyone knew she'd have more. "Rollie, I could use your help in the kitchen. Let's give these kids time to talk."

Kyle nodded after them. "As usual, I've been reduced to a snot-nosed kid. You owe me, Dawson. If I weren't around, they'd be picking on you."

Charlie laughed. "You know what they say about the people who tease you?"

"Yeah, they're mean." Kyle kicked back on the sofa.

"You're not fooling me, Yates. You love it."

Sarah nudged her husband. "Don't give Charlie a hard time." Her voice cracked when she asked, "Have the dates for Juliette's services been set yet?"

"Between the days needed for the autopsy and the Memorial Day weekend, the wake won't be until Tuesday, the funeral Wednesday. I think inviting you two over for dinner is Grams' way of keeping my mind off everything."

As if that could happen.

"Whatever the day, Chief Eason has assured me I'll have shift coverage," Kyle said.

"That reminds me, any reports of break-ins in this area? I caught a kid sneaking around my house this afternoon. He gave me some lame story that didn't add up."

"No break-ins, a few domestic calls. Got a description?"

"White, longish, dirty blond hair, skinny, maybe six-two. Late teens, early twenties. Dark green hoodie and a Pittsburgh Steelers knit hat."

Kyle cracked his knuckles. "Well, since there's been no announcement about the services in the papers, I doubt he was an obituary thief."

Sarah tilted her head. "An obituary thief?"

Kyle took a minute to explain how thieves choose their targets by reading funeral notices.

Sarah's eyes were bright with temper. "I can't believe there are people who would actually want to hurt those already suffering."

Kyle tickled the back of her neck. "Apparently I haven't been talking about my job enough."

Charlie mused, "The kid might've been a newbie in crime circles, 'cause he wasn't very good at lying."

Eleven days went by before Charlie could hold Juliette's services.

When he first saw his wife's obituary in print, the pain sharpened the reality, stabbing his every sense. He felt like he did when bully Johnny Buford had shoved his head under the ice at Widgeon Pond when he was a kid. Reading about the woman he knew in the third person shocked and burned and stole his breath away.

Edy and Grams and Pop escorted him to the family viewing Tuesday night. His in-laws joined them, as did Kyle and Sarah. He was ready, or so he thought. But the scent of flowers mingling with foreign odors made him sick to his stomach. Did all funeral homes smell the same?

Unlike the colonel, who stood as if he were inspecting cadets at West Point, Charlie's knees failed him, and he broke down at first sight of his sweet Juliette in the silver pearl casket. He didn't want to be strong; he wanted to weep, he wanted to yell, he wanted to wake his wife up.

Oh, Lord, give me strength.

The three-hour viewing passed like six. People tiptoed in plush carpeting and whispered as if Juliette were sleeping. He responded the same way to them all: "Thank you for coming"—he'd state their name—"I appreciate it."

Just when Charlie thought he couldn't handle one more condolence, someone would recount a kindness Juliette had shown them. A teenage girl said, "When my running shoes gave out, Juliette gave me a brand new pair. She told me they didn't fit her anymore. But who outgrows shoes when you've stopped growing?"

An older man choked up telling Charlie how Juliette had sat with him in the hospital when his wife was sick. "Sometimes we didn't even talk. We just sat there. But I wasn't alone."

"I was a tomboy growing up," said a woman from their church. "When my daughter was invited to the prom, I had no clue how to help her find the right dress. Juliette acted as our personal shopper."

Apart from those unexpected moments to savor, the wake was all very civil, crowded, and lonely.

The morning of the funeral, Charlie checked his appearance in the mirror. Would Juliette have approved of his attire? His shirt was bleach-white and starched. His tie was one she'd bought him a few birthdays back. And his charcoal gray suit came straight from the dry cleaners. He'd polished his black wing-tips that morning and made sure his socks matched, which is hard when your vision is cloudy.

The limo driver pulled up behind the hearse at the entrance to the sanctuary. Charlie, Juliette's parents, Grams and Pop, and Edy followed behind the casket. He was mentally prepared for the pews to be packed with friends, coworkers, and fellow congregants. But the contingent of fellow athletes and fans who took up the last three rows caught him off guard. He nearly broke down at the sight of them.

Pastor Westfall shined a light on Juliette's acceptance of Jesus Christ as a pre-teen, her walk of faith as an adult, and her assurance of eternal life. Charlie knew his wife would've been pleased when he included the complete gospel message as part of his eulogy.

Sarah, however, shared stories about her best friend.

"Juliette was a runner. She tried to teach me how to run but was unsuccessful. I got even. I tried to teach her how to walk, but she failed."

Those who knew Juliette best laughed the loudest.

"A few winters back, we decided to learn how to knit. What a fiasco. We'd get talking and forget to count stitches. The scarf I knit ended up twice as long as Juliette's. I couldn't brag, though, because hers was twice as wide."

The laughter seemed to put Sarah at ease.

"And a few times a year, we'd take these marathon bargain-hunting trips to outlet stores across three states. Juliette couldn't pass up a deal. By our next shopping excursion, Juliette would've already donated most of her purchases from the last trip to charities like Best Foot Forward.

"People tell me I will have another best friend someday. But I'll never have another one like Juliette. I'll miss her.… No. I already do."

After a brief graveside service at Vine Hills Cemetery, they returned to the church for a mercy meal. What more could Charlie say to the two-hundredth condolence? And why is the time you least feel like eating the time people want to feed you the most?

After Edy drove him and his grandparents back to his house, he excused himself and went back to Vine Hills. He carried his camping chair from the back of his Jeep and sat facing Juliette's grave. It was the first time he'd been alone with her in days.

"You should've heard all the nice things people said about you, Jules. Maybe you did, who knows? … Grams and Pop held it together. I was so proud of them.... Sarah's eulogy was touching and funny. She misses you a lot."

He reached for the handkerchief in his breast pocket. Damp from his earlier tears, he wiped his eyes again.

"Your mom will need more time. She's just so sad.... Not sure about your dad. He pretty much holds everything in.... Franklin Morris was at the wake. Is your boss always that strange? He acted odd when I mentioned coming by the office to get your things. Maybe it was just me ... Not sure if I told you the last time we spoke, but you're the best wife a man could have ever hoped for."

As Charlie returned to his car, an elderly man passed by and nodded hello. He carried a plaid blanket, a cooler, and an old-fashioned boom box. When Charlie circled the loop to the exit, he saw the man seated on the blanket, under a tree, near a gravestone. He had a sandwich in one hand and an iced tea in the other. The sound of folk music, maybe Greek, filled the air.

Lord, help me. I don't ever want to get that bad.

CHAPTER FIVE

That night at home, Pop pulled Charlie aside. "Our tenants said the house will be ready for us tomorrow. But if you need us to stick around a while longer, just say the word."

He put his arm around his grandfather's shoulder. "Aren't you the man who used to say 'prolonging the inevitable is never a wise thing to do?'"

Pop smoothed the wrinkles in his forehead. "Words have a way of coming back to bite a person, don't they?"

"That they do." Charlie smiled. "I appreciate the offer, but I need to deal with a big part of my grief alone. Understand?"

"I do, Bud."

Edy came by for Grams and Pop early Saturday morning. "Ready to go?" She planned to get them reasonably settled back in their home by the end of the day.

All three of them had refused Charlie's offer to help.

"What's your rush, Edy?" Pop drained his coffee cup. "We rented the place fully furnished, so there's nothing to do."

"Tell that to your wife," Edy scoffed. "You know she's going to want to re-clean every corner."

A full hour later, Charlie finally waved them off. He settled into the peace and quiet they'd left behind. Being alone gave him a chance to think straight. But he wasn't sure he wanted to or what he would think about.

A familiar verse from Psalm 46 brought comfort. *Be still and know that I am God.*

He stared out the French doors and obeyed, eventually dozing off …

The colonel shouted at Juliette, "At the starting line, cadet! I already have an out-of-shape wife, I don't need an out-of-shape daughter!"

Natalie grabbed his arm and pleaded, "Wick, don't make her run again!"

"Discipline is good for her." He turned to Juliette and yelled. "West Point's motto, cadet. Now!"

Juliette stood at attention. "Duty. Honor. Country."

"Don't forget it!" He looked at his stopwatch. "On your mark! Get set! Go!"

Juliette sped down the high school track, dressed in a black and white botanical print dress and pear-green bolero jacket. She carried her black flats in her hands.

All the while Charlie sat in his canvas chair at the edge of Vine Hills Cemetery, eating a sandwich and drinking iced tea. When Juliette called out to him, he didn't respond, too distracted by the music ringing in his ears. Besides, he never cared that much for confrontation …

With a start, Charlie woke in a cold sweat.

Kyle stopped by mid-afternoon. "Come on. I'm getting you away from this house."

"Where're we going?"

"The driving range. Get your clubs."

They were on their way in minutes.

Kyle turned onto Route 3. "Nice service Wednesday. Ted and the other speakers did good, huh?"

"Yes, especially Sarah. Thank her again. Juliette would've loved those stories."

"I'll tell her."

A thought rolled around Charlie's head. "Odd how the funeral reminded me of our wedding day."

Kyle stole a glance. "How so?"

"A few clear moments inside one big blur, just like the day we got married."

"Still, it was nice. Everyone said so."

There were only a few people in line ahead of them at the range. They got their bucket of balls and walked to the mats.

Charlie pulled out his driver. "Sox playing tonight?"

"Yup. Against the Braves." Kyle smacked one a good distance. "Thanks to their bullpen, they're off to a decent start."

Charlie took a practice swing. "Hard to believe after last year."

"Just like I've been saying, the pitchers just needed some time."

"Time, yeah." Charlie's eyes didn't budge from the ball. *Thwack!* It went straight down the middle and neared the 250-yard marker.

Kyle looked hard at him. "Where've you been hiding that?"

Charlie shrugged. "Freakish, huh?"

After a pause in their conversation, not awkward or unusual for them, Kyle blurted, "Really sucks about Juliette."

"Yeah, it does," Charlie said, "I still don't get why someone who took such great care of herself could be gone."

Kyle didn't answer.

Of course, Charlie got that his wife couldn't have died apart from God's will, but he was grateful Kyle didn't say that.

"No history of heart problems in her family?" Kyle asked.

"None." Not that finding that out would make any difference, but it was still hard to accept.

Buckets emptied, they picked up their clubs and made their way to the car.

"Want to stop for a burger on the way home?" Kyle asked.

"Either that or a casserole from one of the church ladies. I think the next one in the queue is made with Spam and sweet potatoes, but it's hard to be sure under all the burnt marshmallows."

"I'm surprised Grams didn't leave you with a ton of meals."

"She did, but they're all in the freezer. I haven't eaten such rich food in ages. Juliette was in training. No carbs, no sugar, no gluten, no preservatives—the whole shebang."

Kyle shook his head. "I don't know how she did it."

"Me either."

They grabbed some fast food before Kyle dropped him off.

Back in the house, Charlie turned the TV on for company. He and Juliette had never needed noise in the background. Now, the quiet without her seemed way too loud.

He sorted a week's worth of mail into three stacks: bills, junk, and sympathy. The one-off envelope from the Plymouth County Medical Examiner & Coroner stood out. He sank onto the bar stool before he unfolded the report and skipped down to Final Diagnoses and Findings. The cause of death was listed as "Heart failure. Undetermined cause." Something about the pending toxicology report. He backed up to the top and read every word. It was succinct, impersonal, and cold. What did he expect to find in an autopsy report—poetry?

His stomach burned. Blaming the jalapeno peppers he'd put on the hamburger, he searched the cupboard for Juliette's Tums. He popped the cap and shook some tablets into his hand. One was a different size. He looked at the imprint: "OC 20."

Months had passed since Juliette had needed painkillers for her ankle surgery. Why would she put an Oxycontin in with the antacids? If anything, he was surprised she hadn't thrown them all out.

He tossed the pill then popped a couple of fruit-flavored tablets into his mouth. They did nothing to settle his stomach.

CHAPTER SIX

After another long week of hanging around the house and the cemetery and trying to work from home, Charlie returned to the office on Monday. He was the first to arrive at Dawson-Landau, the design-build firm he and Hank Landau had formed five years earlier.

Charlie had worked summers as a construction laborer for Hank during high school and college. Once he got his BA in architecture from Northeastern, he'd apprenticed while getting his master's. When he passed the state exam and was registered, Dawson-Landau was born—due in large part to the trust money Charlie's parents had left him.

He and Hank had found an old hipped-roof colonial on Samoset Street, a few blocks from the center of town. The sizeable warehouse out back clinched the deal. Their interior renovations included four glass-partitioned offices surrounding the main reception area, a kitchenette, and a large, private conference room.

Hank handled purchasing, employees, and subcontractors. Charlie's job was to keep clients happy by turning their wish-lists into plans in line with their budgets.

He planted himself at his desk behind his twenty-seven-inch monitor. If he looked busy, he might stave off the staff's sad looks and sympathy. Working behind see-through walls didn't help. Though Juliette seldom visited him here, the office felt strange without her. Much like every other place: home, the grocery store, post office, his in-laws', Kyle and Sarah's, even their regular gas station.

He closed his eyes tight then opened them, hoping to clean the slate in his mind.

His inbox held mostly junk, except for two change orders for Oliver and Vanetta Quinlan's house plans which he'd been working on before. *Before.* That's how he broke down his calendar now: before and after Juliette's death.

He clicked open the AutoCAD file to change out a spacious library for a walk-in pantry and a hidden panic room. Charlie seldom panicked, but a grief room would come in handy. After a few false starts, he hit undo.

If only life had an undo button.

He shook off the self-pity and refocused.

The outside door swung open, and Hank yelled across the reception area. "Charlie! What are you doing here? There's nothing that can't wait until you're ready."

"Those your words? 'Cause I doubt they're Oliver Quinlan's."

Hank took his ball cap off and ran his hand through his thinning hair. "Yeah, well, Quinlan will understand."

"I've met Quinlan, remember? The only thing he understands is us finishing his house on schedule. Anyway, I'll go nuts if I stay home much longer."

"You might go nuts here. Penny will mother you, and Dee will psychoanalyze you when you're not looking."

Before Charlie could respond, Penny bustled in. "Oh, Charlie, I had a feeling you'd be here today." She held up an aluminum foil-wrapped plate. "I made my maple-walnut coffee cake." She set the plate down. "Just so sad about Juliette. Let me know what I can do for you."

"How about a piece of that cake?"

She smiled. After tossing her coat on her chair, she raced to the coffee machine. "I'll slice you a big piece as soon as the coffee's finished brewing."

Hank gave him a sidelong glance and mouthed, "Told you."

Charlie shrugged.

Three months after he and Hank had become partners, they'd hired upbeat Penny Tilden as their administrative assistant. A happy wife and proud mother of twenty-year-old twins, Penny supported her daughters, both enrolled in Bold Look Beauty Academy, by letting them practice on her hair. Today, her signature spikes were royal blue to match her nails and eyeglasses. Or was it vice versa?

A couple months later, Dee Jennings came on board as business manager and took one of the remaining two offices. About the only thing the staff knew about Dee's personal life was that she was not married and had a son named Zach who stopped in now and again.

The two women complemented each other—Penny, the maternal social director, and Dee, the loyal protector of business interests.

Dee entered, put her briefcase down, and hung up her trench coat. Though every day at Dawson-Landau was "casual dress Friday," Dee preferred to wear suits. Today's was a charcoal gray pinstripe, an almost perfect match to her hair.

She approached Charlie and made eye contact. "As long as you're up for it, I'm pleased you're back. If you need any assistance, see me."

"Yes, ma'am." Charlie often felt like he worked for her.

"Penny,"—Dee reached into an insulated bag—"I brought the whipped cream you requested."

Hank crossed his arms. "This isn't a celebration, ladies."

Horrified, the two women looked at each other, then Charlie.

Dee fiddled with her starched collar. "Sorry, we didn't mean anything by—"

"Ignore Hank. He's just jealous 'cause he's not gettin' any cake."

"Hey, whaddya mean?" Hank slapped his ball cap on his desk in mock protest. "As equal partners, Landau's entitled to whatever Dawson gets."

Are you sure you want that? Instead, he said, "While we're waiting, Hank, maybe you could fill me in on what's been happening around here the past few weeks."

"Sure. We can do that at the staff meeting. Artie's on his way."

Artie Wayne had come on board as foreman around the same time as Dee. He ran crews made up of a dozen or so carpenters and laborers, usually working on three or four jobs simultaneously—most of them residential. Although his was the fourth office, he operated mostly out of his truck.

Nodding to Penny and Dee, Hank said, "You ladies set for the meeting?"

Dee adjusted her jacket and smoothed her skirt. "I need a few minutes to print my reports."

Penny leafed through a folder on her desk. "I'm ready. Just have to slice the cake."

Artie arrived as the coffee machine beeped done. "Hey, Charlie, good to see ya. Not the same without ya."

Not the same without ya either, Jules.

"I hope you meant that as a compliment." Charlie smiled then gestured to Penny. "We've got cake."

Artie put his hands in the pockets of his overalls. "Cake's always good."

Yeah, pretty much another awkward conversation. When people brought up Juliette, he wished they hadn't. If they didn't, he wondered how they could be so insensate.

Dee clicked by in her pumps with a stack of papers in her hand, heading for the conference room. "I'm ready when the rest of you are. Grab your java."

Penny followed the hot beverage parade with her file folder tucked under one arm, carrying a tray of sliced coffee cake and a container of whipped cream.

When they were all seated, Hank said, "Let's open with a word of prayer."

Early on, Charlie and Hank had determined their firm would put God first. They brought their needs to him in prayer daily and tithed on their income. Even though some staff members were not believers, they responded to the company policies without complaining. At least to Hank's and Charlie's faces.

"Lord, this is a real tough period for Charlie. Help him, please, and help us support him. None of us can imagine the grief he feels, but you know, Lord. Comfort him, strengthen him, and give him peace. Amen."

A lump blocking his voice, Charlie took a few seconds before he spoke. "Thanks, Hank. I appreciate it."

Hank nodded once then addressed Penny. "Okay, what's up first?"

She passed out copies of the agenda and progress reports. "The punch list Artie gave me on the Oldham renovation is here too."

"The foundation's been poured on the Quinlan job. We start framing soon," Hank said. "Penny, have you called the power company about the temporary panel?"

"Yes." Penny checked her notes. "The installation is scheduled for tomorrow."

"Good. And make sure the security camera system is up and running before any material or equipment is delivered. People would steal dirt out of a hole if they thought they could get away with it."

They discussed the various phases of each project. Charlie was relieved he hadn't fallen too far behind. Once he finished the changes to the Quinlan plans, he'd set up a meeting with the new prospect Hank mentioned. "Hank, what can you tell me about the new client?"

Hank looked at him like he was speaking pig Latin. "Uh, don't you know?"

Charlie was confused. "Know what?"

"Your in-laws?"

Charlie thought he'd heard wrong. "Juliette's parents? What about them?"

"Um, uh, the colonel contacted me last Friday about renovating their house. I assumed you knew."

Last Friday? His daughter dies, and the week after the funeral he decides to renovate a house he's owned for some fifteen years? Was there no end to this man's bad timing?

"My father-in-law neglected to mention it." He heard the sarcasm in his tone but tried to remain professional. "I'll talk to him."

The Annandales had purchased their house on Widgeon's Pond years before Charlie knew Juliette. After the colonel retired and they moved to Plymouth fulltime, brief rumors of renovations circled, but nothing was ever mentioned to Charlie. And he hadn't pushed. On the one hand, he'd been afraid the colonel wouldn't hire Dawson-Landau. On the other hand, he'd been afraid he would. Either way, Juliette would've been in the middle.

What was so important that her parents couldn't wait a while longer? Besides, didn't the colonel's unspoken obligation to use his son-in-law's firm end with the loss of Juliette? Why had he chosen to undertake this project now?

The meeting was interrupted when Dee's twenty-something son Zach stopped by. She met him at her desk. He handed her a newspaper and tapped the front page. They chatted a second before she ushered him out. A minute later, she came back for her purse.

Penny shook her head. "When's she going learn to say no to that kid?"

Charlie stared at Penny's *blue* hair, but he knew what she meant. The buzz in the supply closet was that Zach had a problem with drugs.

In years past, Dee always had a pile of ready excuses: "Poor kid's going through a rough patch." "It's so hard for kids to make it in this economy." "That program wasn't for him. It's for *addicts*." "He's my son, what am I supposed to do?"

No one dared answer her until she was ready to listen.

When Dee returned, she made no mention of Zach but moved on to the company's budgetary report. She ended her presentation by saying, "Let me put it simply—"

"Please do," Artie said, with a hang-dog face. "Numbers give me a headache."

Dee faked-scowled at him. "As I was saying, we're in the black."

Hank stood. "Then meeting adjourned."

On the way back from rinsing his cup in the kitchenette, Charlie was taken aback by a full-color photo of Juliette on the front page of a weekly paper on Dee's desk. The headlines read: "Mourning a Beloved Triathlon Star."

Dee rushed over. "Oh, Charlie, I didn't mean to upset you. Zach brought the paper by this morning. He recognized Juliette from the picture but didn't realize she was your wife until he read the story." She paused. "He sends his condolences."

The last part sounded more like Dee than Zach, but Charlie didn't quibble. "Tell him thanks. Do you mind if I take a look?"

"You're welcome to keep the paper. The article is a fitting tribute to a lovely person so many admired."

Charlie didn't trust his emotions enough to go by his in-laws' on his way home. He didn't want to talk about their building project but went straight to Vine Hills instead. After replacing the wilted flowers on Juliette's grave with fresh ones, he opened his chair and sat.

"First day back at work. Penny made a coffee cake. Hank prayed. You know how he is. Almost made us cry." … "You made the front page of the local paper." … "Did you know your parents wanted to renovate their house? What's the colonel up to, Jules? I'm not sure I can deal with him now."

He didn't expect answers, and he didn't get any.

The late afternoon sun opened a memory like petals on a flower. Tenth grade French II class. Charlie had struggled with French I, and he was dreading this advanced course. Until he sat next to the girl with the sun-streaked, caramel-colored hair and the creamiest skin he'd ever seen. Her aquamarine eyes took his breath. The first time he heard her ask, "Puis-je aller aux toilettes?"—"Can I go to the toilet?"—he knew why they called French a romance language.

Juliette and her mother had moved to Plymouth to take care of a great aunt while the colonel was on tour in the Middle East. A few months into their sophomore year, they started seeing each other, mostly meeting up at their church's youth group. When Juliette was allowed to date formally, they attended homecoming and prom together. When college time came around, the colonel put his foot down. He and Juliette were not to attend the same school. Probably for the best. Charlie wouldn't have been able to concentrate.

Later, after a supper of cold pizza and Pepsi to settle his nerves, Charlie called his in-laws.

Natalie answered. "Hi, how did you fare your first day back at work?"

"Okay, I guess." He steadied himself. "I wanted to speak to you about your plans to renovate your house."

"Plans? Charlie, I'm not sure we're ready to talk about that now."

He cringed. So, the colonel had gone ahead without his wife's knowledge. Oh, well, saving this man's butt wasn't his job. "Hank said the colonel called the office Friday to make an appointment."

Silence for a few seconds, then a terse reply. "I'm handing the phone to Wickford now."

Not the colonel, not my husband, but *Wickford.* Uh, oh.

His father-in-law was abrupt. "Let me call you back, Charlie. Natalie and I have a few things to discuss." *Click.*

I bet you do.

If he'd ever dared make a major decision without consulting Juliette, there would've been a come-to-Jesus meeting. Charlie wondered how his father-in-law would make out trying to explain his reasoning to Natalie.

He chuckled. Not well, he guessed, since he didn't hear back from him that night.

CHAPTER SEVEN

Charlie's extension rang around nine the next morning. He hoped his voice reflected the smile he pasted on his face. "Charles Dawson speaking."

"Hi, Mr. Dawson, this is Heidi Vincent. I used to work with Juliette."

"Yes, Heidi, of course."

"I have some of Juliette's things. Can I come by your office today around twelve-thirty?"

"Uh, sure. Do you know where we're located?"

"Yeah."

"How about I meet you in the parking lot by my white Jeep Cherokee?"

"Okay. Again, that's twelve-thirty."

"Right. I hope this isn't putting you out, Heidi. I planned to pick her things up myself."

"No, I *want* to do this. Juliette asked me to."

"I'll see you then." He hung up before he realized what she'd actually said. *Juliette asked me to*? What was this girl talking about?

About mid-morning, Zach came by while both his mother and Penny were out. He poked his head into Charlie's office. "Mr. Dawson? Just want to say I'm so sorry about your wife."

"Thanks. And it's *Charlie*. I'm not old enough to be called mister."

Zach turned down the collar on his camouflage jacket. "If my mother hears me call her boss by his first name, she won't be pleased."

The guy didn't look so bad—clean clothes, combed hair, clear eyes. He certainly didn't seem high. "Then let's keep the informality between us, okay?"

A shadow of a grin appeared. "On your say-so." He shoved his hands deep into his coat pockets. "So, you back to work fulltime already?"

"Yes. Keeps me out of trouble."

"I know what you mean." Zach looked down at his feet. "I'm job hunting myself."

"What kind of work are you looking—"

Before Charlie could finish the question, the main door flew open and Oliver Quinlan entered. His wiry build and steel-gray, Julius Caesar haircut signaled no nonsense. Marching straight through the reception area to Charlie's office, he bellowed, "Dawson, what's this about these change orders costing me more money?"

"Better let you go." Zach glanced at Quinlan then whispered to Charlie. "Good luck."

Charlie stuck out his hand. "And to you too."

Zach looked puzzled as he shook Charlie's hand. "Me?"

"On your job search."

"Oh, right." Zach nodded to Quinlan on his way out.

"Come on in, Oliver. Let's have a look." Charlie brought up the plans on his monitor—even though he didn't need to.

"The square footage hasn't changed," Quinlan grumbled, "so there shouldn't be any additional costs."

"Hm." Charlie pretended to study the specs. "You want to convert the library into two separate areas—a laundry room with built-ins and a sink and a panic room with a half bath. Am I correct?"

"Yes, but each of these two rooms is half the size of the library."

"You're right, they are." He could never tell if Quinlan was shrewd or dense. "New interior walls, custom cabinetry, plumbing, and electrical don't come cheap. It's not too late to scrap the changes. Do you want to let Vanetta know or should I call her?" By now, Charlie knew Quinlan couldn't say no to his wife.

Quinlan's teeth clenched. "Never mind, just make the changes." He stood. "By the way, who was that man in here before? The one with the military jacket?"

"His name's Zach. His mother's our business manager. Why?"

"Looks familiar, that's all."

Charlie doubted Zach Jennings, out-of-work suspected drug user, and Oliver Quinlan, Private Wealth Manager, frequented the same social circles.

It was quarter past twelve by the time Quinlan left. When Hank walked in seconds later, Charlie said, "How'd you manage to avoid Oliver?"

Hank smirked. "I have my ways. There's something about that guy."

Charlie checked the time. "Besides the arrogance factor, you mean?"

"I'm not sure yet."

"Let me know when you figure it out." Charlie grabbed his keys. "Be back in a few."

As he waited by his car, a bit of hope floated in on a sun's ray, and the scent of salt air soothed his nerves. June—the end of spring, the beginning of summer—had been one of his and Juliette's favorite months.

A faded-baby-blue compact pulled in and parked two spaces over. The girl inside held a just-a-second finger up, then finished a two-thumb text. Skinny legs in skinny jeans atop high-heeled sandals exited the car. One hand brushed wisps of light brown bangs out of her eyes, the other held her phone.

When a gust of wind came out of nowhere, he feared the girl might topple over. He walked toward her as she popped her trunk. "Heidi?"

"Hi, Mr. Dawson."

Mister again. He was feeling older by the minute. "Charlie, please."

"What? Oh. Sure." She rearranged a few items in the cardboard carton. "There's just one box, but it's kind of heavy."

He lifted the box out of her trunk. "I appreciate you doing this." The aloe plant he'd given Juliette to help with her blisters sat on top.

"No problem. I promised Juliette."

The gears in Charlie's brain jammed. Was this some kind of a ghoulish last-will-and-testament company exit strategy? "I'm sorry. What do you mean 'you promised Juliette'?"

Heidi closed her trunk. "She asked if I'd pack up her things."

What kind of wacko was this girl? "I'm not sure I understand."

"Well, I don't like to talk unkindly about those who've passed away, but she was pretty mad when she left."

"Why would Juliette have been mad when she left work?"

"Other than Franklin firing her, you mean?"

Charlie fumbled the box. "What did you say?"

Heidi froze. "You knew she was let go, didn't you?"

Stalling to think, he put the box in the back of his Cherokee. "Uh, I don't ... when did you say that happened?"

"The first week in May, I think."

He could feel his face getting hot. "I didn't ... she didn't ..."

She fidgeted with snaps on her denim jacket. "She was probably waiting to tell you after she got a new job."

Heidi trying to make him feel better didn't make him feel better.

Not that knowing the reason would help but he asked anyway, "Do you know why Franklin Morris fired her?"

She took a step back toward her car. "You'll have to ask him."

"I understand." That was a lie. He didn't understand any of this—other than why her boss had acted so strange at the wake.

"I'm real sorry about Juliette." She stuck her hands in her pockets. "Um, I'm sure being back at work will help you."

What could this girl possibly know? "Well, thanks for dropping off her things, Heidi."

She hung her head. "I hope I didn't upset you, Mr. Dawson."

"Not your fault." He slammed the tailgate of his car. "I hope you'll excuse me. Taking a half day sounds good about now."

"No, don't do that!" She rushed a few steps toward him. "I mean, you'll make me feel guilty. Anyway, I need to tell you how to take care of Juliette's plant. She was quite specific in her directions."

He retrieved the aloe plant from the back of his car and handed the plant to Heidi. "Since my wife trusted you with this, I'm sure she'd like you to have it."

She stared at the plant in her hand. "I don't know what to say." She checked her phone again. "Is there any chance I could come in for a drink of water?"

He gripped the handle of the driver's door. "Sure. Just tell my partner I said it was okay."

Her phone beeped, and she checked the screen. "Sorry, Mr. Dawson. I don't have time right now." She got in her car and drove off.

Franklin had fired his wife yet kept this scatterbrain?

Juliette had gotten a sizable bonus all six years she'd been a sales account manager at the Morris Companies. What could've happened? And why didn't she tell him? Did she think he wouldn't understand? And what had she been doing the weeks she was supposed to be at work?

Confusion, anger, and sadness fought for his attention. He ended up staying at work until closing but didn't get much done. Emotions wreaked havoc on his mind, gut, and ego.

He skipped the cemetery and went straight home.

CHAPTER EIGHT

The ride home was a blur until Charlie pulled into his driveway and pressed the garage door opener. His mind cleared as he braked fast and hard. The garage was a mess—boxes emptied, their contents scattered. What was going on? The door into the kitchen was ajar. He put the car in reverse and backed out slowly. He drove around the corner and called Kyle.

"Kyle, are you patrolling near my neighborhood?"

"In the vicinity, why?"

"Someone broke in. They might still be inside. I'm parked on a side street, but I can see my house through the trees."

"Stay put! I'll call for backup and head over."

Within minutes, Kyle's patrol car skidded to a stop in front of the house. A second unit pulled up behind him. By her height, sturdy build, and dark brown no-nonsense bun at the nape of her neck, Charlie knew the second officer was Sergeant Glenna O'Neil. The two approached the house, guns drawn. Kyle went around back; Glenna entered the garage.

Not long after, Kyle waved him over. "All clear!"

Charlie drove back to his house.

"Whoever did this is gone," Kyle said. "Maybe you can tell us what's missing."

O'Neil nodded at him but said nothing.

Inside looked like the aftermath of a Great Plains tornado. In disbelief, he stepped over pots and pans, plastic ware, and utensils. Cabinets and drawers were wide open and empty, dry goods spilled out. Juliette's quackology bottles had been tossed about. Even the refrigerator had been pillaged.

The bookcases flanking the living room fireplace were bare, everything was strewn across the area rug. Every room had been ransacked. Their two flat screens and modest collection of original art had not been taken. It didn't make sense.

"Maybe I'll discover what they took when I clean up the mess." Charlie put the couch cushions back in place.

O'Neil snapped, "Mr. Dawson, let me get some photos before you start rearranging things."

"Oh, sorry." *Mister* again. And she was his senior by at least a dozen years. He dropped to a chair and pressed his temples, without inviting her to call him Charlie. "I always lock the house up. How'd they get in?"

"Broke the window in the garage," Kyle said, "then jimmied the interior door."

Waving his hands around at the mess, Charlie asked, "Why? Not like we have a wall safe full of cash and jewels."

Kyle rested his hands on his utility belt. "Could be someone looking for booze or drugs."

Charlie huffed. "Then they sure picked the wrong house."

O'Neil narrowed her eyes. "It's hard to tell if they left when they heard you or after they found what they were looking for. What do you suppose that was, Mr. Dawson?"

What was that tone in her voice? "What makes you think I'd know what they were looking for?"

The senior officer folded her arms. "Twenty-two years on the force, that's what."

Behind her back, Kyle grimaced.

She continued. "Mr. Dawson, what reason did you have for calling your friend first instead of 911?"

Charlie shot back, "Twenty-two years as my friend, that's what."

Kyle smirked, and O'Neil packed up her camera and walked out.

Sarah came straight from her job at the Philharmonic to help Kyle and Charlie put the house back together. They began in the kitchen.

She picked up a torn box of granola. "Pure meanness, that's what this is."

Charlie surveyed the scene. "O'Neil was right, wasn't she? They were looking for something specific."

Kyle grunted. "Probably, but I didn't like what she was insinuating."

Sarah's face brightened. "Maybe the thieves left a clue behind?"

Kyle said, "Like a tee shirt stenciled AA Breaking & Entering Co.?"

Sarah scowled at him. "Are you making fun of me?"

"Not at all, dear."

"Well, I say you never know what you might find in this mess." She gathered up the vitamins and supplements on the counter. "Where do these go?"

Charlie pointed to the second shelf then changed his mind. "Just toss them in this basket for now." He picked up a bunch of scattered envelopes and advertisements. "I'll go through them later, along with the mail." Something occurred to him. "Hey, Kyle, what about that kid I caught in my backyard?"

"He did cross my mind. We don't have much to go on, but maybe you can come down to the station to look at some mug shots."

All the food went back in the cabinets or refrigerator unless the packages had been ripped open. Sarah wiped the counters down. Kyle swept then wet-mopped the kitchen. They moved on to the living room, which was a little easier to straighten. By eight o'clock, the rooms on the first floor were in order.

Sarah pulled the vacuum cleaner to the bottom of the stairs. "Kyle, bring this up to the master bedroom, okay?"

Already feeling violated, Charlie hesitated inviting Kyle and Sarah into his and Juliette's private space. When he thought about the mess awaiting him, he decided he'd rather have the help. "Are you sure you're up for this tonight?"

"We are if you are," Sarah said. "You can't possibly sleep in there the way it is."

Kyle chin-pointed to his wife and picked up the vacuum. "What she said."

First, the guys muscled the mattress back on the box spring. Once the bed was made, they piled the clothing from the floor on top.

Sarah lifted a white sweater with a pearl neckline from the pile. "Charlie, how 'bout you do your clothes and I do Juliette's?" She hung the sweater back in the closet.

Although her offer was kind, re-hanging Juliette's clothes seemed unnecessary and awkward. Did he need to keep them? Was he ready to let them go? This housebreak gave him the opportunity to complete at least one task he'd been dreading. "Sarah, could the women at Best Foot Forward use some of Juliette's clothes? I know she donated items to them in the past."

"She sure did. Anything you want to give would be a blessing." Sarah lifted a dress from the bed. "But are you sure?"

"No, I'm not, but I think Juliette would be pleased." He motioned to Kyle. "Mind checking the garage? I bought some large leaf bags a while back. Maybe we can fill a few of them for Sarah to take with her tonight." If they'd noticed the catch in his voice, they didn't let on.

"No problem." Kyle dropped a pair of Charlie's unfolded shorts on the bed. "Be right back."

With all that'd had happened since he'd gotten home, Charlie had forgotten what he'd learned from Heidi Vincent. If Juliette had confided in anyone other than him, it would've been her best friend.

"Sarah, I need to ask you something, and I want you to tell me the truth."

She stopped folding and stared at him. "I would never lie to you, Charlie."

He took a deep breath. "Did you know Juliette had been let go?"

"Let go?" Her face screwed up. "You mean from her job?"

"One of her coworkers told me she was fired at the beginning of May."

"How can that be? We talked about work a few days before she died. She would've told me."

It was silly, but Charlie would have felt worse if Juliette had confided in Sarah and not him. "That's what I thought too. She'd never been fired before. My guess is she was embarrassed."

Kyle came in on the tail end of the conversation but said nothing.

Sarah studied her husband's face. "What do you know about this?"

He shrugged. "Nothing, really. I saw Juliette at the high school track a few times mid-week, but she told me her hours were flexible."

"We had a few awkward moments in our chats,"—Sarah shook her head—"but I attributed them to Juliette's disappointment at not getting pregnant as soon as she'd hoped."

Kyle exchanged a look with his wife. "No sense second-guessing now."

Sarah dropped the subject and went back to work.

Charlie appreciated how Sarah handled every article of Juliette's clothing tenderly—baptizing a few with her tears. She placed them in the bag as if she were tucking away fond memories.

After patting down a suit jacket, she pulled out a small bottle. "Charlie, trash or flush? I'm never sure how best to dispose of medications."

He reached for the bottle. "Something to ask my sister the good doctor, I guess." He put it on his dresser.

"Got another one," she said a few minutes later, then tossed the bottle to Charlie.

Two half-empty prescriptions? He shook his head. Jules never did like taking medication. But he was surprised how careless she'd been about where she'd kept them.

Sarah said, "I'm almost done, except for this bunch of gloves, hats, and scarves."

"You've done enough already." Charlie pointed to a canvas bin nearby. "Chuck 'em in there. I'll sort them later. Thanks, guys. This would've taken me days."

"Who are you kidding?" Kyle snorted. "Your big sister would've put everything back together for you."

"You're right." Charlie pointed at Kyle. "That's why I'm not going to tell her, and neither are you."

Sarah put the cleaning supplies in the cabinet under the kitchen sink. "Edy's a good big sister, Charlie. She loves you."

"And I love her too. But, since Juliette's death, I get the feeling that if I asked her to, she'd move back in here—at the expense of her own personal life. And that wouldn't be healthy for either of us."

It was ten o'clock when they left. Sarah had been right. With his room back in order (and a flashlight and baseball bat by his side), he'd sleep better that night. Right after he figured out why Juliette hadn't told him about being fired and what the vandals were looking for in his house.

CHAPTER NINE

After a fitful night, Charlie rose before daybreak. He dragged himself to the kitchen, flipped on the coffeemaker, then plopped on a bar stool and waited.

How long had their landline voice mail light been blinking? Days? Weeks? He sighed and punched in the code. There were three earlier messages for Juliette: the Apple Store, probably trying to sell her an upgrade; the bank about an overdraft on her account; and a pharmacy in Hingham saying her prescription was ready.

Hingham? She must have changed to a branch closer to her office.

He continued to listen: "It's Ethel Rivers, dear. What's a convenient time for me to bring a meal over this weekend?" … "Pastor Ted here. Let's get together after service this week." … "Mr. Dawson, this is the County Medical Examiner's office. We were unable to reach you regarding Mrs. Dawson's toxicology report, so we mailed you a copy of our findings."

Charlie checked his cell and found the multiple calls he'd dismissed as spam because he hadn't recognized the ME's number. He pawed through the basket of mail and found their letter. He filled his coffee mug before reading the first page.

Various compounds were listed under the heading Positive Findings: Clonazepam, hydrocodone, methadone, meperidine, estrogen, and progestin. He was an architect, not a chemist. He wasn't sure what all this meant. Had Juliette taken a painkiller—one with multiple ingredients—shortly before she died? Maybe by accident … from the Tums bottle? Could some of the compounds listed be generic names for her supplements? What did any of this have to do with her heart?

He needed to see Edy.

Charlie: Need help reading tox report. U free this am?

Edy: Can u b at my office by 8?

Charlie: Ok.

He finished off his third cup while mulling over scenarios. Neither his coffee nor his scenarios sat well. "Lord, keep me from jumping to conclusions. Help me find a logical explanation."

He showered and dressed. Since he was going to see Edy anyway, he grabbed the two prescriptions bottles on his dresser, making a mental note to ask her about disposal. He decided to check the prescription names against those in the tox report, but the labels were peeled off—except for the corner of one. He squinted to read what was left of it.

Why would Edy Dawson, M.D.—a pediatrician—write a prescription for his wife?

One of the bottles slipped out of his hand and rolled under the bed. When he knelt to retrieve the bottle, his hand brushed against something. He pulled it out—one of Juliette's old birth control pill containers. His throat constricted.

We'll never have our babies now, will we, Jules?

He tucked all three items in his briefcase along with the report.

Ten minutes later, Charlie strode into Edy's office and dropped the prescription bottles on her desk. "What's this about?"

She removed her glasses. "And good morning to you, too, brother."

"Why would you be writing prescriptions for my wife?"

Her brow wrinkled. "What are you talking about?" She picked up one of the bottles.

"Your name's on one of the labels." He planted his feet in front of her desk. "Maybe both of them."

Glasses back on, she read the partial label, then examined the tablets from both bottles. Sitting back, she stared off in silence for a long moment. "I never—"

He crossed his arms. "Never what?"

Her hands fell to her lap. "I never suspected—"

"Suspected what?"

Edy sank deeper into her chair. "About three months back, Juliette came by my office before our girls' night out. She told me about a friend of hers who had a problem with painkillers. I directed her to a website which outlined the short- and long-term dangers of addiction."

"And you think she was talking about herself?"

"I didn't then." Edy hesitated. "I left Juliette alone in my office for a few minutes. I put my script pad in the pocket of my lab coat before I hung it on the back of my door. When I couldn't find it the next morning, I thought I was mistaken. Since the pad was almost depleted, I let it go."

"You're accusing Juliette of stealing your prescription pad?"

She held up one of the bottles. "That's the only way she would've gotten a prescription for painkillers filled under my name."

Charlie dropped to the chair without a word then handed her the tox report.

Following each word with her finger, her amber eyes darkened. "According to their findings, Juliette most likely died from a combination of drugs mixed with supplements which taxed her heart over a period of time. Mostly, painkillers and anxiety medication."

Confusion zigzagged through his mind. "Anxiety?"

"Those might have been easier to get." With a sober expression, she read off the long, official names in the report.

Studying Charlie's face, she added, "However, the estrogen and progestin mentioned are common ingredients in birth control pills."

Birth control pills? Stunned, he reached inside his briefcase for the container he'd found under the bed. The label was marred, but he could still read the date it was filled.

There must be some mistake.

They'd been trying to get pregnant for months. According to the date on the label, the last pill Juliette had taken was the Friday before she died. The same day she'd added two more names to their baby book.

"There's something else," Edy said. "Juliette's 'friend' was concerned about getting pregnant while using." She started around her desk toward him.

With one hand raised, he stopped her. "Please." He couldn't handle any more consolation. "Just let me go."

Minutes later, he was at Vine Hills, tearing flowers off Juliette's grave. He sank to his knees and buried his face in his hands, begging for answers. "Were you in that much pain? Why did you lie to me? Did you think I wouldn't understand?"

One thing Charlie knew, anything built on a faulty foundation would fail. Is that what they'd done? Gloom overtook him. His belief in their relationship didn't square with her behavior. His trust in her words wobbled and cracked. His memory of their love buckled.

He would never know the answers, and that hurt almost as much as her lies.

At the sound of gentle weeping, his ears perked. He hadn't noticed the woman standing by a headstone twenty feet away. Had she seen him? He wanted, no needed, this time alone with Juliette. The woman's presence irked him. Maybe because her tears sounded loving while his tasted bitter.

He stalked back to his car. Already an hour late for work, he shoved his emotions aside and headed for the office. Falling apart could wait until he got home. This was *his* problem. He wouldn't make it Dawson-Landau's too.

Weeks passed as Charlie took on work like a robot. He made the changes to the Quinlan plans, met with potential clients, and designed the Clarks' garage. Much of his time was spent researching federal, state and local agency regulatory requirements for pond-front construction in preparation for the dreaded meeting with his in-laws.

He mentally dodged nagging questions, but they kept coming back: Who knew about his wife's drug use? How long had it been going on? When Edy's prescription pad ran out, where did she get what she craved? Did the colonel know his daughter was using painkillers? More recently, a chilling question surfaced: As her trainer, could he have been behind it?

In the past, Charlie always bounced his troubles off Kyle. Now, he wasn't sure if he was more embarrassed or ashamed to admit to his best friend how little he'd known about his wife. Besides, if the break-in at his house was about drugs—and what else could it be?—dragging Kyle into this mess might prompt a police investigation.

On his way home, Charlie decided he'd deal with this alone, beginning with a more thorough search of their home than the creep who broke in.

Pulling into his driveway, he was startled to see Juliette's Rav4 parked in its usual spot. Almost six weeks had passed since she died. The plan on that day had been for her to give her father a ride home. The colonel had had the car since then.

Whenever Charlie thought about retrieving the vehicle, he felt petty bringing the subject up.

Realizing her SUV was one place the thieves hadn't searched, Charlie checked under seats and floor mats and in every compartment. Except for her gear bag, everything else was ordinary stuff found in any vehicle. He unzipped her bag. Other than workout clothes and a helmet, all he found was her dead cell phone and charger. The only thing suspicious was that the car was clean.

Shrugging off incriminating concerns, he pocketed the cell and charger and took her gear bag to the garage. When he spotted the cardboard box Heidi Vincent had delivered to him, he brought the box into the house for a more thorough look at its contents.

The box held more emotions than surprises. The stack of books reminded him how impossible it had been for his wife to sit and wait anywhere without something to read. The pink Red Sox cap brought back memories of their first game at Fenway Park. The half dozen framed employee-of-the-year certificates raised more questions. He traced the line of Juliette's face in their wedding photo until his head ached. His knees weakened at the "I'm Charlie's wife. What's *your* superpower?" coffee mug he'd put in her Christmas stocking last year.

Composing himself, he piled everything back in the box, then plugged in Juliette's phone.

He searched the house for potential stashes. The secret bottom drawer in Juliette's antique dresser held her "vacation" lingerie and the love letters they'd written each other every year on their anniversary. He picked up the lavender-scented pack, tied with a blue ribbon. Juliette had always said she placed more value on these letters than on any other material thing they owned.

"And what kind of value did you place on the truth?" He dropped the letters back in the nightstand and kicked the drawer shut.

Nothing was hidden atop the kitchen cabinets or behind the major appliances. He even peered through hollow curtain rods and inside paper towel and bathroom tissue rolls, a trick he'd read about in a mystery novel. He lifted toilet tank covers, checked behind drawers, and on the bottom of furniture. He discovered no false baseboard heaters or fake switch plates like he'd seen on reruns of *CSI New York.*

Not sure if he felt defeated or relieved, he sat at the kitchen island. Maybe the thieves who broke in *had* gotten what they came for. How would he know? More than drugs, Charlie was looking for reasons. He found neither.

Her quackology supplies mocked him from the basket beside him. He glared at the healthy collection. Maybe he'd just flush 'em all down the toilet. What did he care?

He fiddled with the pile of supplements, wondering which ones were partially responsible for killing his wife. He popped the cap on a bottle of vitamins. The contents looked normal to him, and he found nothing out of the ordinary in the next few bottles. While examining a few others, he discovered tablets which didn't match the description on the labels. And there were more OxyContin in with the Tums.

Stunned, he stared at his discovery. "Jules, how did this happen to you ... to us?"

He went online for images to help identify the drugs. He compared size, color, and shape but found no matches. A peculiar marking, or maybe a logo, was found on some. But he couldn't be sure what the pills were.

He clicked on a "How to dispose of drugs properly" link and found a few options. He wasn't willing to risk the DEA drug take-back program, so he chose option two. He dropped every pill and bottle he found in a plastic bag, sealed it, then buried the bag in the trash bin for pickup next Tuesday.

Juliette's phone had charged during his search. But to read her messages, he'd need a password. When had she needed a password?

He glanced at the open cardboard box. His and Juliette's smiling wedding photo stared up at him.

The memory of that day came back so clearly …

Charlie woke the morning of his June wedding to the clearest day Plymouth had seen in months. Every color looked brighter. The sun was warm, the breeze, gentle. It seemed all the birds sang in harmony as the trees swayed to their rhythm. He was certain he'd heard God whisper, "This day is holy."

He and Juliette had honored the colonel's wish—more like a command—that she wait to marry until they both received their college degrees. They'd scheduled the wedding for the second weekend in June—only because the first week at the church had already been booked.

Charlie smiled as he read the clock. In six hours, his wait for Juliette would be over. He called his bride-to-be. "I know I'm not supposed to see you before the ceremony, but is there any rule against speaking?"

Her lilting laugh quickened his heart.

"If you hadn't called, I would've called you. Charlie, just think …"

"Oh, I've been thinking."

"I bet," she teased. "Not going to wimp out, are you?"

"Do you think I'm crazy?"

"A little," she said.

"A lot crazy over you."

If it was possible to hear her smile, he did. "What do you have planned for your last morning as Juliette Annandale?"

"The usual secret bridal stuff. First, Dad and I are going for a run."

"A run? Don't tire yourself out, Jules. I've got plans for us for the next sixty years."

Charlie didn't know much about dresses, but when Juliette walked down the aisle, he couldn't imagine a bride as beautiful or a gown as perfect. Juliette's mother and great aunt had succeeded in creating a one-of-a-kind for their one-of-a-kind girl.

As they recited their vows, he was glad they'd decided on a traditional wedding ceremony complete with "To have and to hold, from this day forward, for better for worse, for richer for poorer, in sickness and in health, to love and to cherish, till death us do part, according to God's holy ordinance ..." The vows taken by generations of couples before them seemed more special than anything they could have written themselves.

When Pastor Ted said, "I now pronounce you husband and wife," it felt more like a blessing. Their first kiss was tender—a token of how Charlie planned to treat her.

Before the reception, they posed for wedding photos. After a few shots, the photographer straightened Juliette's veil. "Let's try a romantic shot now, you know, show fewer teeth."

"Sure," Juliette said. "No problem." She stuck out her lip and crossed her eyes.

Charlie laughed. "You want serious? I can do that." He snarled his lips and frowned.

The photographer's camera clicked on and on. "I don't think you two know how not to smile."

Juliette's grin grew wider. "Is that such a bad thing?"

Charlie tightened his hold around her waist. "I just married the girl I've been in love with since I was a high school sophomore. I can't help but smile!"

In the end, there were no serious photos ...

He silenced the memory and turned the photo face down. Not smiling hurt way too much.

CHAPTER TEN

Hank came into the office on Monday, grumbling to himself and anyone else who would listen. "I told Artie that guy wouldn't last!" He threw his keys on his desk. "Any thirty-year-old who needs his mother to take him to work and has to borrow tools is not a good candidate for Dawson-Landau."

Penny scolded, "Now, Hank, everyone has to start somewhere."

Charlie stifled a laugh. He knew exactly what Hank's response would be.

"Yeah, somewhere else!" Hank's voice got louder. "I majored in business, not social work. How soon can you get an ad in the paper?"

Penny sighed. "Same one as usual?"

"No. This time add 'Must have own tools and transportation.'"

"Will do." She picked up the phone.

After Hank left for the job site and Penny for the Town Hall, Dee approached Charlie's office. "I hate to put you in the middle, but what do you think about hiring Zach to replace the guy who didn't work out?"

What did he think? So many answers raced through his head, starting with Zach's history of drug use, moving on to family working together never being a good idea, and ending with Dawson-Landau losing their business manager. And Dee was right. He hated being put in the middle.

But what he said was, "Hmm. That's an idea. Tell me, does Zach have any carpentry experience?"

Dee stepped over the threshold. "Not a lot, but he's a natural like my father. He's holding down two part-time jobs now, but the work is menial. He's desperate for a position working at something that matters."

Sounds a lot like social work. But again, he said, "I can understand that."

Dee uncrossed her arms to plead her case with her hands. "Look, I can't ask Hank, but you can. He'll listen to you. Zach's been clean for a long while now, and he has his own transportation and hand tools. What do you say?"

He wanted to say, "Hank will never agree," but instead he said, "I'll run the idea by him."

And that, Charlie, is the reason your partner does all the hiring and firing.

"When?"

He realized Dee was still talking to him. "Let's give him a few days to cool down. Timing is everything."

She jotted down Zach's phone number and handed the slip of paper to him. "Thank you, Charlie." She seemed appeased when she went back to her office.

Yes, timing is everything. Charlie couldn't delay meeting with Juliette's parents much longer either. Once he revealed the cause of their daughter's death, he doubted the topic of their renovation project would even come up. He called before his nerve gave out.

Natalie answered. "Charlie! The colonel and I were just talking about inviting you over for dinner."

Nothing could make this conversation easy, but at least their home would be private. "Sounds good. When did you have in mind?"

"Are you free around six tonight?"

Tonight? Charlie was free every night. "Sure. What can I bring?"

"Yourself will do nicely."

Not quite true, but Natalie's words were always kind.

Charlie was on time, knowing promptness would set the right tone with the colonel.

His father-in-law greeted him at the door. "Six o'clock sharp."

"That's me. Sharp." There was a little less stiffness in the older man's stance and a little less starch in his shirt.

"Good to see you, Son." He patted him on the back.

Did Juliette's father plan to call him *son* from now on?

Natalie came around the corner and hugged him then took a step back. "Have you lost weight?"

Charlie couldn't recall when he'd weighed himself last. "Not that I know of."

She adjusted his shirt collar. "I worry about you."

He made no remark about the dark circles under her eyes and her less-than-coiffed coiffure.

"Now stop fussing, Nat. The man doesn't want to be interrogated."

"You're right, dear." She took Charlie's arm. "Come have a seat."

The three of them settled in the front room. Charlie got as comfortable as he could, considering his in-laws' formal furniture and ornate style.

Natalie motioned to a tray of beverages and a plate of cheese and crackers. "Help yourself. Dinner won't be ready for another forty-five minutes."

Silence ensued. Charlie broke in before the mood got any more awkward. "By the way, thanks for dropping Juliette's car off."

"No problem." The colonel raised his glass and took a sip. "Hm. Good lemonade, Nat."

"We would've brought it back sooner," Natalie said, "but Wick insisted on cleaning the car, inside and out."

Charlie chuckled. "Sorry about that. Your daughter was neat at home, but her car was another matter."

"She was like that as a teen too." Natalie shook her head. "Never could figure out why."

The colonel cleared his throat. "Charlie, I was wondering, have you decided what you're going to do with Juliette's triathlon bike?"

"Hadn't thought much about it. Why?" Was this man more sentimental than he'd imagined?

His father-in-law leaned forward and clasped his hands. "Well, I'm working with this young woman and—"

"*Working* with?"

"Yes, training her for a triathlon coming up in August."

Did he hear him correctly? The colonel had replaced Juliette already?

"Anyway, she's got a road bike,"—he leaned back—"but I think she needs to upgrade to a triathlon-style so she can better handle the steeper grades."

Less than two months had passed since Juliette died. Charlie's first inclination was to tell him to go suck eggs. For some reason, his sister's words came back to him. *Don't be too hard on him, Charlie. People handle grief in different ways.* He said a quick, silent prayer. "Tell me about her, Colonel."

"Mandy is her name. She's been a fan of Juliette's for years. Followed her around at events like a little sister. Juliette always told me to talk loud enough for her to hear so she could benefit from some coaching. I think she'd approve."

Juliette had mentioned Mandy more than once. "Does *free* work for you and your new student?" Charlie still detected a pinch of nasty in his own tone.

"Thanks, I appreciate it." The colonel drained his glass. "I'll let her know."

It was Charlie's turn to clear his throat. "I received the final results of Juliette's toxicology test."

The colonel stood and turned away from Charlie and his wife, staring out at the pond through the large bay window.

Natalie moved to the edge of the sofa. "And? Did they confirm her heart was at fault?"

"Yes, they did." Charlie first held then let his breath out. "But they found pharmaceuticals in her system, which they believe contributed to the heart failure."

Natalie looked back and forth between her husband and Charlie. "What do you mean? Juliette didn't take drugs."

"You're right, she didn't … as a rule." Charlie leaned forward and clasped his hands. "But she did take pain medication when she had that bad ankle break."

"But her ankle was fully healed." Natalie looked puzzled. "She was back to running and cycling. She didn't need the medication anymore."

"I know." *Lord, please help me.* "There's a strong possibility she became dependent during the months she *did* need them."

"Is that what they're saying? Juliette was addicted? Wick?"

He didn't answer her.

Charlie steadied himself. "They didn't find performance-enhancing drugs, but they did find anti-anxiety meds."

The colonel dropped to the sofa and covered his face with his hands.

"Wick?" Natalie pressed his arm. "What do you know about this?"

"*Nothing*, that's the thing." He shook his head. "As her trainer, I should have seen the signs earlier."

Charlie sensed he was holding back? "Earlier? You suspected, didn't you?"

"Not right away. At first, I blamed her sluggishness and irritability on her long recuperation period. Juliette always hated being cooped up. I thought she'd bounce back once she got into her regular routine."

Natalie's jaw tightened. "Not all weaknesses are physical, Wick. Maybe if you'd said something to me, I could have helped."

His father-in-law rose and paced the room. "I'm sorry, Nat. I would have, but my suspicions weren't confirmed until the day she died."

A thought came to Charlie. "Is that why you opposed the autopsy?"

"Yes." He lowered his head. "Nat dropped me off at the state forest that morning. Juliette was already there, talking with some young guy off to the side. I didn't like the looks of him."

"I remember," Natalie said. "Longish hair, a bit scruffy. His jacket looked like one a soldier would wear."

He continued. "She was squirrelly and had trouble focusing. After practice, I confronted her. She didn't deny using drugs but insisted she had everything under control. When I asked if the guy I'd seen earlier was her supplier, she got angry then took off down the trail again. I thought she needed some space." He slumped on the sofa beside his wife. "I should have gone after her."

Charlie didn't miss the tears in the colonel's gunmetal gray eyes, and he understood how he felt. "I was her husband, and I didn't see a problem either. No one did. She was as good at fooling us as she was at fooling herself."

Natalie held her husband's hand. "He's right, dear. She and I spent the previous Saturday shopping, and I saw nothing in her behavior to alarm me."

"There's more," Charlie said. "Our house was broken into a few weeks ago. The police suspect the perpetrator was looking for drugs."

The colonel stared at him. "How would they know that?"

"Kyle said a good sign is when everything in the house is torn apart but nothing stolen." Charlie hesitated but decided to tell them the rest. "He also told me if the police department gets autopsy and toxicology reports from drug-related deaths, they might have cause to get involved."

Natalie adjusted her sweater. "Would they take any further action?"

Charlie shrugged. "I have no idea. Meanwhile, I've been through the house and found every pill Juliette had ever hidden."

"Not every pill." The colonel went to the hall closet and returned with a small, white plastic bag. "I found these in her car."

Natalie's mouth fell open.

Charlie surveyed the weariness on his father-in-law's face. The man looked like he'd aged ten years. Reaching for the bag, he said, "Let me take care of that for you."

Sadness seemed to settle over them and prevailed throughout dinner. The few remarks his in-laws made about their building project were less than enthusiastic. In the end, they shelved the discussion for another day.

CHAPTER ELEVEN

Charlie reread Binnie Westfall's text from the previous day, inviting him to dinner after church. He had yet to respond.

Truth was he hadn't been back to church since the funeral. The thought of people fawning over him and making him feel sadder than he was already made him shudder. What would he say if they asked questions he couldn't or didn't want to answer? And if one more person hugged him, he thought he'd fall apart, maybe for good.

No, he needed to grieve in his own way and process everything he'd learned since Juliette's death. And that was better done alone.

Really? Have you tried telling God that?

Exhaling loudly, he surrendered to God's prompting and accepted Binnie's invitation before he could change his mind.

Charlie pulled into the parking lot of Heritage of Faith Church. The 3,000-square-foot pre-fabricated building was more a testimony to the church's limited budget than architectural design. Only recently had the church been able to afford an interior designer to make updates to the foyer and sanctuary and to build-out new office spaces and classrooms. He'd contributed his architectural services while others had lent a hand with construction.

He waited in his car until the service began—mainly to avoid stilted conversations with well-meaning people. He tiptoed in and sat in the back, far away from his and Juliette's usual section.

Despite his plan to maintain a modicum of self-control, the hymns and choruses melted his resolve. They washed over him like a soothing spring shower. Too weak to move, Charlie didn't sing or stand or clap or pray. Resting in God's presence was all he could do.

Pastor Ted's sermon was on God's grace. Charlie wondered if Ted had him in mind when he ended with, "Remember, people, fixing others is the Lord's job, not ours. Now let's share his grace by giving each other privacy to come before God."

Charlie couldn't walk to the altar. Instead, he rested his arms on the chair in front of him and put his head down. He made no eye contact, and no one approached him. Coveting this precious time alone with God, he stayed until the church was almost empty.

Ted patted him on the shoulder. "The ushers will be here for a while, so take all the time you need. See you at the house."

Charlie hadn't felt this much peace since before Juliette died. He realized a few things while waiting on the Lord. One, he wasn't mad at God. Two, he *was* mad at Juliette. He decided to take that as progress.

Although not billed as such, Sunday dinner was Binnie Westfall's ministry. If you'd ever met her, chances are you'd been invited to one of her guess-who's-coming-to-dinner events. The last time he and Juliette had been there, they'd dined with a trio of cranberry harvesters, the two cousins who owned the Happy Sushi Bar, a town selectman, and the conductor of the Plymouth Philharmonic Orchestra. Binnie had also entertained her share of clergy, including priests, ministers, and rabbis, some orthodox, some not so much. She'd fed more than a few atheists and tax collectors too. Thanks to her hospitality and witness, many of those dinner guests now worshipped in various congregations around town.

Now she could add a widower to her growing list.

To ease into the noisy company of others, Charlie left his Jeep in the church lot so he wouldn't get blocked in by the cars of the other guests. Thankfully, a light breeze had his back as he walked the quarter mile to the Westfall home. He needn't have bothered. Besides Ted's car and Binnie's minivan, there was only one other vehicle in the driveway—a shiny black Chevy Impala.

The front walk was lined with every shade of petunia and zinnia. The porch was deep enough to hold full-sized wicker furniture. Baskets of purple and red bougainvillea hung above the rail. To the left of the front door, a welcome sign hung, the size of which screamed, "And we mean it!"

Ted opened the door before Charlie could ring the bell. "Glad you came."

"To church or dinner?"

"Both." He smiled. "You know Binnie. She always makes enough for all twelve tribes."

"And how many tribes is your wife expecting today?" Hoping for some private time to speak with Ted, Charlie preferred a short guest list.

"Just a few besides us. One's here already. Do you know Glenna O'Neil?"

"*Sergeant* O'Neil?" The news did not whet his appetite.

"Yes. She and Binnie serve together on the Plymouth Drug Task Force."

"Is that so?" He internally replayed his testy back and forth with O'Neil on the day of the break-in. "Does the sergeant attend Heritage now?"

O'Neil answered from the dining room. "I'm a good Irish Catholic woman myself. I go to St. Patrick's."

Charlie forced himself not to flinch at her voice. "Good afternoon, Glenna. How're you doing?"

"Doing fine, and you, Mr. Dawson?"

He didn't like the way she said his name. Like he was hiding something behind it. "I'll be doing even better once I get you to call me Charlie, and after I enjoy some of Binnie's cooking." What could O'Neil say to that?

Binnie entered and set down a tray of glasses. She hugged him. "You're a flatterer, Charlie Dawson, but I'll forgive you."

O'Neil snarked, "So forgiveness is what you need, eh, *Charlie*?"

He smiled like she wasn't getting to him. "I believe everyone needs to be forgiven at one time or another."

"That's why we Catholics have confession." Her eyes were black and hard. "Good for the soul, don't you agree?"

A remark Kyle had once made came back to Charlie. *Contrary to popular belief, the biggest hindrance to O'Neil making detective is not her gender but her personality.* Her miserable countenance probably didn't help much either. Maybe if she loosened that bun of hers, she'd be able to relax.

Ted answered, saving him a response. "I agree, and isn't confession part of the recovery program the task force supports?"

"You're right, Ted," Glenna said. "Step Five reads: 'To admit to God, to ourselves, and to another human being the exact nature of our wrongs.'" She turned to Charlie. "You familiar with the Twelve Steps?"

"Not sure I could recite them, but yes." When would dinner be ready? Maybe she'd stop talking once her mouth was full. He called out, "Binnie, need a hand in there?"

Binnie came through the swinging doors carrying a pitcher of iced tea. "I'm all set, thanks. You three sit and chat. Everything should be ready when our remaining guests arrive."

Having more guests to deflect O'Neil's attentions sounded like deliverance.

Binnie reached into the hutch for dinner plates. "Glenna, I'm so glad you suggested I invite that other couple. They're fairly new in town, so they probably don't know too many people other than those they've met through the task force."

Glenna raised an eyebrow. "Oh, but they know Charlie."

"*Me?*"

"Yes, I believe Oliver and Vanetta Quinlan are your clients."

Two awkward coincidences in one Sunday dinner? More than awkward—unpleasant. Before he could figure out what was going on, the doorbell rang.

Binnie hustled toward the front foyer. "Come in! So pleased you could join us."

The open floor plan of the Westfall home allowed Charlie to see and hear from the living room.

Oliver Quinlan stepped inside with his wife. "We had to see what your famous Sunday dinners were all about."

Ted met them in the foyer. "Ted, Binnie's other half. I hope we don't disappoint you. Other than my wife's cooking, we're pretty simple around here. Our guests are the ones who make our dinners interesting."

Charlie waited with Glenna, who seemed to stare at him like a cat would a bird. When the Quinlans reached them, they didn't look surprised to see him. "Oliver, Vanetta, nice to see you outside of the office."

"Right." Prompted by a sharp elbow from his model-thin wife, Oliver opened the pre-dinner conversation. "By the way, have you ordered the slate for the roof yet? Vanetta wants to make sure it matches what she has planned for the hardscape. Don't forget, my wife has final say on the finishes."

Despite their harping, Charlie was glad for the subject change. "Wouldn't have it any other way. Your wife has excellent taste." He winked at Vanetta. "Ever thought of working for a design-build firm when your house is complete?"

Looking less intense, she actually smiled at the compliment, her pale face softening against the severity of her straight, black chin-length hair. "My marketing consulting practice keeps me quite occupied, thank you."

Marketing practice? Up until that point, Charlie wasn't aware she worked.

Not one person had yet mentioned Juliette or his grief. He wasn't sure if that made him feel better or worse. Before the subject could come up, he steered the conversation in a less emotional direction. "Binnie, do you remember when you had the Pilgrims and Wampanoag Indians and the children's Sunday school class over for a meal together?"

"How could I forget?" She chuckled, then paused in front of him with a small platter of appetizers. "The cast of Plimoth Plantation came and *stayed* in character. The parents gave me grief for weeks because their kids wanted to sit on the floor and eat with their hands. So much for my attempt at blending cultures."

Charlie breathed easier at the guests' laughter.

Then Ted had to go and say, "Oliver, I hear you're a West Point man. Is that right?"

"Yes. Most valuable experience of my life."

"Navy man myself. Stationed in Norfolk for four years." Ted laughed. "Most *painful* experience of my life."

Great, the subject of military service was trending. This didn't bode well for him.

"Twenty years serving in the National Guard," O'Neil boasted. "What about you, Charlie?"

Charlie didn't dare bring up his father-in-law's West Point connection. He suspected O'Neil would accuse him of coat tailing. "Me? Got my BA in architecture before Juliette and I married. Then I worked in the field a few years before getting my masters. Afraid I was never called to military life."

"*Called?*" O'Neil cracked. "Good thing everyone doesn't wait to be *called* or this country would be under the control of terrorists."

Sheesh. Charlie refused to let the insult stick. Instead, he toasted them with his iced tea. "More reason to thank you all for your service."

"I have to agree with Charlie on this one, Glenna," Ted said. "Not everyone is *called* to be a police officer or a pastor either."

Glenna mumbled a vague agreement.

When their hostess bid everyone to the table, Charlie was the first to his feet.

He didn't remember if the Westfalls had found a dining room to fit Binnie's ministry or started a ministry to fit the huge room. With all the leaves in, the long, hand-scraped table could seat up to eighteen comfortably. Thankfully, with only six guests, Charlie's seat was a safe distance from O'Neil's.

Then Ted spoke up. "Honey, before we get comfortable, why don't you let me take a few of these leaves out for a cozier feel."

Great. Within minutes, he was seated directly across from his personal *grill* sergeant.

If the spicy pork tenderloin with blackberry sauce was as good as it smelled—and all her meals were—maybe their chitchat would be limited. In the meantime, Charlie took a risk and broached the subject of the drug task force like he would any other mammoth in the room—head on, but carefully. "So, tell me about this task force. What exactly do you do?"

Binnie passed the potatoes. "Our main mission was to get out ahead of the opiate crisis. Unfortunately, by the time we got organized, the crisis had a sad and sizable lead."

"No one likes to talk about the facts," O'Neil added, "but the addiction rate and death toll have actually risen since the committee's formation."

Ted laid his knife on the edge of his plate. "That may be true, but those numbers are a reflection of the disease, not of those trying to help. Isn't that right, Sergeant?"

"I agree—to an extent," O'Neil groused. "But there's plenty of blame to go around."

"What do you mean?" Vanetta bit into a bare celery stick as if it were a juicy Italian sausage.

O'Neil's voice got a few decibels louder. "Pharmaceutical companies lobbying Congress. Drug cartels with international leverage. Lazy, uninformed physicians over-prescribing pain meds. Not enough Narcan or clean needles to go around."

Charlie couldn't help himself. "What about personal accountability? Isn't that one of the twelve steps you mentioned?"

She glared at him. "Would that personal accountability include friends and family coming forward instead of covering up for those addicted?"

What was she inferring?

"The problem is complicated." Binnie sighed. "Throwing loved ones in jail or in a twenty-eight-day rehab that doesn't work isn't much of a motivation for people to report those who need help."

Ted refilled his glass. "Maybe if the state had better programs and treatment facilities. According to recent studies, 87% of the graduates of faith-based programs are living drug-free lives."

Oliver helped himself to a roll. "I know you're a minister and all, Ted, but bringing religion into the mix only complicates policies, not to mention state and federal funding. My belief is that success can be achieved by better managing the current resources and manpower."

"My husband knows what he's talking about." Vanetta pushed some food around her plate. "Under his leadership on the Waco, Texas, task force, drug sales plummeted."

Oliver chuckled. "My wife may be a tad prejudiced."

"Yes, but is it true?" Binnie asked.

Oliver cleared his throat. "Yes, but Waco and Plymouth are two different towns."

O'Neil lit up. "But if the ideas you implemented lowered drug use in a city the size of Waco … What's their population anyway? Over 100,000, I bet."

Vanetta interjected, "Close to 125,000 when we moved."

O'Neil practically frothed at the mouth. "Just imagine what you could do as head of the task force in this town of 62,000!"

Oliver held his hand up. "Hold on now. I'm fairly new in town, remember? I don't want to step on anybody's toes."

Of course, you do.

Charlie scolded himself for being cynical.

Binnie put her fork down. "Glenna, we can't exactly boot out the chairman without giving him a fair chance. Let's go at this as a team."

O'Neil frowned. "Maybe."

"Binnie's right," Oliver said. "But I'm happy to offer suggestions based on my experience."

I bet you are.

Charlie gave himself an imaginary slap for backsliding again.

"We can start where you did in Waco, dear," Vanetta said. "Look for common denominators in the lists of repeat offenders and drug-related deaths."

"That's right," Oliver said. "There's often a connection between them—like neighborhood, family, friends, workplace—that might otherwise be overlooked. Numerous times, that knowledge helped us put dealers out of business."

O'Neil's frown disappeared under a creepy grin. "I think that's a perfect place to begin."

Was it Charlie's imagination or had she narrowed her eyes at him?

"Aha!" Oliver raised a finger in the air. "Speaking of connections, Charlie—now I remember where I've seen that young man who was in your office. His mug shot is on the sheet of repeat offenders."

"Really?" He played dumb. "Sorry, I don't know enough about him yet to comment."

O'Neil put her elbows on the table. "Is there anything you *can* comment on, Charlie?"

He steadied his breathing. His plan to go on the offensive with that topic had backfired. "Seeing as I'm not a member of the drug task force, guess not."

A bombardment of questions he dared not ask taunted him. Did everyone on the task force get reports of drug-related deaths? Were names included? Did O'Neil know about Juliette? How about the Quinlans and Westfalls? How long could he keep Juliette's probable cause of death a secret?

While the others continued their discussion of how best to rid society of the evils of drugs, Charlie's big contribution to the cause would be to put Juliette's stash out with the trash on Tuesday.

CHAPTER TWELVE

This was the first time Charlie had *not* enjoyed a Westfall Sunday dinner. Who could blame him, considering Glenna O'Neil's accusatory undertone and Oliver Quinlan's false humility? More so, he felt like he was teetering on the edge of some big unknown, even bigger than the secrets surrounding Juliette's death. He had to get out of there.

As soon as they finished their final course of chocolate mousse and coffee, he used the first polite excuse that came to mind to make his exit.

Ted led him to the door. "I regret we didn't have much chance to talk, Charlie."

He shook Ted's hand. "That's okay."

"No, it's not okay." He stepped out onto his porch, closing the door behind him. "Sergeant O'Neil acted a bit bristly toward you. Do you two have a past I don't know about?"

He sighed. "If we do, I'm not aware of it."

"Well, I apologize for her behavior. No guest in my house should be treated that way."

Finding some consolation in Ted noticing, Charlie said, "Not a problem. See you next week, Pastor."

"Maybe we can find some time before Sunday."

"Sure." Charlie didn't hang around to set a date.

The jaunt back to his car in the church lot helped clear his head. He knew what he needed to do next. Seated behind the wheel, he called Kyle. "Hey, it's me. You guys home?"

"Yeah, why?"

Charlie took a deep breath. "I need to talk."

"We're here for ya."

"Be there in ten." He pulled out into the road. As he rounded a corner, he caught sight of Glenna O'Neil's black Chevy Impala creeping up behind him. *Coincidence?*

Forty minutes later, Charlie knocked at Kyle and Sarah's side door.

Kyle answered. "That was a long ten minutes."

Charlie glanced up and down the street before he slipped in. "I was making sure Sergeant O'Neil wasn't still on my tail."

"What?" Kyle cocked his head. "Why would she do that?"

Charlie shrugged. "I have no idea. But something tells me her actions have something to do with Juliette."

Sarah hugged Charlie then leaned back to look into his eyes. "Come sit. I made a fresh pot of coffee."

Charlie joined them at the kitchen table, his hands shaking.

Sarah poured them each a cup. "Would you like to explain what you mean, Charlie?"

"I don't know if I *can* explain."

He spent the better part of an hour telling them about Juliette's tox report, the drugs he'd found at the house, the colonel's suspicions, and O'Neil's innuendos over dinner. He died a little with every word.

Sarah sat open-mouthed through most of his story, occasionally rubbing her temples. "How could we have missed all this? I never saw any signs of Juliette using drugs. She always hated taking meds."

"I know." Charlie hung his head. "I used to scold her for not following the doctor's orders."

Kyle's knee bounced up and down. "I should have said something when I saw her in a less reputable part of town in the middle of the day."

Charlie opened his hands. "It wouldn't have made any difference."

Sarah dabbed the corner of her eyes. "Tell us again about Sergeant O'Neil."

Charlie clutched his coffee cup with both hands. "I think she knows how Juliette died."

"How could she?" Sarah looked at her husband. "Did you hear anything about it at the station?"

Kyle shook his head. "Other than condolences, not a thing."

"O'Neil's a member of the Plymouth Drug Task Force," Charlie said. "Maybe they get information you don't. All I know is she acts like she's on some sort of a medieval crusade—and her trebuchet is aimed at my head."

Sarah choked on a sip of coffee. "She can't possibly think you had something to do with your own wife's death?"

"It's not that so much," Charlie said. "She acts like she's angry about Juliette's death." He paused for a moment. "More specifically, angry with *me* for allowing her to die."

Kyle chewed on his lower lip. "My memory's kind of fuzzy, but I seem to recall O'Neil being concerned about her kid brother using drugs."

Sarah's brow lifted. "And you think she might be projecting her feelings as a defense mechanism to cope?"

Kyle appraised his wife. "I thought you gave up watching Dr. Phil?"

Charlie rapped his fingers on the table. "Do you think knowing more about O'Neil's past will help?"

"Can't hurt," Kyle said. "Let me look into it."

While getting his juice Tuesday morning, Charlie noticed the neon green sticky note on his refrigerator. Trash Tuesday! He hurried through the house, emptying wastebaskets and gathering recyclables. Even though he'd forgotten last week, there was still room in both bins. One of the unheralded benefits of living alone.

A wave of heat greeted him when he opened the overhead garage door. He dragged the recycling to the end of his driveway. For some reason, getting bins out to the road had become an unspoken competition among his neighbors. Even Juliette had reveled in her frequent victories. She wouldn't have been pleased with his recent performance.

He took another look, hoping he hadn't come in dead last. That's when he spotted the black Impala parked a few houses up. Keeping his normal pace, he reached the garage and went straight for his phone. "Gotta question for you, Kyle."

"Shoot."

"Any idea what Sergeant O'Neil hopes to gain by staking out my house?"

"Is she there now?"

"Yep. Parked up the street, hiding between black and blue bins."

"There's a possibility she's responding to a domestic call. Hang on, let me check." Kyle came back a minute later. "Nope. Dispatch says no calls for that area."

"What does this woman have against me?"

"I don't know … Black and blue? Is it trash pickup day?"

"Yeah. I noticed her when I was putting the recycle bin out."

"Throwing out anything that might interest her?"

Charlie told Kyle about the bag of pills in the trash, still sitting in the garage. "Doesn't she need a warrant to go through my stuff?"

"Once it's on the street, your trash is considered public property."

Charlie moaned. "Should I confront her?"

"No. Find the bag and hide it—and not in your car. Put your trash out as usual, then leave for work."

"How will I know what she does?"

"You won't, but I will. I'm on my way. Call you later with my findings."

Charlie buried the pills in a large bag of potting soil, then dragged the barrel to the street.

Kyle phoned him before he got to his office. "I was right. A few minutes after you left, O'Neil clawed through your trash."

Charlie rubbed his forehead. "Did she find anything?"

"Nope, went away empty-handed."

He sank into his seat. "What am I supposed to do now?"

"I've got your six, Charlie. Don't worry. Let me do some more digging—in her trash this time."

CHAPTER THIRTEEN

Charlie dreaded the next thing on his day's agenda: approach Hank about hiring Zach—the same guy whose mug shot was on the task force's sheet of repeat offenders.

Great. This could turn out bad for everyone.

He decided to call Zach first—either to warn him or quiz him, he wasn't sure which. He found the scribbled phone number Dee had given him, then closed his sliding glass door.

"Yo! You've reached Zach Jennings live."

Charlie had to think for a second. "Zach? This is Charlie Dawson."

"Hey, what's up? Mom okay?"

"She's fine. Although she's partly responsible for my call."

"Not sure what you mean."

"Can I be straight, Zach?"

"Uh, sure."

"Your mother asked if we'd consider hiring you. Hank does the hiring and firing, but I value your mom's opinion enough to hear you out before we get to that point."

"*Mom* asked? I'm sorry about that. I planned to do that myself."

"To be candid, family working together isn't usually a good idea."

Zach cleared his throat. "And then there's my history of drug abuse to consider."

His bluntness surprised Charlie. "Yes, how're you doing with that?"

"I was a mess when I got back from Afghanistan. It took a bad year to hit bottom before I entered a fifteen-month recovery program. I've been clean and sober two and a half years now."

"Impressive." Charlie's mind wandered. Juliette hadn't been taking prescription drugs for that long. Why hadn't she been able to stop? He refocused. "Tell me why you want to work here."

"I'm not putting my carpentry skills to good use in the jobs I have now. And there's no chance for advancement."

"How about hand tools and your own transportation?"

"Got both."

"Good. As I said, Hank does the hiring, and mandatory drug testing is part of that process. If you're still interested, I'll give him your number. But I can't promise anything. Understand?"

"I'm interested, Charlie. Thanks."

When Hank came in, Charlie spelled it out.

"What am I supposed to do now?" Hank grumbled. "If I say yes, we could be hiring trouble. If I say no, we could lose our business manager."

Charlie leaned against the door jamb and crossed his arms loosely. "Well, I doubt Dee would suggest anything that would put Dawson-Landau at risk, but it's your call, Hank."

Hank dropped his hat on his desk and sighed loud enough to make his point. "I'll ask Penny to set up an interview."

Once Zach's employment was official, he came by the office the following week to fill out tax forms and get his orders from Hank.

Sergeant Glenna O'Neil walked in right behind him.

Charlie didn't flinch at her presence, refusing to give her the satisfaction of seeing his ire. Instead, he took extra time fixing his coffee.

Penny greeted her. "Good morning. How may I help you?"

"Is Dawson here?"

Charlie sauntered over. "Need some house plans, do you, Sergeant?"

"Not on what the town pays me. I was in the area and thought I'd stop by."

"Right." He took a sip.

"I need to speak with you." Glenna eyed Zach then turned back to Charlie. "In private."

"Follow me." Once they were in his office and the door was closed, Charlie spoke before she could. "If you have something to say, Glenna, say it. Or do you plan to insult me with insinuations like you did at the Westfalls'?"

She glowered at him. "I don't know what you're …"

"Of course, you know. Everyone knew."

"Look, I'm just doing my job as a police officer and a member of the drug task force."

"And what does that have to do with me?" Charlie sat, leaned back in his chair, and folded his hands behind his head. "Have a seat, Glenna."

She didn't sit. "I think you know."

"Why don't you tell me."

"Have it your way." She stiffened. "Your wife died with drugs in her system. The guy in the next room is an addict, maybe even a pusher. The connection is easy enough to make."

"Anyone can make a connection … if they jump to conclusions."

Her black-Irish eyes pierced the six-foot space between them. "Are you accusing me of doing that?"

"No accusations, just facts." Leaning forward, he casually rested his elbows on his desk. "I had no foreknowledge of my wife taking drugs. I'm still not clear what killed her. As for Zach, he's been clean for more than two years."

"Druggies lie, and so do those who enable them."

"But drug tests don't." Charlie slid the door open and stepped aside. "Good day, Sergeant."

Her face reddened, and her tight bun seemed to pull her face taut. "This isn't over."

Charlie stared her down. "You bet it's not."

As she walked by Dee's office, her glare almost bore a hole in the back of Zach's head. On her way out the door, she bumped shoulders with Hank.

Hank's head spun around as the door slammed. "What're the cops doing here?"

Zach came out of his mother's office. "Might be my fault, sir. Sergeant O'Neil's been after me for years. There was a time she had good reason. I don't think she believes a person can change."

"Well, then, we'll have to prove her wrong, won't we?" Hank tossed Zach a Dawson-Landau hat. "Let's get to work."

Once Zach and Hank were gone, Dee approached Charlie. "Thank you."

He shrugged. "Everyone needs a second chance." *Even your wife, Charlie?*

Penny sputtered, "The nerve of that woman! She stopped my twins once and gave them a lecture. Said their goth hairstyles were 'telling a story that wouldn't end well.'"

"Sergeant O'Neil's *modus operandi* seems to exclude the presumption of innocence." Charlie winked at Penny. "But we both know your girls will prove her wrong."

A proud-mother look erased the outrage from her face.

Charlie went back to his desk. Before focusing on the day's project, he whispered a prayer, "Help, Lord. There's a lot on the line for all of us if Zach doesn't work out." Then he made a call. "Kyle, you might need to speed up your investigation. Glenna O'Neil harassed me in person at my office this morning."

"You've got to be kidding."

"Nope. Gotta give her credit. She's relentless if not pleasant. And she knows about Juliette."

"Figured. Hang tight. I'll step up my snooping. Hey, how 'bout first thing in the morning I fill you in on what else I find out, and you help me move a file cabinet at Best Foot Forward? I promised Sarah."

"Fair enough."

If Charlie ever admitted to Kyle how much he valued his friendship, his big head would bust out the windows of his cruiser. Of course, chances are he suspected already.

Charlie went by the cemetery after work. He wanted to make sure Juliette knew he was still mad at her. After all, who else could he tell? He got his camping chair out of the car and sat, brooding in silence. Once he felt he'd made his point, he spoke.

"First, I practically bit Edy's head off when I found the prescription bottles with her name on them. I can't believe you'd do that to her of all people … Now I've got Glenna O'Neil on my back … You literally left me holding the bag, Jules. And it's filled with pills in our garage … Dee's son, Zach, managed to clean himself up. Why couldn't you? And why didn't you trust me? That's what hurts the most."

His grumbling continued until he was interrupted by a stocky, older man stomping across the cemetery.

Is this the guy I saw before, the one having a picnic?

The man bestrode a gravesite then leaned over and shouted. "I LOVE YOU!"

Why was he yelling? Didn't he know nothing was ever really loud enough to wake the dead?

Oh, and your idea of speaking to your wife in a normal volume makes sense?

Maybe not, but that guy had a few loose parts.

Right.

Once shouting-man left, crying-woman showed up—the same auburn-haired one he'd seen *and* heard a few times before. He didn't want to stare, but she looked so sad when she placed her hand on the top of a headstone. Before he could turn away, she slumped to the ground, her head barely missing the stone.

He hurried over, then knelt and patted her cheek. "Are you okay?"

Her green eyes fluttered before opening. "Where am I? Who are you?"

"You're at the cemetery. I think you fainted."

"I did?" She looked around then tried to sit up.

"Slow down a bit. I'll be back in a second." He scrambled over to get his chair, then helped her up. "This'll be more comfortable."

"Thanks."

"Does this happen often?"

"Hope not. But I was told to expect the unexpected while expecting."

"Expecting? Uh, congratulations. Is there someone I can call? Maybe your husband?"

"Are you like that man who yells to his wife in the ground?"

"Uh, no, why?"

"Well, my husband's right there." She pointed to the grave. "You can call him, but he won't answer."

"I'm sorry. I didn't know." He paused, trying to think of something to say. "My wife's over there."

She looked where he pointed. "How'd she die?"

"Heart failure, most likely caused by drug use." This was the first time he'd spoken the truth out loud. Why did telling a stranger seem easier? "And your husband?"

"Stupid joy ride on his cousin's Harley. I'm still mad at him. We moved here all the way from Iowa because Roman got the job of his dreams. Even had great benefits. He was killed before his first day of work. Now I'm trying to figure out how to live without a husband or a decent income or health insurance—all with a baby on the way in a town I know nothing about."

Charlie didn't have any words that would fix her problems. "Are you sure there isn't someone I can call for you?"

"I'm all right, really. I'm staying in town with the Harley owner and his wife. They work the three to eleven shift."

"Will you be okay to drive?"

"Pretty sure." She looked down at her hands. "Look, I apologize for my whining. I'm probably overtired."

"I understand." And he did. Before Juliette died, he wouldn't have. Something popped into his mind. "Did you say you're looking for work?"

"Yes, why?"

"My friend volunteers at Best Foot Forward, an organization that helps women in difficult situations find employment. If you're interested, I can give you their address."

"I've heard of them." She sat up a little straighter. "Thanks, I'd appreciate the help."

"Ask for Sarah Yates." He scribbled the address on the back of his business card, then handed it to her. "Tell her Charlie sent you."

She glanced at his card. "Thank you, Charles Dawson, Architect. If you talk to your friend today, tell her Ashlyn Reid will come by tomorrow."

"Will do." Having been on the receiving end of charity lately, giving back felt good. "Well, I'd better get going."

"Oh, wait,"—she stood—"your chair."

"Tell you what, Ashlyn Reid, why don't you keep it. I've got another one like it at home."

"No, I can't do that."

"Why not? It'll save me from having to pick you up off the ground again."

She chuckled. "Okay."

On his drive home, his self-pity waned under the realization that others were worse off than he was.

CHAPTER FOURTEEN

Charlie arrived at Best Foot Forward ahead of Kyle. He was surprised when his mother-in-law greeted him. He gave her a hug. "I didn't expect to see you here, Natalie."

"Well, Juliette always talked about this place, so I decided to volunteer. Started a few days ago."

"I can't think of anyone more perfect for the job."

"You're sweet to say that." She adjusted a few items on the counter. "Charlie, before Sarah gets here, may I speak to you about something?"

"What's up?"

"Well, I'm sure you wondered how the colonel could begin coaching Mandy so soon after Juliette." She paused to clear the catch in her throat. "Wick believes taking on this task is his penance for missing Juliette's, um, problem."

"What Juliette did wasn't his fault."

"When someone you love dies there's always guilt, even if the feeling is misplaced. We're human. I didn't want you to think he'd moved on already."

Which was exactly what Charlie had thought.

The bell on the door jingled, and Sarah entered. "Hey, Charlie! Kyle's parking the car." She hung her jacket on the coat tree. "Thanks for opening, Natalie. Having you here now is such a blessing."

"That's what I'm here for, dear."

Kyle blew through the door. "Glad you remembered, Dawson 'cause I need some muscle."

He rolled his eyes. "Right. Muscle. That'd be me."

"File cabinet's in the back office." He moved past Charlie. "This won't take long."

Anxious to press him about O'Neil, he followed.

Kyle shut the door behind them. "O'Neil lost her kid brother about eight years ago. They were really close. Word is he got into drugs. She's been on the hunt for drug users and dealers ever since."

"You'd think she'd have empathy for those going through the same thing."

"Apparently, she refused to see the department shrinks, but those who were around back then said she was a mess. Rumor is she might've been on the outs with the kid when he died. The desk sergeant, who's been on the force for decades, thinks guilt's gotten the best of her."

Guilt again. "Now that part I *can* understand."

"Anyway, she turned into a bloodhound, following every whiff of drugs on the street. She keeps a file locked in her desk at the station. No one's ever read it, but they've seen her inserting notes and clippings. The sergeant said her whole mood changes when she's in that file. I'll try to get a look-see when I have a chance."

"Whoa, Kyle! Don't get fired over this. Just knowing her motivation might give me the upper hand."

Kyle tipped the file cabinet on its end. "I doubt that."

"Tell you what, let's see how things go. If I have to, I'll confront her again." Charlie bent to pick up his end.

They slow-stepped sideways to the far wall, then set the cabinet in place by a desk.

Kyle studied him. "Don't tell me you feel sorry for her?"

"Let's just say I know a little of what she's going through."

"One day that soft heart of yours is gonna backfire on you."

Don't you know it already has?

On his way out, Charlie told Sarah and Natalie about their new prospect. "Her name is Ashlyn … Reid, I think she said. Sad case. She may come by today."

"Someone from church?" Sarah asked.

"No, from the cemetery."

He didn't miss the worried looks Natalie and Sarah exchanged. "What? She's a real person."

Natalie walked around the counter and hugged him. "Of course, she is, dear."

Did they think he'd gone bonkers?

Charlie had one more thing to take care of before he went to the office.

Something had been gnawing at him since Heidi Vincent returned Juliette's things. He wanted Franklin Morris to tell him, in person, the full reason he'd fired Juliette. He didn't understand why knowing why mattered so much but it did.

He and his Jeep idled in the Morris Companies' parking lot in Hingham while he decided whether to go in. The four-story half brick, half glass office building with its manicured lawn and trimmed shrubbery looked out of place in the wooded setting.

When Franklin pulled into a reserved space, Charlie exited his car before he could talk himself out of confronting him. "Mr. Morris!"

Franklin's brow furrowed on his tanned face. "Yes?"

Charlie extended his hand. "Charlie Dawson. Juliette's husband."

"Of course, of course. What can I do for you?"

"I know you're busy, so I'll be brief. Specifically, why did you fire my wife?"

"*Fire?* Who told you that? Juliette asked me for a leave of absence."

Now *that* he hadn't expected. "Heidi Vincent told me you fired her in early May."

His eyes grew wide. "I have no idea why she'd say that. Juliette told me she had some personal issues to work out."

Charlie's mind tried to grasp that piece of news. "Then why would she be the one to return Juliette's personal belongings to me?"

"That doesn't make any sense. I helped Juliette carry a box to her car myself. I remember because that's when I told her to come back whenever she was ready."

Now he understood why Morris had acted so strange at the wake when Charlie told him he'd be by to pick up Juliette's things.

Charlie's face got hotter as his temperature rose. "Is Heidi in yet?"

"No." Franklin chuckled. "The irony is she's the one I fired."

"Mind telling me why?"

"The official reason was her inability to perform her tasks in accordance with the job description."

"And unofficially?"

Franklin switched his briefcase to his other hand. "Off the record? I suspected she was dealing drugs but had no proof. And from what I saw of the guy who stopped in occasionally to see her, he might've been her best customer."

His brain flinched at the news. *Had Juliette been one of Heidi's customers too?*

At Charlie's request, Franklin called HR for Heidi's address. "You sure you want to pursue this?"

"I am." Charlie shook his hand. "And I appreciate your help."

"One thing puzzled me." Franklin rubbed the back of his neck. "Your wife was a model employee, as accomplished at her job as Heidi was *not*. But when that girl was around, Juliette's confidence seemed to slip." He shrugged. "Probably nothing. I'm not even sure why I brought the matter up."

Franklin had put his trust in Juliette. Charlie couldn't bear to tell him he may have been wrong. Besides, what good would his knowing do now?

Twenty minutes later Charlie pulled up in front of a dilapidated farmhouse in a rural section of Plymouth. A weathered sign by the mailbox read, "Apt for Rent." The front door held a scribbled note: "Use side entrance."

He knocked three times before an elderly woman cracked the door.

"You here about the apartment?"

"No, ma'am, I'm here to see one of your tenants."

"Got no tenants. That's why the sign."

"I was given this address for Heidi Vincent." Charlie pressed. "Did she live here?"

"Yeah, why?"

"She worked with my wife, and I need to speak with her."

"If an' when you find her, let me know. She and that boyfriend of hers skipped out on their rent."

Although disappointed, he wasn't surprised. "Sorry to bother you, ma'am."

Charlie pulled into work around eleven o'clock. On his way across the parking lot, their foreman Artie waved him over from the warehouse.

"Hey, Artie, what's up?"

"You've gotta do something about Quinlan. He wants Zach fired. The kid's good, and I need him."

Why hadn't he seen this coming?

He pinched the bridge of his nose. "I'm surprised Oliver hasn't complained to me in person."

"Oh, he will soon enough. I told him Hank was out of town, then I stalled him, saying you'd be in late. Which wasn't exactly a lie since you just got here."

"Thanks for the warning."

Artie saluted him. "I'm outta here before the prima donna shows up."

Charlie poked his head into Dee's orderly office. "Trouble's on the way. If you want to leave while Quinlan rants, you better do it now."

"That narcissist doesn't scare me."

Not much did scare Dee.

She squared a stack of files to the left of her keyboard before a frown appeared. "Does this have anything to do with Zach?"

"This time, yes, but if he weren't complaining about Zach, he'd be whining about someone or something—"

"Dawson!" Oliver Quinlan barged in. "I'm paying you too much money to have a drug addict working on my house!"

Charlie rolled his eyes at Dee then took a deep breath. "Oliver, join me in my office and tell me what this is all about."

Without waiting for privacy, Oliver jabbed his finger at Charlie. "This is about you hiring a guy whose mug shot is on the drug task force list!"

Doing things discreetly wasn't Oliver's style.

Charlie ushered him into his office and closed the door. "If you mean Zach Jennings, then the task force needs to update their list. He's been clean for years." He offered Oliver a seat, which he doubted the man would accept.

Oliver remained standing. "So? If he's not using, he's dealing. Get rid of him or my contract with Dawson-Landau ends."

"Your project is high-end and complex. Hank assigned Zach because he needed a craftsman rather than another laborer. However, if you prefer, we can put him on another job—"

"No! Sacked and out of town."

Out of town? Did he think this was the wild, wild West?

Quinlan took a bully stance, filling up most of the space in the office.

"Hank handles the crew. Let me see if I can get hold of him." Charlie stretched out and relaxed in his chair before he picked up his phone. He spoke in a casual tone to match. "Oliver's here. He has an issue with Zach Jennings working on his house … Yeah, I know he's one of our best workers. Anyway, I offered to move him to another jobsite, but Oliver wants him fired or he'll cancel his contract with us." He addressed Oliver. "Is that an accurate assessment?"

"Quite."

Charlie went back to his call. "A lawsuit? … Based on what grounds? … Let me look it up." He typed, one-handed, into a search engine. "Got it. I'll read it to you. 'The Americans with Disabilities Act prohibits discrimination against drug addicts based solely on the fact that they previously illegally used controlled substances.'"

He stole a glance at Oliver, whose stance wavered.

"Would Zach have any chance of winning? … You're right. The lawsuit could tie the job up in court for months, maybe years … What? Why would our liability carrier insist we sue our client?" Charlie made sure Quinlan saw the concern on his face … "Sure, I'll let him know … Look, if Oliver decides to proceed, how soon do you want Artie to pull the crew off his job and put them on Belichick's beach house?"

The smug look on Quinlan's face vanished. He sputtered, "He can't do that!"

"Wait a second." Charlie put his hand over the mouthpiece. "Sorry, did I misunderstand you?"

"Put that druggie on another job, then finish my house on schedule!" Oliver turned on his heel and left.

Artie chuckled on the other end of the phone. "*Belichick* as in Coach? Nice touch."

Charlie smiled. "Thought you'd like that."

CHAPTER FIFTEEN

Charlie swung by Vine Hills on his way into work the next day. His phone rang as he parked. "Morning, Edy." Since Juliette died, not a day had gone by without her calling him.

"Hey, little brother, have any plans for Sunday afternoon?"

"What do you have in mind?"

"Your minister's wife invited Grams and Pop and the two of us over for Sunday dinner. They accepted, but I'm not going unless you are."

"The Westfalls don't bite, you know." Charlie wasn't sure if his sister was a skeptic because she was a scientist or because God took their parents so early. She'd never confided in him.

"I don't trust the whole scenario. How do I know you won't all gang up on me?"

He chuckled. "And do what? Baptize you in their birdbath? Binnie loves people and loves to cook. Nothing more."

"Okay, but I'm not going to church. I'll meet you at their house after."

"You can run, Edy, but you can't hide if God decides to get you!" He knew she'd hang up on him, and she did.

Charlie called to RSVP for himself and Edy.

Ted answered. "Binnie thought a little welcome back dinner for your grandparents was in order. And in case you're wondering, Glenna O'Neil is not on the guest list."

Charlie chuckled. "Good to know." Now he could relax.

The morning sun roused Charlie from a deep sleep. He turned over. Today was Saturday. He didn't have to or *want* to get up. But even with his eyes shut, he could see tiny bouncing beams of light. What good were eyelids if they couldn't keep things out?

Sounds like a spade scraping through dirt came from his yard. He could almost smell the rich soil.

What's Juliette doing up so early?

A bucket of cold reality hit him in the face. Fully awake, he groaned then rolled out of bed. From the window he could see a figure kneeling by the flower bed that lined the patio, garden tools scattered around.

He opened the window. "Is that you, Edy?"

His sister's face turned up. "Sorry if I woke you. I wanted to get the weeding done before it got too hot."

Charlie threw on his jeans and an old T-shirt and joined his sister out back. "You don't have to do this, you know."

"If I want the flowers to live, I do. Besides, I have to keep the tradition going."

"What tradition?"

Edy dropped her digging knife to throw a small pile of weeds into a cart. "Tell me, what kind of flowers do you see here?"

"I don't know … pink ones, yellow ones, purple ones."

She pointed to various plants. "Those are Gloriosa daisies, asters, and dahlias. Juliette took over gardening where Grams and Mom left off. Taking on the mantle is up to me now."

Charlie was acquainted with his wife's planting and even Grams', but he'd been too young to remember his mother doing the same. "How can I help?"

"You dig out the troublemakers. I'll toss them and rake the soil smooth around the beds. We should be done in an hour or so."

As they worked together, Edy rattled on about how *they'd* plants bulbs in the fall, how *they'd* protect the shrubs against the winter, what *they'd* plant in the spring, and what annuals *they'd* need to fill in. Was she taking this mantle thing too literally?

She'd get back to her own life soon, wouldn't she?

Truth was he kind of resented her for thinking she could so easily replace his wife. Of course, he'd never tell her that because it would hurt her feelings. His thoughts even made him feel small-minded.

He tried another tactic. "So, what's going on with MIT Matt?"

She shrugged. "Not much. We've both been busy."

"So, he works Saturdays too?"

"No, why?" She sat back on her haunches.

"Well, if you weren't *here* this morning, you could be with him."

She gave him the *look.* "Just keep pulling those weeds little brother and let me worry about my social life."

The thing is she wasn't worried at all about her life because she was so entrenched in *his.* Charlie hated to admit it, but he might have to call in a big gun—Grams.

As his grandparents parked, Charlie waited on the church steps.

"I loathe being tardy for Sunday service." Grams gave him a quick peck on the cheek. "On the other hand, my husband here doesn't know how to read time." She made a beeline for the entrance.

Pop winked. "Your grandmother's mad because she likes to check out what the other ladies are wearing as they come in."

She called over her shoulder. "Come on, you two! The music's starting."

The few times Charlie had been back to church since Juliette died, he'd sat in the back out of sight. Sitting with family was another thing he'd taken for granted. When Grams and Pop held hands while they sang, wobbly voices and all, Charlie nearly broke down. Still, being emotional was better than being lonely. He smiled when, after all their years of marriage, the two elbowed each other during the sermon from Ephesians on the duties of wives and husbands.

Would he and Juliette have been like that after fifty-two years of marriage?

When the service ended, Charlie didn't rush his grandparents' chatting until Ted was ready to leave. Then, one after another, the trio of cars made its way to the Westfalls'. After the week of drama and mystery, Charlie planned to unwind and enjoy the pleasant company over dinner.

Right up until Grams said, "Looks like Wick and Natalie got here ahead of us."

His shoulders sagged, and he grumped, "I thought Edy said it was just gonna be family?"

Grams scolded, "Wick and Natalie *are* family, Charlie. You'd do well to remember that."

"Yes, ma'am." He felt like a ten-year-old boy again, being reprimanded for not giving a tenth of his allowance to God.

Edy showed up out of nowhere and entered with them.

Charlie whispered, "Hiding in the bushes, were you?"

She shrugged. "Good timing is all."

"Right."

After the initial greetings, Natalie approached Charlie. "Did Sarah tell you the young woman came by?"

"Young woman?"

"Ashlyn Reid, auburn hair, sweet girl."

Charlie nodded. "Oh, you mean my imaginary friend from the cemetery?"

"Touché." Natalie chuckled. "She already has a job interview this Tuesday."

"That's great." Since Natalie hadn't mentioned the girl's pregnancy, Charlie didn't either. "She seemed like a good candidate for BFF."

"Your intuition was correct. By the way, Ashlyn's looking for a place of her own. You don't know anyone with an apartment for rent, do you?"

Heidi Vincent's former landlady popped into his head, but he quickly tossed that idea. "Nothing suitable, I'm afraid." He noticed the lift to his mother-in-law's countenance. "Working there seems to suit you, Natalie."

She smiled. "I agree."

The colonel stepped up. "I've warned my wife about getting too involved with the clients. Natalie can be too soft-hearted for her own good."

"Ha! Coach Colonel, may I remind you of Mandy, the young athlete you're coaching? Besides, volunteering isn't about *our* own good. It's about the good we can do for others."

Grams teased, "Hard to argue with charity, right, Wick?"

His eyes narrowed. "I'm only trying to protect my wife from getting in over her head."

Pop wisecracked, "Too late now. She married you!"

Charlie couldn't believe Pop said it. But he was even more surprised when the colonel laughed.

Grams took Edy by the arm. "Come, dear, why don't we give Binnie a hand in the kitchen?"

Natalie stepped in between them. "I'll help, Lana. That way the good doctor can visit with the gentlemen."

As the two women walked away, Natalie turned back and winked at Edy.

"I like that woman," Edy said. "I think she gets me."

Charlie teased, "Your aversion to cooking may have come up once or twice in conversation over the years."

She chuckled. "The more people who know, the less they'll expect of me in the kitchen."

"Ah, but you have other gifts," Ted said. "I know that because a lot of your patients are my congregants. The kids and parents alike rave about Dr. Dawson."

Charlie nudged her. "Finally start giving out better lollipops?"

Edy ignored him but responded to Ted. "Is that so?" She looked pleased.

"Are you kidding?" Ted said. "I thought about sneaking in for a checkup myself to see what all the hoopla was about, but Binnie wouldn't allow me to."

Pop put his arm around Edy's shoulder. "Our Edy is one of the best and brightest pediatricians in her field."

"Said the man without one prejudiced bone in his body." Edy kissed his cheek.

"You may be my granddaughter, but your record speaks for itself."

"I'm going to see if I can at least help the ladies set the table," she said. "You flatterers are up to something."

Ted led the men into his home office to show off the desk he'd gotten at a recent auction. "All mahogany, not a single scratch. Only set me back $135."

Pop opened and shut the drawers and ran his hand over the finish. "You got a steal."

A large cork board filled a good portion of one of the walls. Four maps of the Town of Plymouth were tacked to it.

The colonel commented, "Looks like a military operation."

"You're close." Ted moved over to the board. "One of the drug task force members is a former West Point man like yourself. The idea was his."

Charlie knew it was Quinlan but didn't comment.

Ted pointed to the maps at the top. "These pins represent the known and/or suspected locations for drug transactions in the past two quarters. The pins in the bottom maps mark the drug overdoses for the same period."

The colonel traced the pins with his finger. "Looks like there's been a decrease in point-of-sales, but not in the number of overdoses."

"That's what has the Board stumped," Ted said. "The drug pushers don't exactly put up a 'We've Moved' sign with their new location. And a lot of people from neighboring towns use our hospital, so discerning where they got the drugs is difficult."

"Young people today!" Pop shook his head. "In my day we didn't have time or the money to fool with drugs. We were too busy working."

For a nanosecond, Charlie locked eyes with the colonel.

"Mind my asking the name of the West Point fellow?" the colonel asked.

"Not at all," Ted said. "Oliver Quinlan. He's one of your son-in-law's clients."

"Really?" The colonel addressed Charlie. "You never mentioned him to me."

Charlie shrugged. "No, I guess I didn't." *Why would I?*

Thankfully, Binnie rang the dinner bell before his father-in-law could start his repertoire of West Point war stories.

"You sure do set a beautiful table, Binnie." Grams shook out her napkin.

"Thanks." Binnie placed a platter of roasted vegetables next to a chafing dish filled with beef stroganoff. "Your prowess in the kitchen is legend, Lana, so the pressure was on."

"I assure you, it's a welcome change for this old woman to be on this side of a meal."

Charlie wanted to believe his grandmother, but his years of being fed by her wouldn't permit it.

Of all people, Charlie hadn't expected his grandfather to continue the conversation about drugs.

"Tell me," Pop said, "since the town has a whole task force dedicated to stomping out drugs, what's taking them so long?"

No one said a word.

Grams added, "Rollie and I don't even like to take aspirin. Why would anyone want to take the sort of pills that would harm them?"

Charlie certainly didn't have the answer.

"I say lock 'em all up and throw the key away." Pop sounded like he had the perfect solution.

Charlie didn't risk a glance at his in-laws.

Binnie was gentle in her response. "Being on the task force has taught me a lot. First, drug addiction is no respecter of persons. We've seen male and female drug abusers of all ages, all social status, all cultures, all races, and all walks of life."

Ted built on her platform. "No one ever expects to be addicted. Hardest of all is to get them and their loved ones to admit they have a problem."

Grams interjected, "The Bible says, 'Train up a child in the way he should go, And when he is old he will not depart from it.' What we need is more Christians raising children."

Ted rested his hands on the table. "I agree with you, Lana. But even children raised by Christian parents have to come to a personal knowledge of Christ on their own. And when they do, they're not immune to temptation and trouble."

Pop stuck his fork in a Brussels sprout. "Well, at least they'd know better than to get tangled up with drugs!"

The discomfort around the table seemed palpable—but not to Grams and Pop. Ted and Binnie's manner convinced Charlie they, like O'Neil, had learned how Juliette died—probably from the task force. He felt like the others were waiting on him to act. His whole body tensed.

Edy must have sensed his anguish. She squeezed his hand and whispered. "They can handle it."

He took a sip of water before speaking. "Grams, Pop, there's something you need to know." He looked to his father-in-law. Was that a nod of consent?

Grams' smile faltered at his tone. "What is it, dear? You sound so serious."

He swallowed the lump in his throat. Not wanting to repeat himself, he broke the news up into manageable bites. "The Plymouth medical examiner … attributed the cause of Juliette's death … to a dangerous combination of prescription drugs and dietary supplements. Over time … those drugs taxed her heart, which eventually gave out."

Charlie paused to gauge how they were doing. Stunned silent, Grams and Pop sat motionless.

He continued, "Between the toxicology report and what we've learned since then, we believe Juliette became addicted to prescription painkillers after her ankle surgery. She hid her problem so well none of us suspected."

His grandparents remained still a moment longer, their faces etched with sorrow.

When tears came to Natalie, Grams got up to console her. "I'm sorry for acting like a self-righteous old fool."

The two women embraced.

Natalie wiped her eyes. "You didn't say anything we haven't said ourselves. We've just had the chance to process the facts."

"I spoke out of turn." Pop's voice cracked. "You're right. If this could happen to our Juliette, then it could happen to anyone."

The colonel reached over and grasped Pop's forearm. "Thanks, Rollie. Your saying that means a lot."

CHAPTER SIXTEEN

Months of emotional upheaval had Charlie praying for some drama-free time. Since the dinner at the Westfalls', God had blessed him with three decent days in a row.

Grams and Pop had handled the news about Juliette without counsel or questions—an amazing feat of self-control for them. The Quinlans had settled down now that their house was weathertight and the interior work had begun. Even Sergeant O'Neil seemed to have tired of stalking him.

As for Charlie's unanswered and painful questions about Juliette, he decided to "let go and let God." Of course, *deciding* wasn't the same as doing. What he wanted most was to type "Why?" into a search engine and find all the answers he needed, listed in chronological order. Instead, he conducted multiple online searches for "Heidi Vincent," "drug addiction," "Glenna O'Neil," and "Plymouth's drug task force."

He found about two dozen Heidi Vincents in almost as many states. The closest possible connection was to a Paul Vincent of Pittsburgh, Pennsylvania. None of the other candidates matched the girl's approximate age. When he phoned Franklin Morris to ask if he would check Heidi's personnel file for previous addresses, this time Franklin refused, citing privacy laws and liability issues his attorney had pointed out. Charlie weighed coughing up fees for a professional background check or a private investigator against his common sense. He decided to pray instead. *God, once I get my questions answered, I'll move on, I promise.*

"Glenna O'Neil" yielded another middle-aged woman of the same name who wrote children's songs. His search for the phrase "drug addiction" drowned him with a flood of links. None of what he learned was uplifting.

Most everything he gathered on Plymouth's drug task force came from a few repetitious news articles and outdated press releases. The rhetoric was devoid of any real information. As usual, politics trumped transparency. Until the public was allowed into the meetings, he feared it would stay the same.

Maybe I could wheedle insider info out of Binnie? If so, would her answers—or those from anyone else—bring Juliette back? Would I be any closer to acceptance?

Before he could answer his own questions, his phone rang. "Afternoon, Grams."

"Hi, sweetie. Pop and I are dying for seafood tonight. Want to join us?"

Thankful for an easy question to answer, Charlie didn't think too hard. "Sounds good. Where do you want to go?"

"Maybe a place in town near the water? You pick. They all have their good points."

"Okay. Meet me at my office. Is six o'clock good? I'll make reservations."

"Reservations on a Wednesday? My, my, Plymouth has gotten kind of hoity-toity since we've been gone."

He chuckled. "Do you want to risk having to wait for a table? You know how impatient that husband of yours can be."

"You said it, not me." Before she hung up, Grams snuck in, "And dinner's on us, so don't argue."

No sooner had he put the phone down than Oliver Quinlan roared. "I need to see Dawson. Vanetta has more changes."

Is that it, God? My run of drama-free days is over?

Charlie called out his office door. "Come in, Oliver. Take a seat. Let's discuss them."

Quinlan marched down the hall and dropped some pamphlets and magazine clippings on Charlie's desk, neon pink sticky notes peeking out from the batch. "Nothing to discuss. Just give her what she wants."

"Okay. I'll check with our suppliers to see if they're special orders."

"You should know by now, Dawson," Quinlan snorted, "my whole house is special order."

And you're a special order, too, Ollie. Charlie sighed internally. "There's nothing wrong with getting what you want. But I'm responsible for telling you that some of these changes might hold things up."

"I didn't put up with excuses in Waco, and I'm not putting up with them here." He turned to walk out then called over his shoulder. "If you have any questions, talk to Vanetta."

When the door closed behind his least favorite client, Charlie dropped to his chair and banged out "Quinlan + Waco + Drug Task Force" on the keys. The first page brought up links to news articles in which Quinlan was praised for his "savvy leadership and insight." Even arrests had been attributed to the "proactive programs" he'd implemented. Everything seemed to point to Quinlan being the hero who'd single-handedly wiped out drug abuse in Waco, the seat of McLennan County, Texas.

So why would a narcissist like Quinlan move almost two thousand miles away from a people who lauded him as the next great giant in Texan history?

And why do I let him get under my skin?

He could feel a nasty mood coming on and didn't like it. At Dawson-Landau, his duty was to play good cop to Hank's bad. When clients needed hand-holding, Charlie's hand was the one they held. When employees wanted favors, they came to him. When people had to vent, his door was always open.

He needed an attitude adjustment before he caused a break in the ranks.

Lunchtime came around. He grabbed his jacket and headed for the cemetery. Sitting by Juliette, he contemplated his mood and mumbled his main complaint. "Quinlan is a pompous pain and an egotistical blowhard."

A bit of Juliette's preaching came back to him. *It's hard to dislike people when you're praying for them.*

"Really? You tell me this now that you're gone?" Charlie kneaded his face. "It's too late to pray for us though, isn't it? But then, you'd know that by now."

Not off to a good start on that attitude adjustment.

He bowed his head. "Lord, please forgive me. The stress has me wound tight. I need your help."

Instead of hearing God's still, quiet voice, he heard tires on pavement. He glanced over his shoulder. Ashlyn Reid climbed out of a silver SUV. She opened the back and pulled out his camp chair.

Charlie acknowledged her arrival with a nod but didn't engage her in small talk. A minute after she got her chair set up by her husband's grave, an old Ford pickup rattled in. The driver's door creaked open. Shouting-man jumped out then shuffled over to his wife's plot.

The three gravesites formed an equilateral triangle, with Juliette's plot being closest to the edge of the cemetery. Shouting-man's wife was to the right, Ashlyn's husband to the left.

Shouting-man leaned over and yelled, "I LOVE YOU!" He paused to take a big breath then cupped his mouth with both hands. "DARLIN', I JOINED A LEAGUE. WHERE D'YA PUT MY BOWLING SHIRT?"

What did he say? Charlie wasn't sure he'd heard him correctly. The guy shouted louder. "I CAN'T FIND IT."

He looked to his left and caught Ashlyn's wide-eyed expression.

Neither of them moved while the older man still bent over, turned an ear to his wife's grave.

Was he waiting for an answer?

Next, Shouting-man boomed, "I KNOW YOU PUT IT WHERE IT BELONGS! WHERE IS THAT EXACTLY?" He paused again then slapped his thigh with his cap. "Well, I'll be." He tromped back to his truck, climbed in, and took off in a cloud of dust.

Not wanting to appear insensitive, Charlie attempted to stifle his laughter. He failed. When Ashlyn's own hearty chuckles reached his ears, they could hardly ignore each other.

As he walked toward her, he cracked up all over again. Ashlyn, holding her sides, had a tough time catching her breath.

With his thumb pointing to the man's wife's gravesite, he said, "Do you think she really answered?"

"He heard something." She shrugged. "Maybe we should take our cues from him."

Charlie shouted, "How LOUD DO WE HAVE TO BE, D'YOU THINK?"

Ashlyn covered her ears. "I don't think it works like that."

"No?" Charlie feigned innocence.

She smiled then lowered her eyes, fiddling with the zipper on her coat. "I owe you an apology."

"You do?"

"I never thanked you for connecting me with Best Foot Forward. Sarah and Natalie have been so helpful. After losing out on a few places to rent, they advised me to find work first. Soon after, I found a job and an apartment in one!"

"How does that work?"

"Jillian McGee, the owner of Partyscapes, hired me. She runs a small craft and party décor shop off Main Street in a big old house. I'd only been working there a few weeks when the apartment over the shop became available. The place even has an alcove off my bedroom, perfect for the baby. And Jillian has a two-year-old, so she understands all about babies."

"So glad things worked out for you." A church bell rang in the distance. Charlie checked his watch "Speaking of jobs, I'd better get back to mine." He tipped an imaginary hat and winked. "You two take care now and don't wake the neighbors."

Her face lit up as she put a protective hand over her growing belly. "Thanks."

Charlie's throat closed, and his eyes filled on the way to his car. Trying to imagine the children he and Juliette might've had ached so much.

He corralled his emotions before he exited Vine Hills onto Samoset Street. In his rearview mirror, he caught a glint of a shiny, black Chevy Impala.

Unbelievable. Even my visits to the cemetery are suspect?

With O'Neil tailing him and Quinlan's outburst fresh in his mind, Charlie worried the meal with his grandparents would be more than they'd suggested—and more than he'd enjoy.

He had an idea. "Edy, it's me. What are you doing for dinner tonight?"

"Matt's coming down. I owe him a meal at the Blue Lobster. I could cancel if you—"

"You will not. I hear they're jammed every night. Better make a reservation."

"I'm way ahead of you, brother, dear."

Charlie thought fast. "Would you mind if I joined you?" Since she'd claimed she and Matt were only friends, he knew she wouldn't dare refuse.

After a long second or two, she said, "Um, sure, uh, if you want."

"Sounds like fun. What time?"

"Well, uh, the reservation's for six-thirty."

"Okay, six-thirty, then." He hung up before she could change her mind. Edy was gonna kill him but seeing her face would be worth it. After two years of hiding the mysterious Matt, tonight was his sister's turn to be in Grams' hot seat.

"Reservation for Dawson," Charlie said as he reached the podium.

"Good evening." A hostess grabbed three menus. "Follow me, please. The rest of your party is waiting."

Pop said, "What did she say?"

Grams looked at Charlie. "Rest of what party?"

Charlie held off responding until he was standing over Edy and Matt. "Surprise! Look who I brought with me."

Edy blinked. "But … you …"

Charlie jumped in. "You must be Matt. I'm Charlie, Edy's much younger brother. These two good-looking people are our grandparents, Lana and Rollie Somers." He extended his hand. "Nice to finally meet you."

Matt's face split into a grin as he stood to shake hands. "The pleasure is all mine." He pulled a chair out for Grams then looked down at Edy. "Why didn't you tell me this was 'meet the family' night? I would have worn a better shirt."

Edy shot Charlie a hard glare when Matt wasn't looking.

He pretended not to see it. "That's my sister. Full of surprises."

"Does this nice young man have a last name, Edy?" Grams shook out her napkin. "And why haven't we met him before?"

Matt answered while Edy took a deep drink of her water. "It's Brock, ma'am. Matthew Brock."

Charlie covered for his sister. "How was Edy supposed to introduce you to each other while you were in South Carolina?"

Grams waved her question away. "Of course. How silly of me."

"So, what do you do for work, Brock?" Pop asked while buttering a roll.

Edy recovered her voice. "His name is Matt, Pop. His last name is Brock."

Pop looked confused. "Yes, Brock. Isn't that what I said?"

Grams patted his hand. "Let the man talk, Rollie."

"I teach Applied Mathematics at MIT."

Grams perked up. "MIT in Boston?"

Matt nodded. "That's the one."

Pop scratched his chin. "Let me get this straight. You don't teach math. You teach students how to apply the math someone else taught them?"

Matt chuckled. "The course is a little more complicated than that, but—"

"Then let's keep it simple." Pop picked up his menu. "Now who's hungry?"

"Your parents must be so proud of you." Grams straightened her flatware. "Do you live with them in the city?"

"No, Mom and Dad live in Connecticut, have all their lives. I've got a condo not too far from campus."

"So, when *applying* math," Pop asked, "which is better, to own or to rent in the city?"

"They both have their advantages, Mr. Somers—"

"Call me Rollie, son."

Grams adjusted her eyeglasses. "I imagine renting or owning depends on whether or not you plan to raise a family—"

"Maybe someday." Matt glanced at Edy.

Edy hid behind her menu. "Is everyone ready to order?"

"As institutions go,"—Pop put his arm around Grams— "marriage is a pretty solid one. Right up there with MIT, I'd say."

At Pop's last comment, Edy gave Charlie a swift kick to his shin and a nod to the foyer.

He excused himself. "Be right back."

She caught up with him in the lobby. "Do you think this is funny?" Her fists rested on her hips. "I told you, Matt and I are just friends."

"Apparently you haven't seen the way the guy looks at you. He adores you, Edy."

"You have no right to butt into my business!"

"You're right, I don't. But that's what bratty brothers do." Charlie sighed. "Tell me, what are you so afraid of?"

She controlled the anger in her voice. "I'm not afraid of anything!"

"Matt seems to want this relationship to move forward. Why don't you?"

"Marriage isn't for everyone, Charlie. Things happen. Look at Mom and Dad. People get hurt. You of all people should know that."

"I wouldn't trade one minute of my life with Juliette, even knowing all I know now." He realized he meant what he said.

"Not everyone is like you, Charlie."

"You're right. Then I better tell Matt this family get together was *my* idea, not yours." He turned to walk back to the table.

She grabbed his arm. "No. Don't. Please."

He smirked just a little.

"Charlie, do you really think he adores me?"

They both looked over at the table.

"Would he be laughing that hard at Pop's jokes if he didn't?"

Later, when Charlie dropped his grandparents off at their car, Grams said, "Now that you're done messing with your sister, we'll meet you back at your house. We want to discuss this news about Juliette."

Of course, you do. What was I thinking?

CHAPTER SEVENTEEN

Just when Charlie thought the colonel and Natalie might put off the idea of a renovation, they called to make an appointment. An hour before their arrival, he checked the water level in the Keurig. "Penny, is this ready to go?"

She looked up from her keyboard over the top of her hot pink eyeglasses. "Yes, all set."

He sniffed the Half-and-Half in the refrigerator. Satisfied, he put the container back. "Do we have any of those sugar-free sweeteners?"

"On the shelf six inches from your nose."

"Oh."

Penny pushed her glasses atop her head and leaned back in her chair. "Relax, Charlie. They're family. Besides, fidgeting doesn't project confidence."

"You don't know my father-in-law."

"But I know you. Now, let's see some of that body language you use to soothe the beast in the likes of Oliver Quinlan and Sergeant O'Neil."

Her comment surprised him. "You noticed that, huh?"

"We all have." Penny stood. Her matching pink hair spikes meant business. "Look, you've got forty-five minutes before they get here. Why don't you walk down to that new bakery on Court Street and buy something to sweeten them up? I'll handle the coffee when they get here."

He sighed. "Have I told you lately you're a godsend?"

"Sounds like a country-western song to me. Now giddyap, cowboy, while you still have time."

As Charlie walked the two blocks to Court Street, he thought back on that body language documentary Juliette had insisted they watch. He mused aloud, "Probably should have told you, Jules, how much that show helped. Too late again."

The aroma of freshly baked bread led him straight to the door of Pilgrim Bakery & Café. His first time there, he perused the goodies in the glass cases, reading the handwritten cards—Massasoit Molasses Cookies, John Carver Cranberry-Apple Turnovers, Priscilla Alden Pumpkin Spice Cupcakes, William Bradford Butterscotch Bars—until a familiar voice interrupted.

"I've got some news for you." Kyle pointed to an item in the case. "It's gonna cost you one of those John Carver turnovers right there."

"Isn't a real bakery a little rich for you? I thought cops preferred the pink and orange franchises."

"I was on my way to your office when I saw you cross the street."

Charlie selected an assortment, then told the girl at the counter to wrap the turnover separately. He handed the pastry to Kyle. "Tell me what you have before you take a bite."

"Well, seems like O'Neil's brother, Garrett, was pretty tight with Zach Jennings when they were kids. The two were inseparable before Garrett disappeared."

Charlie put his wallet back in his pocket. "Disappeared? I thought he died?"

"Yeah, that's a fair assumption since he's been gone eight years. Glenna was a teenager when he was born, so she was like a second mother to the kid. She waited five years before having him declared dead. And even then, she only agreed so she could settle her deceased parents' estate. Not that there was much to settle other than paperwork."

They exited the bakery.

Charlie made certain the box of pastries was upright. "Hm. I wonder why Zach never mentioned any of this to me. Their being friends explains a little about O'Neil's behavior."

"They were in high school." Kyle took his pastry out of the bag. "A lot has happened since then."

"Didn't you tell me there were rumors of Glenna and her brother having a falling out before he died? If that's true, why doesn't she blame herself?"

Kyle held the turnover to his lips. "You've met her. She prefers to blame others."

"Well, I'm still not clear on what she hopes to accomplish by targeting Zach. Not like he can bring her brother back."

You do realize your amateur sleuthing won't bring Juliette back either?

"Some say she's twisted the story to gain a scapegoat." He brushed pastry flakes off his shirt. "Zach's a good fit for her purpose."

"After all he's been through?" Charlie shook his head. "The guy served four years in the army. He admits to struggling with addiction after he got out, but he entered a recovery program, and he's been clean and sober for two plus years. I hear he even mentors others."

"Even if she believed all that," Kyle said, "she'd resent him because her brother never had the same chance."

"And what do I have to do with any of this?"

"Haven't completely worked that out yet. Somehow, she's connected you to her crusade against drug abuse. Won't let it go." He took another bite. "Mm, this is good. Anyway, the latest bit of news is she's been lobbying for your client, Oliver Quinlan, to replace the current chair of the drug task force."

Charlie groaned. "That guy's ego is as big as his construction budget."

"Anyway, thought you'd like to know." Kyle stopped at his cruiser. "Want a ride?"

Charlie declined, then took his time walking back, mainly because the road was all uphill. As he reached the parking lot, one of the Dawson-Landau crew trucks passed him on their way to the warehouse out back. The driver honked hello; he waved back.

His in-laws pulled in behind them, so he waited for them to park. When they reached him, he removed his ball cap and bowed grandly from his waist.

Natalie smiled. "Such service."

The colonel nodded, took a few steps then stopped abruptly. "Hey, you! Hold up!"

The look in his eyes scared Charlie. "What's the matter?"

He pointed to the trio of workers standing outside the warehouse. "That guy near the truck. The one in the camouflage jacket. He's the one I saw talking to Juliette the day she died."

Charlie's stomach sank. *Zach Jennings.* "Are you sure?"

"Yes, I'm sure."

Charlie could hear Zach and the other crew members joking back and forth as they loaded the truck.

Natalie put a hand on her husband's arm, holding him back. "Wick, we were in the car, a good thirty feet away. All we saw was his jacket and long scruffy hair. We never saw his face full on. How can you be certain?"

"Maybe." The colonel grumbled. "Now that I think about it, the guy wore his hair much longer."

"He's one of my guys," Charlie said. "How about I check into it, Colonel?"

Another grunt from his father-in-law.

With a confrontation avoided, Charlie ushered them into the conference room, where Penny served coffee and set out plates for the pastries.

He sketched as his in-laws presented their ideas for their new first-floor layout and second-story addition. "This is a substantial project." Charlie phrased his next question in his head before asking. "Where will you stay during construction?"

Not with me, I hope.

"Friends of ours are traveling abroad," Natalie said. "The timing was serendipitous. They needed a house-sitter, and we needed a house."

While Natalie was receptive, even excited, about his design ideas, the colonel grew pensive as their meeting progressed. Funny, Charlie had expected the opposite reaction from his father-in-law since the whole idea had been his to begin with.

He gave them some ideas to ponder.

Except one.

Before Zach started at Dawson-Landau, Dee had insisted her son get a "proper haircut."

CHAPTER EIGHTEEN

The last few weeks, Charlie's mind had gotten stuck on Heidi Vincent and the lies she'd told him. He retrieved the box of Juliette's stuff, hoping he'd missed something the first time around. How had Vincent gotten her hands on the box and why? And did she find what she was looking for?

He examined each item more thoroughly than before. The pink Red Sox cap and coffee mug held no clues. He checked inside the frames of the employee-of-the-year certificates as well as their wedding photo. *Nope.* He flipped to the inside cover of each book and to the back, then shook them upside down, hoping something would fall out. *Nada.*

He hadn't been able to get into her phone because of the password. Maybe her computer would reveal something. Where *was* her Mac anyway? He hadn't seen her laptop in the house or in her car. And it hadn't been in the box from her office.

I'm missing something but what? Think, man, think!

Later that afternoon, he vaguely recalled a voice mail from an Apple Store, maybe two or three months back, but couldn't remember what the message was. He contacted the closest store in Hingham.

"Yes, Mr. Dawson, we were wondering what happened. Mrs. Dawson dropped her Mac off on … let me see… on May 10. She wanted us to check the battery. It's ready and waiting."

May 10. The day before she died.

"And you only called once?"

"Uh, no, sir, but we've left a number of messages."

"Right. I'll be by to pick it up in about an hour."

If her phone was password-protected, what about her laptop?

After waiting his turn for a good long while at the Apple Store, he finally reached the service counter. When the technician brought Juliette's Mac out to him, Charlie asked if he needed a password to access the files. He prayed the kid wouldn't tell him he needed Juliette's permission.

The tech pointed to a pink sticky note on the service order. "Right here, Mr. Dawson."

Charlie recognized Juliette's hand.

By the time he got home, he was too tired to scroll through a zillion computer files, but he did find a file containing her passwords, including one for her phone. Where had he put her phone after he charged it? He found it, dead again, in the basket on the counter. He plugged it in then unplugged himself for the night.

"Charlie, you up?"

"Hank?" He looked at his alarm clock. "It's 6:00 a.m."

"We've got a problem."

"One that can't wait a few hours?"

"Sergeant O'Neil arrested Zach Jennings last night on possession of illegal drugs."

Charlie bolted up. "What? Did he call you?"

"No, Dee did. They'll be in after she figures out how to post bail."

"Poor woman must be a wreck." He slid out of bed.

"She is. And with your way with people and all, I want you here when they get in."

"Gotcha."

His head was spinning. Charlie would've bet money this guy was clean. Of course, he would have said the same thing about his wife.

A quick shower left him enough time for a cup of coffee. Juliette's phone sat on the counter all charged. How long could it take to look through texts and listen to messages? He turned on the phone and punched in the password he'd found on the list.

There were a dozen voice messages in all. Three from him, two from the Hingham Pharmacy about a prescription; one from the bank about an overdraft; three from the Apple Store; and the last three were hang-ups from numbers he didn't recognize. Other than the overdraft, nothing stood out as alarming.

The texts were another matter altogether. He read them through once. Dazed from shock, he read them again. Fuming, he pocketed the phone and stormed out of the house.

Why would you do this, Jules? How could this happen? Who can I trust if I can't trust you?

Charlie had just joined Hank in the conference room when Dee arrived. She looked tired and a little less put-together than she normally did.

Penny had a cup of tea ready for her before Dee could take a seat.

"Thanks, Pen, I needed this."

Charlie tapped a pencil on the table "Tell us exactly what happened."

Dee took a sip then placed her cup back on the coaster. She almost exhaled her words. "Zach is innocent. He was framed."

Charlie tried to respond. "What makes you …"

Dee held her hand up to stop him. "I know what I sound like. I've heard the whispers before. 'Gullible.' 'Overprotective.' 'An enabler.' 'When will she ever learn'?"

Penny lowered her head.

"While I may have been guilty of being naïve in the past,"—she choked up—"I am one hundred percent convinced my son is innocent."

Charlie shot back. "And others are one hundred percent convinced he's guilty."

Dee's eyes filled.

Hank gave Charlie a what-was-that-about look. "Dee, help us to understand why you believe that."

Her hands wrapped around the mug. "First, they found no trace of drugs in Zach's system. For Pete's sake, he's well into his third year of being clean and sober. What more does he have to do to prove himself?"

Charlie wasn't impressed. "Maybe he was dealing."

Hank interrupted. "Dee, Charlie's playing the devil's advocate here. We've got to look at all sides."

"Then look at Zach's," Dee snapped. "O'Neil stopped him because of a broken taillight. He'd just gotten his inspection sticker on his lunch break that day, so we know the light wasn't broken then. And the car was parked in the same spot all afternoon."

Charlie drummed his fingers on the table. "He could have had a fender bender on the way home."

"No!" Dee slapped the table. "When Zach left at the end of the day, he noticed a cruiser parked around the corner from the jobsite. The car pulled out behind him as he drove by."

Zach walked through the door as his mother was speaking. "I'm pretty sure Sergeant O'Neil was waiting for me."

Charlie made eye contact with him. "Maybe she suspected you had drugs on you."

Zach took a seat near Dee. "She did more than *suspect*. She knew right where to look."

Hank asked, "What do you mean?"

"She told me to open the passenger door. The bag was in plain sight, stuck between the door and the seat." He directed a comment at Charlie. "Do you think O'Neil would go as far as planting drugs?"

Even if he thought so, Charlie wasn't about to admit that to *him*. Instead, he grilled him. "Come on, Zach, if your truck didn't move from the jobsite all afternoon, how do you explain the drugs?"

Zach's knees bounced up and down. "I can't."

"Not a very good answer." Charlie leaned in. "And I don't suppose you saw Sergeant O'Neil anywhere near your truck that day?"

"I would have told you and them if I had."

"Really?" Charlie grunted. "Like you told me you were friends with her brother, Garrett?"

"Yeah, when we were teens. What does that have to do with anything—"

"Enough!" Hank kneaded his forehead. "What job were you on yesterday?"

"Clark's garage."

"Okay, let's check with the crew to see if they saw anything. Then we'll go from there. For now, there's plenty of work to keep you busy in the warehouse."

"Thanks, Hank." Zach left the conference room without a word to Charlie.

Dee and Penny did the same.

Hank closed the door. "What's wrong with you? First, you browbeat Dee, then practically call Zach a liar. You behaved more like a prosecutor than a defense attorney."

Charlie shrugged. "A bit hard to know who to trust these days."

Hank shout-whispered, "You were the one who convinced me to hire him!"

"Yeah, well, maybe I was wrong."

"For the record, I believe the guy." Hank shook his head. "No, a person who works that hard and learns that fast can't be doing drugs and has no time to sell them."

"We'll see."

Charlie shut himself up in his office the rest of the morning. Other than reading and re-reading Juliette's texts messages, he didn't get much done. His anger festered until he could stand it no more.

He waited until Hank left then walked out back to the warehouse. "Jennings!"

Zach came around the corner. "Yes?"

"We need to talk."

Zach yanked his work gloves off. "I think I got your message loud and clear in the conference room."

"Not even close." Charlie pulled out Juliette's phone. "Tell me if any of these texts sound familiar. 'Nice to meet you, Juliette. … I've never been that open before. … It's life-changing. … When do we meet next? … Saturday night? … Can't, my husband. … You need to tell him.'"

Zach raised his hands, palms facing Charlie, then took a step forward. "You're misreading those."

"Back off! That *was* you my father-in-law saw at the state forest that day, wasn't it?"

"Yes." Zach spoke in a calm voice. "A bunch of us were hiking there that morning. I saw Juliette warming up and went over to her."

144

The knowledge that Zach had been with Juliette the day she died was too much. Charlie's head pounded, his hands balled into fists. "Did you supply her with drugs? Tell me!"

"No. Hear me out, will ya?"

"Why? So you can tell me more lies?"

Zach pulled up a sawhorse and sat. "I met your wife at the recovery program I facilitate."

Charlie stared at him but said nothing.

"I encouraged her to attend meetings regularly and get a female sponsor. Juliette had a hard time admitting she had a problem. But, after the second meeting, she recognized herself in some of the stories she'd heard from others."

The tension in Charlie's neck eased. "Are you being straight with me?"

"Yes. That morning at the state forest, she told me she planned to tell her husband everything the next day. When her father showed up, she shooed me away."

Charlie sank down on a pile of lumber.

"I had no idea Juliette was your wife until I saw her photo and read the story in the newspaper. I even came by to confirm that fact with my mother."

"I remember that." Charlie breathed evenly. "Why didn't you say something to me?"

"Maybe I should have." Zach sighed. "Over and over, I've asked myself if knowing your wife was ready to accept help would make things better or worse for you. I still don't know."

Charlie didn't know the answer either. "Well, this news certainly fills in a lot of blanks."

"I'm sorry, Charlie. The few times Juliette joined us in the recovery meetings, the one thing we learned about her was that she loved you. No room for compromise there."

"I've been a jerk, haven't I? Forgive me?"

"Done. Now, will you do something for me?"

"What?"

"*Believe* me."

"Done. Now let's prove it."

CHAPTER NINETEEN

Zach's court date was coming up fast. Hank and Charlie had lunch with him in the conference room to go over what they'd learned before he had his final meeting with his attorney.

Hank popped the top on his soda. "Unfortunately, the crew didn't see anything suspicious or anyone near your truck."

"Neither did the Clarks." Zach picked at the label on his water bottle. "They left before noon and didn't get home until late evening."

Charlie pushed some chips around his plate. "Again, why didn't we have security cameras on that jobsite?"

Hank sighed. "Because the garage was an addition to a private home." He paused for a moment, then his eyes lit up. "Wait. Do the Clarks have their own security system?"

Zach shifted in his seat. "If so, Mr. Clark never mentioned it."

Hank held a single finger in the air. "Even if they don't, in that upscale neighborhood, I bet others do."

Charlie went to Google Street View and typed in the Clarks' address. "This will give us a pretty good idea of who has a sightline to their house." He found several homeowners to contact. "Looks like a field trip's in order."

The three of them hopped into Charlie's Jeep and headed out.

Turned out, the Clarks did have a security system, but with all the comings and goings of the workmen, they'd shut the system off. Two of the neighbors had cameras, too, but they didn't cover that section of the Clarks' property.

Running low on hope, they knocked at the next house.

An older woman, maybe mid-sixties, answered the door. "How may I help you, gentlemen?"

Hank introduced himself and the others and explained their dilemma.

She smiled and held out her hand. "Ursula Nixon. I'm sorry, but my husband Bob and I only moved in a month ago. We're still researching our security options."

Zach described his personal predicament in more detail. "Anything, anything at all, you might have seen that Wednesday, sometime between one and five, could help."

"We've been so busy setting up our house we haven't been out in the yard much. I wish I could be of more assistance."

Hank and Charlie thanked Mrs. Nixon for her time, then trudged silently down her driveway.

Zach followed behind, his hands pushed deep inside his jeans pockets. "Well, we're down to my word against O'Neil's. With my history, that doesn't bode well."

Hank slowed to let Zach catch up then slapped him on the back. "We're not done yet."

They climbed back into the Jeep.

"What do you have in mind?" Charlie asked.

Hank buckled his seatbelt. "Prayer."

"Prayer?" Zach asked.

"Yes," Hank said, "and right now." He began before they could object. "Lord, we know you've got this. We've done all we can. The rest is up to you. Thank you. In Jesus name. Amen."

Both guys echoed his amen.

Charlie started the engine and began backing down the driveway.

Hank blurted, "Hold up!"

148

Mrs. Nixon was fast-walking toward them, waving and yelling. She reached their vehicle out of breath.

Hank rolled down his window. "Yes, ma'am?"

"Phew. I don't know if this will help or not, but I just remembered my grandson was here that day. He and my husband were playing with those silly drones of his. They showed me some of the footage, but I was too busy to pay attention. Maybe they got something with their cameras?"

Hank words rolled slowly out of his mouth. "Yes, praise God, maybe they did." He smiled at Charlie and Zach. "When your husband gets home, perhaps he could show us the footage?"

"He's in his workshop now. If you have time, come on in."

Bob Nixon was excited to be part of their investigation. "Despite what the missus says, these drones are not toys. The cameras yield high-resolution aerial imagery and digital elevation models. I use them in my geospatial company ... and occasionally to show off for my grandson a little."

Mr. Nixon was able to play back specific footage on a large monitor. It took an hour or so to review what they'd caught on both cameras. They were able to piece together enough to see a light-colored compact car pull off the side of the road before the Clarks' driveway.

Charlie tilted his head. "I've seen that car before. Does that model look familiar to either of you?"

Hank and Zach shook their heads.

When a tall, thin man in a green hoodie and a Pittsburg Steelers hat rolled out of the car, Charlie blurted, "Hey! That's the guy I caught cutting through my yard some weeks back."

One camera caught the culprit creeping up behind Zach's truck, planting a packet inside the passenger door, then smashing the taillight with a flashlight.

The three of them high-fived each other and shouted, "Yes!"

The second camera filmed him running back to his car. When Mr. Nixon zoomed in to get a partial plate number, they got a clear view of a girl standing outside on the driver's side.

Charlie leaned in closer. "I don't believe what I'm seeing."

"Don't believe what?" Hank said.

He stared at the frozen shot. "That's Heidi Vincent. One of Juliette's former coworkers."

Hank said, "What's the connection to Zach?"

Charlie scratched his head. "I have no idea."

Mr. Nixon gave them a copy of the files, and they drove straight to Zach's attorney's office. By the end of next day, Zach's court case had been dismissed, the police had an APB out on Heidi Vincent, and Sergeant O'Neil had been called in for questioning.

A few mornings later, Charlie and Zach approached Kyle's cruiser as it pulled into Dawson-Landau's parking lot.

Kyle lowered his window. "O'Neil claims she got an anonymous tip about the drugs in your vehicle."

Charlie snorted. "And Chief Eason believes her?"

"She may not be the most popular cop on the force, but she's got a good record." Kyle shrugged. "He has no reason to think she'd lie."

Charlie noticed Zach hadn't reacted. "You're kind of quiet. What's on your mind?"

"I've been thinking," Zach said. "O'Neil wasn't so bad before her brother died. And in the year right after I got out of the army, she had plenty of legitimate reasons and chances to arrest me. So why now?"

Charlie nodded. "So, you think she might be telling the truth about the anonymous tip?"

Zach shrugged. "Well, we know she didn't plant the drugs, but she did know where to look."

"Maybe I can get a few more details out of her." Kyle laughed. "That's if she's talking to me."

Kyle drove away, and Zach went off to load trucks with Artie and Hank at the warehouse.

Charlie's mind was ready to explode. He felt like a pile of building materials had been dumped on his desk, and he'd been told to design a house using them—Juliette's secret addiction and Zach's efforts to help her. O'Neil's anger and bitterness and the anonymous tip. Heidi Vincent's lies and her connection to the guy he saw in his yard and the break-in at his house.

Are these random acts connected? If so, how?

CHAPTER TWENTY

Charlie pulled up to the curb in front of Best Foot Forward where Sarah met him outside with a rolling cart. He opened the back hatch to get at the jackets and coats he'd found stored in their cedar closet.

"Hope I'm not too early dropping winter things off."

"Unlike men, women like to shop a season *ahead*. Besides, my best friend had excellent taste. Our women will be so grateful."

After they filled the cart, he shut the back of his vehicle. "Hey, I thought you closed at noon on Saturdays?"

Sarah grinned. "We do, but your mother-in-law has a private fitting with a client."

"Really? Didn't know you did that."

"It was Natalie's idea. Some women can use the extra attention. Besides, I think being needed helps her."

"I can understand that. Well, I'll let you get back to—"

"Sarah! Charlie!" Ashlyn Reid crossed to their side of the street.

"Ashlyn, I almost didn't recognize you away from our usual Vine Hills setting." Her baby bump was more like a hill now. "How's everything with you and little Master Reid?"

"Great! But he's not so little anymore." She smiled as she placed a hand on her belly. "And he has a name. James Luke."

He nodded. "A good solid one too." *Much like the ones Juliette and I had picked out.*

"I wanted to keep it simple and classic. My husband, Roman, used to tell me he never wanted a junior. His mother, Marlena, came from a long line of soap opera fans. *Days of Our Lives,* I think."

Charlie laughed. "I see."

Ashlyn's face lit up as she turned to Sarah. "Oh, guess what? In a few weeks, I start those Lamaze classes you told me about. Jillian, my boss-turned-friend, offered to be my coach."

"That's wonderful!" Sarah hugged her. "Sounds like your baby boy is off to a good start already."

Ashlyn smiled as she adjusted her shoulder bag. "Well, I don't want to keep Natalie waiting. Thanks again for calling me when the maternity clothes came in. I'm outgrowing everything."

"We're pleased to help," Sarah said. "Tell Natalie I'll join you in a minute."

"Sure thing." She smiled at Charlie. "Good to see you again."

He nodded. "You take care now."

As soon as Ashlyn entered the shop, Sarah whispered, "Just so happens that a half a dozen maternity outfits came in yesterday … all the right size … all with sales tags … all from Natalie's car. She even told Ashlyn she'd do alterations, if necessary."

"Do you think Ashlyn knows?"

"That girl doesn't have a suspicious bone in her body."

"Guess I had a pretty good mother-in-law, huh?"

Sarah tilted her head. "You still do, Charlie."

Instead of going to Vine Hills like he usually did most Saturday afternoons, Charlie found himself on Rocky Pond Road, heading to Myles Standish State Forest. Three months to the day had passed since he'd lost Juliette. He finally felt ready to visit the place where she'd fallen, maybe died.

He exited his Jeep and headed down the trail. Streaks of sun dappled the path, the leafy trees doing their best to add shade, but it was August after all. As he padded along the path, still damp from the previous day's rain, he recalled the colonel saying the spot was a quarter mile up. His stomach clenched with each step he took. What did he hope to find there? Closure? Evidence? Understanding?

What he hadn't counted on finding was the colonel, sitting on a blanket off to the side. He stopped short, not sure whether to proceed, but his father-in-law saw him.

"Charlie! I didn't know you came here."

"First time." He pretended not to see the man wipe his eyes. He'd never seen him cry, not even at the wake or the funeral.

"Have a seat." The colonel moved over a bit.

When Charlie sat, he recognized the blanket as the quilt Juliette had carried around as a child. "Does Natalie know you have this?"

"Her idea, actually." He looked around the area. "Visiting this place overwhelms her, so I come alone and do my thinking. I wanted to set a granite bench here in Juliette's memory, but the State has rules against private memorials. They wouldn't even let us plant a tree."

"In a state forest?"

"I know, right? You'd think complying with regulations would be easy for me. Not so in this case."

A few moments of silence followed until the colonel said, "My daughter was a wonderful girl. She never would've let her problem go on too long. She was stubborn, like me, probably thought she could handle things on her own."

"I remember Juliette saying, 'Why don't addicts just stop?' She never did understand the aspects of addiction. This whole thing must have caught her off guard."

"Ignorance wasn't so much her problem as pride," the colonel said. "Everyone needs help."

Had those words come out of colonel? Before Charlie could stop himself, he said, "Even you?"

His father-in-law made eye contact. "Especially me."

Charlie absorbed the moment. "I learned something big recently. Juliette had been to a couple of drug recovery meetings and was getting ready to tell us." He filled him in about Zach's role in all that.

The colonel yanked a clump of weeds out of the ground. "Guess I had that guy all wrong too."

"We both did."

The older man rested his arms across his knees. "This is the exact spot where I performed CPR on my daughter until the EMTs arrived. Yet, every time I come here, I go over and over every second, asking myself if I could have done more. The haunting never ends."

Charlie felt guilty for having wondered the same thing. "You know, in the early weeks, I didn't want people preaching to me about God's timing and sovereignty. Now, those very truths are what help me cope. He's got a plan for all of us, and that was his for Juliette. We don't have to like it."

I sure don't.

On their walk back down the trail, Charlie decided to trust his father-in-law with his concerns. "Colonel, there are some things about Juliette's case I don't understand. Nothing will change the outcome, but I've got this gut feeling I'm missing something, that I should do more."

"Gut feelings have their place. Go on."

Charlie told him about Heidi Vincent, her male cohort and their lies, the drugs planted in Zach's truck, and Sergeant O'Neil's harassment. "And remember the break-in at my house? I think all these events are connected, but I'm not sure how. Kyle thinks so too."

"Maybe my intelligence training can be of service. Why don't the three of us meet? You set the day and time since you've got your hands full at work."

"You're right about that. Mostly with one gigantic thorn-in-my-side client."

The colonel's eyes widened. "Speaking of clients, I mentioned your Oliver Quinlan to an old West Point crony. He says he's a likable chap who's done quite well for himself in the financial arena."

"He's done well financially," Charlie grumbled, "but I have to disagree with the 'likable' part."

The colonel chuckled. "Is he the thorn you referred to? Maybe if I spoke to him, one West Point man to another."

Charlie grimaced. "Not sure that's a good idea, sir. If he knows I've been complaining about him, finishing his house won't be pleasant."

"Speaking of houses," his father-in-law said, "looks like Natalie and I cleared out just in time. Your demo crew has already torn through our place."

"Yes, you can trust Hank to stick to the schedule."

"I know we can." The colonel laughed. "We wouldn't have hired you otherwise, family or no family."

Mid-week, Charlie went by his in-law's jobsite. Now that the first floor was gutted, finalizing the floor plans would be easier. With the house situated high on a hill overlooking Widgeon Pond, the view from the framed second story would be panoramic.

Though the house was a third the size of the Quinlan's testimony to an overinflated ego, there was enough square footage to accommodate four decent-sized bedrooms and a large open kitchen and living room space. Charlie had always dreamed of living on the water.

Perfect place to raise a family. Maybe two or three kids. We could build a playroom in the basement and a guest suite in the attic—"

We? What was he thinking? He kicked a stray chunk of wood. *Why'd you have to go and spoil everything, Jules?*

CHAPTER TWENTY-ONE

If Charlie were going to hang out with Juliette at Vine Hills on the weekends, he'd need to get there before the sun was high. With so few shade trees, the sun could be brutal.

He recalled the wide-brimmed, straw hat Juliette had insisted he buy on their trip to Bermuda. He'd scoffed at first, refusing to wear it. Once he'd accepted the hat was more about function than fashion, he hadn't taken it off.

Where had Juliette stored their vacation duds? He chuckled to himself. *Shouting man's wife found his bowling shirt. Maybe I should ask Jules.*

After checking the closets in the guest suite and the spare bedrooms, he remembered Sarah asking him what she should do with the smaller articles of clothing she'd found after the break-in. He found a large canvas bin in the master walk-in, filled with hats, scarves, mittens, and gloves. He dumped the contents on the floor. No straw hat.

When he began separating Juliette's things from his, he found items with no match: a rainbow toe sock, a pink leg warmer, and a Pittsburg Steelers glove. He could sort of understand the rainbow sock and the leg warmer, but why a Steelers glove in Patriots country? The glove wasn't his, that was for sure.

A picture flashed in Charlie's mind: the black and gold Steelers' gloves sticking out of the back pocket of Heidi's Vincent's accomplice. Could this glove prove he was the one who broke into his house?

Tossing his stuff back in the bin, he bagged everything that'd belonged to Juliette. He threw a few odd items in the trash but stored the glove for safekeeping. He'd talk to Kyle about his find at dinner that night.

With an hour remaining before he was due at Kyle and Sarah's, Charlie walked around Plymouth Harbor. With multiple restaurants close by, he didn't know where the scent of salt air ended and the smell of fried seafood began. No matter, he liked them both.

More tourists than usual filled the streets. Plymouth's 400th birthday added to the buzz. He joined the crowds as he climbed Cole's Hill to pay his respects to the early Pilgrims buried there and to Massasoit, Great Sachem of the Wampanoags, whose statue stood at the crest of the hill. He walked across Water Street for his millionth peek at Plymouth Rock then stared out at the refurbished sixty-year-old replica of the *Mayflower*.

As he took to the sidewalk along the jagged stone seawall, his eyes were drawn to a woman jogging in and out of shoppers across the street. Her running gear and pink Red Sox cap reminded him of Juliette. She even had the same height, build, and coloring.

Intrigued, he followed her on his side of the street. He slowed when she slowed and sped up when she picked up her pace. Her profile was identical to Juliette's. Mesmerized, he had to see her face full on. Ignoring the cars that honked as he zigzagged across the street, his heart thumped with his every step. The more he gained on her, the more out of breath he became.

This woman *needed* to be Juliette. He refused to think about his wife being dead. Lost in obsession, he argued with his left brain: *What if her death was a nightmare? Even if it wasn't, God's capable of sending her back, isn't he?*

Everything in him cried *If only I could touch her, hold her, and smell her again!* More and more convinced, he called out after her, "Juliette! Wait!"

When he reached the spot where he'd seen her last, she was gone. Frantic, he searched in shops and around corners, to no avail.

What's wrong with me?

Charlie was still numb when he knocked at Kyle and Sarah's later.

"Door's open!" Kyle yelled.

He entered without saying a word, his brain still stuck in disappointment.

"Charlie?" Kyle said. "You okay?"

Sarah moved a pot off a burner, then came over and hugged him. "What's wrong?" She pulled a chair out. "Sit. You look like you've just seen a ghost."

His mind snapped shut. "No, just tired." He wasn't ready to accept Kyle and Sarah's logical explanation of what had happened to him.

"One strong cup of coffee coming up," Sarah said.

"No falling asleep over dinner." Kyle grabbed three plates. "We've been slaving away to impress you with our gourmet creations."

Charlie pretended not to see the empty Stouffer's containers sticking out of the kitchen trash. "I'm sure dinner'll be great." Then, storing his unnerving experience in a safe place, he changed topics. "I bumped into the colonel over at the state forest near where Juliette … fell. We had a good talk."

"I'm impressed," Kyle said. "Sounds like things are thawing between you two."

"Seem to be." It was sad that it took Juliette's death to effect that change. "I told him about Heidi Vincent, O'Neil, and Zach. He even offered to help us investigate."

Sarah grabbed her oven mitts. "How?"

"Not sure exactly," Charlie said, "but he mentioned his military intelligence background."

"Seriously?" Kyle stood at attention. "Will we have to salute him too?"

Sarah placed the hot dish on a trivet before she whacked her husband with a mitt. "Be nice and say grace."

Kyle did as he was told.

"Who knows?" Charlie shrugged. "Maybe he'll see something we missed."

"I suppose his need to be involved is understandable," Kyle said. "Besides you, me, and the colonel, who else should we include?"

Sarah put down her fork, then dabbed her lips with a napkin.

Charlie nudged Kyle's boot under the table. "Other than Sarah, you mean?"

"Goes without saying." Kyle took his foot out of his mouth to make room for a roll.

"I was thinking of asking Ted and Binnie since she spends a lot of time with O'Neil on the task force." Charlie looked from Sarah to Kyle. "And what do you guys think about Zach?"

Sarah nodded. "I'm sure he's anxious to get to the bottom of O'Neil's harassment."

"And he might be able to give us an insider's view into the local drug scene." Kyle switched gears. "Speaking of O'Neil, I talked to an older woman who used to live next door to her family. Glenna claims she was raised in Plymouth, but the woman said the O'Neils didn't move here from Peabody until Glenna was around fifteen."

"Peabody's a good sixty miles north of Plymouth." Sarah put the empty dinner plates in the sink. "Why would someone lie about where they were raised?"

"A variety of reasons, I suppose." Kyle shrugged. "But I don't know why Glenna would."

"Did the woman say anything else?" Charlie asked.

"Just that the O'Neils mostly kept to themselves early on. Once their son was born, she'd chat with Mrs. O'Neil, even Glenna, when they took him for a walk. Eventually, the two women became good friends."

"Nothing strange about that." Charlie sipped his coffee. "I don't know some of my neighbors, and I've lived in the same house all my life."

Kyle's forehead creased. "You're right, but something's a little off. I just don't know what yet."

Sarah scooped strawberry ice cream into three bowls and placed them on the table. "Kyle, do you remember my father's cousin, Trudy?"

"Uh? Why? Am I supposed to?"

"You met her at my family reunion a few years back. Anyway, she lives in Peabody and works at the town offices—at least she did—but I'm not sure what department. Maybe she could help."

He leaned over and kissed her on the cheek. "I knew you'd make a good member of our team."

"Your wife's a treasure, Kyle. And you weren't even treasure-hunting when you found her. What are the chances?"

"Chances?" Kyle winked at Sarah. "More like divine intervention."

Sarah laughed. "Besides, *I* found *him*."

She tried calling Trudy after dinner but got no answer. "I left a message. I'm sure she'll get back to me."

Charlie had stayed late at the office all week. First, because he was afraid he'd see Juliette again. Second, he was afraid he wouldn't. Third, he needed to keep his mind occupied until he and the others got together to pool their information. They'd agreed to meet after Labor Day at Binnie and Ted's. If anyone asked about their group, they decided to refer to it as a "search committee."

Now, seated at his kitchen counter, he jotted down random facts about all those involved, wondering how or if they fit together. After a few hours of this, he pushed his paperwork aside and piled a week's worth of newspapers on top of Juliette's Mac to make room for his ten o'clock bowl of Cheerios.

I should probably cancel the paper if I'm not going to read it.

While munching, he scanned the latest edition, not focusing on anything in particular: *Senate budget aims to collect $300 million in new revenue. Authorities drag river for missing dog. Plymouth boasts decrease in drug trafficking.*

He muttered, "And I'm sure Quinlan's taking all the credit."

Disgusted at the depressing news, he got up and tossed the unread stack in the recycle bin and vowed to cancel the paper the next day.

Back at the counter, he stared at Juliette's computer and wondered why he still hadn't looked through her files.

What am I afraid to find?

CHAPTER TWENTY-TWO

This obsession to *see* Juliette again needed to stop. The thing was, he didn't want it to. Ever since that day downtown, he'd been looking for her everywhere. Since he felt close to Juliette at the cemetery, now his early morning visits to her grave boosted his hopes. After all, if she was going to show herself again, why not there?

This morning was no different, only hotter. He sat in his chair by her plot. "Jules, could that have been you I saw? Did I ruin everything by trying to hold on? Are you trying to tell me something? Will you show yourself again? Am I crazy?"

"We're all crazy, aren't we?"

Charlie jumped up. "Ashlyn! You caught me talking out loud again."

"Nothing I don't do myself. At least you weren't shouting." She smiled briefly then fanned herself with both hands. "Outright sweltering today, as my granny used to say."

"Sure is. But when winter gets here, I'll complain about the cold."

She rested her hands on her belly. "I've got four and a half months to go before I meet my son. All I know is some days the wait seems like forever."

"James Luke, right?" Charlie wondered what waiting for a son would be like. "And everything's good?"

"We're both fine, thanks." She got a faraway look in her eyes. "Roman died not knowing he was going to be a father. I wanted to wait until I was a little further along before I told him. One of my biggest regrets."

"Do you know for sure he doesn't know now?" Why did he ask that?

She tilted her head. "Do you think he does?"

"I don't know. I guess I'd like to think so." Charlie wanted to make her feel better, but he also wanted to believe. "Can I get your chair for you?"

She checked the time on her phone. "No, I can't stay long. I have to be at work early today."

"The party decorating company?"

"Same one. Partyscapes. My boss, Jillian, even lightened my work duties so I can work throughout my pregnancy."

"That's good." Charlie chuckled. "Not that I'd know, since I've never been pregnant."

And Juliette and I never will be.

When he refocused on Ashlyn, she seemed distracted. "Why don't you take my seat for a minute? I need to stretch my legs."

She sat without protesting. "Charlie, may I tell you something?"

"Sure."

"You might think I'm crazy."

"Yes, I will, because we're all crazy, right?"

She half-smiled then looked down at her hands in her lap. "I saw my husband yesterday … on a motorcycle. I chased him and even got mad at him for leaving me." She tugged at her coat again. "Has that ever happened to you with your wife?"

He breathed in deeply then exhaled. "Yes. Last week. Except my wife was jogging past Plymouth Rock."

She peered at him. "Are you just saying that to make me feel better?"

"No, I'm not." He scuffed his shoe against a clump of dead grass. "That's what I was just talking to her about."

166

"I felt like I'd lost him all over again."

"I know." He nudged her shoulder with his arm, then worried he'd been too familiar. "At least now, we're not going crazy alone."

She smiled. "Thanks, Charlie."

He put his hands in his pockets, glad to have made her smile.

"I miss the silliest things about being married." She shook her head. "Like having someone to scratch my back."

"I miss not hearing Juliette sing in the shower. She never could carry a tune. Always made me laugh."

For a moment, they sat in the quiet of their thoughts. Just as Ashlyn stood to leave, Shouting-Man showed up.

The quick and stocky rumpled man walked over to them. "Hey, folks, I apologize for talking so loud when I come to visit the wife. That woman is as deaf as she is stubborn. Refused to get a hearing aid."

Charlie muddled through his response. "No, uh, problem."

Ashlyn, wide-eyed, nodded like she understood.

The man tromped toward his wife's grave. "I'm comin', Peaches. Hold your horses."

Charlie led Ashlyn to her car before their resolve gave way to laughter.

She whispered, "I don't feel so crazy after all."

Charlie smiled. "Yes, I'm pretty sure we're doing just fine."

CHAPTER TWENTY-THREE

Holidays weekends only meant Charlie had three days to fill instead of two. Labor Day weekend was no different. Thankfully, Grams and Pop opted to work in their yard, and Matt had Edy's attention, so Saturday and Sunday passed without pressure. Other than a cookout at Kyle and Sarah's on Monday, Charlie's only plan was to visit the cemetery.

In the early morning hours at Juliette's grave, Charlie sensed his former notion of grief wasn't accurate. People talked about "processing it," "getting through it," and "overcoming it." After almost four months of pain, he felt like Sisyphus, rolling an immense boulder up a hill, only to have it roll back down on him. Under the weight, Charlie wondered if he would endure this grief forever.

That conclusion didn't upset him. Maybe because the pain felt more like a tribute to Juliette's worth.

Is that normal, Lord?

The following day, a cross-section of society—a minister and his wife, an ex-military man, a former drug user, a cop, Juliette's best friend, and Charlie—gathered at the Westfalls' home at seven p.m. They had two things in common—their faith and their desire to connect the dots of their case—or cases.

The table was set up with legal pads, pencils, and coffee cups. A large, magnetic whiteboard, borrowed from a Sunday school classroom, straddled the opening between the dining and living rooms.

Once coffee was served, Ted opened in prayer. "Lord, we're ignorant and confused. But you know everything. Please help us understand what's happened. If there are connections to be made, help us make them. If we have misconceptions, reveal them to us. Let us make no assumptions based on our feelings. Reveal the truth for your glory. Amen."

Everyone echoed "Amen."

Binnie stood in front of the whiteboard. "Since I was invited to be part of this group because of my experience on the task force, I thought we could start with some concept mapping."

Sarah raised her hand. "Could you please explain what that is?"

Charlie was glad someone asked.

"No problem," Binnie said. "I didn't know either until I joined the task force. In concept mapping, you organize facts and ideas on a particular topic in circles or squares. Once you find how they connect, you link them with a line." She held up a graphic with connecting circles. "Here's a sample. We should have something like this when we're done."

Zach readied his pencil. "Sorta like connect the dots. Cool."

Sarah, with her hand up again. "And our main focus is on …?"

Kyle said, "Did I mention my wife was an A student in school?"

Binnie uncapped a blue marker and wrote "Curious Incidents" at the top of the board. "Throw out your concerns, no matter how strange they seem. I'll put them in circles while you jot them down on the legal pads to refer to after our meeting."

Charlie glanced at the notes he'd been keeping. "Sergeant O'Neil blames me for Juliette's taking drugs. Why? Heidi Vincent, Juliette's coworker, lied to me. Why? Then she and a male accomplice, the same guy I caught in my yard, planted drugs in Zach's truck. Why again?"

Binnie scribbled as fast as she could.

"Who hired them to plant the drugs?" Zach looked at the board. "Does it have anything to do with O'Neil blaming me for her brother's death?"

"And who called in the anonymous tip?" Kyle asked.

The colonel sat quietly studying the board.

"I don't know if this has to do with drugs," Sarah said, "but why would Glenna O'Neil lie about where she was raised?"

Ted shook his head. "What has made that poor woman so bitter?"

Binnie added, "And does her staunch support of anti-drug lord, Oliver Quinlan, stem from guilt about her brother's death?"

"Another thing," Kyle said, "how does the break-in at Charlie's house fit?"

In rapid succession, three dots connected in Charlie's mind. One, Heidi's odd behavior the day she dropped Juliette's box off at his office—the box she must have stolen from Juliette's SUV. Two, the gold and black gloves sticking out of the back pocket of the guy in his yard. Three, the alien Pittsburgh Steelers glove he'd found in his closet. "I'm pretty sure this guy is the same one who broke into my house while Heidi distracted me."

Binnie was quickly running out of space. "I'm gonna need a bigger board."

Sarah bit her lip. "I saw that glove when I was helping you put the house back together. I should have said—"

"How would you have known?" Charlie asked.

Kyle squeezed his wife's hand. "Only a matter of time before we pick her and her partner up. Logic tells me neither of them is the head of any drug cartel. They'll talk if the DA offers them a deal."

Charlie remembered something else. "Kyle, the police might want to look in Dormont, a suburb of Pittsburgh. When I searched for Heidi Vincent's phone number, I found that name in connection to a Paul Vincent in the area."

His father-in-law rubbed his arms. "What does any of this have to do with my daughter's death?"

"We don't know that it does, Colonel." Binnie capped her marker. "But we need your analytical skills."

The colonel sat up straighter in his chair. "I'm sorry. Sometimes the frustration is too much to handle."

An hour passed with no one making any more definitive connections. Circles covered the board, but all Charlie could see were questions. The others were quiet—he suspected they felt the same.

Ted pushed back his chair. "Unless anyone has anything else, I say we break for tonight and get back together in a few weeks."

"One other thing." The colonel stood. "Until we know what we're looking for and who we can trust, I suggest we avoid sharing what we learn with anyone outside this room." He looked from Kyle to Binnie. "Including members of the local police and the drug task forces."

Binnie nodded. "I agree."

"Me, too," Kyle said. "Especially since O'Neil is on both."

Around mid-morning the next Saturday, Charlie sat peeling an orange at the counter when his kitchen door flew open, and Kyle walked in. "Hey, what'd ya do with that stash?"

"Do come in, please." He continued peeling. "I'm gonna have to start locking my door."

Kyle didn't react to his crack. "The pills you hid in your garage, what'd you do with them?"

Charlie thought for a second. *Argh!* How could he have forgotten about the bag he'd stuffed in the potting soil? "Uh, they're still in the same spot."

"I was hoping you'd say that. We might be able to trace the dealer by looking at the tablets. Drug dealers like to brand their product much like any other manufacturer or distributor."

"You mean like Pfizer or Bayer?"

"Exactly." Kyle grabbed an orange out of the refrigerator.

"How're you going to explain those pills to the chief? And won't O'Neil wonder where they came from?"

"I have another source. Remember Theo, the DEA agent I met at the conference in New York?"

"Isn't he the guy I met at Blue Lobster with you?"

"That's him," Kyle said. "He's a drug specialist, so to speak. One I can trust. He offered to look at the drugs for us—on the QT."

"Yet another piece to the puzzle." Charlie stepped into the garage and pushed the button to close the door. "Can't be too careful. O'Neil's probably spying on us from a rooftop across the street." He dug in the potting soil then handed the plastic bag to Kyle. "Hope you don't get in trouble over this."

"Me, too. I like getting a paycheck." Kyle pulled a Styrofoam cooler down from a shelf. "Can I borrow this to transport the stuff?"

"Keep it." Charlie knew he'd never see the cooler again anyway.

Kyle placed the bag inside the cooler and covered it with ice from Charlie's freezer. "Oh, speaking of O'Neil, Sarah's cousin Trudy called back. Found out something interesting. Turns out she knew the O'Neils from church."

"How's that interesting?"

"The O'Neil family's move out of Peabody was sudden. When Trudy heard they'd settled in Plymouth and had another baby, she was shocked."

"Why?" Charlie asked. "Families move, and women have babies all the time."

"Yes, they do." Kyle clicked his tongue. "But women don't have babies five years after they've had a hysterectomy."

"What?"

"Trudy was a member of the women's guild. They provided meals for the family when Mrs. O'Neil was recuperating from her surgery."

Charlie pieced his thoughts together. "Do you think the baby was Glenna's? Didn't you say she was only fifteen when they moved here?"

"Hey, things happen. Until we know more, what we have now is just speculation."

Charlie scratched his day-old whiskers, pleased with his new plan not to shave on weekends. "Sure would explain a lot about Glenna's behavior, though."

"I know." Kyle whipped his phone out and called Theo. They made plans for the handoff.

The call over, Charlie asked, "Where're you meeting him?"

"At an independent lab he uses in Groton, Connecticut. They should be able to tell us something in a few weeks."

"Again, this will lead us to the dealer?"

"I'm not sure," Kyle said," but something tells me this trail's worth following."

When Kyle left, Charlie drove to Vine Hills, wanting to share what was happening with Juliette.

When he got in his car, a bag stuffed under the front passenger seat caught his attention. His memory failed him—he looked inside—the bamboo backscratcher he'd bought on a whim in the odd lots store after his last conversation with Ashlyn.

Without overthinking the gift or her reaction, he walked over and leaned the bag against Roman Reid's gravestone.

CHAPTER TWENTY-FOUR

Charlie switched his phone to his other ear so he could finish gathering his notes. "I'll be there in five, Vanetta."

He rushed past Penny's desk, her matching purple highlights and polka dot glasses catching his eye. "I'm on my way into the lion's den. Pray I make it out alive."

"Quinlan?" She checked her calendar. "You're not scheduled to leave for another hour."

He shrugged. "Vanetta wants what she wants when she wants it." On his way out the door, he called back, "By the way, tell your twins the purple's my favorite look so far."

Penny's smile made him feel like he'd done a good thing.

Charlie pulled his Jeep onto the Quinlan jobsite. Vanetta's Escalade was there, but no sign of Oliver's none-too-subtle metallic-gold Mercedes-Benz S-Class Maybach. With any luck, he'd be spared the man's pomposity this morning.

He climbed the temporary steps and entered the cavernous foyer. Above the din of a half a dozen subcontractors, he called out, "Morning, Vanetta!"

The reed-thin woman entered on spiked heels. Her straight black hair was tucked behind perfect ears, causing it to flip under her perfect chin. "Oh, good, you're on time."

No point reminding her he was early. "Will Oliver be joining us?"

"No, he's working."

Pure curiosity got the best of Charlie. "Where exactly is his office anyway?"

Vanetta's lips pursed. "As Oliver is given to say, 'To make money in wealth management, you go to your clients, they don't come to you.'"

"I see." Sounded nothing like the Oliver he knew.

She crossed her arms. "I want to talk about flooring."

"Sure." Charlie perused the spacious entry. "Why don't we start here? What material did you have in mind for the foyer?"

"A collection of 16th century Italian Renaissance era marble." She pointed to a page in a high-end design magazine. "Although similar to this pattern, my design will be original."

Original. Of course. Charlie estimated the marble flooring she wanted might cost as much as Oliver's Mercedes.

"And I don't care about cost."

Had she read his mind?

She crossed her arms again. "I won't be cheated like I was in Texas."

"They weren't able to get the marble you wanted there?"

"They got the marble all right, but I never got to move in to enjoy it."

"So, your move north was unexpected?"

Vanetta stiffened, then waved his comment away. "Let's get back on topic." Her footsteps echoed as she paraded across the plywood underlayment to the main living room. "Other than the kitchen and baths, I want Brazilian mahogany, maybe walnut, throughout. I'm going to commission a mosaic artist to do the guest baths, but I haven't decided on the flooring for the master bath or kitchen yet."

Charlie looked up from his notepad. "I'll send my rep over with some samples. We need to get this ordered as soon as possible if we're to make the deadline."

She did a sharp about-face. "My husband may be concerned with deadlines, but I care more about the work being done right. *Capiche?*"

178

"Then we're on the same page, Vanetta." Charlie pocketed his pen. "Are we good for now?"

A voice bellowed from the front door. "No, we're not good!"

Charlie held back a cringe. *So close.* "What can I do for you, Oliver?"

Oliver stomped the dust off his shoes. "What's going on with that investigation?"

"What investigation?" Charlie feigned ignorance.

"That couple who planted drugs in the druggie's truck?"

Charlie ignored his slur. "I'm not privy to police matters. You being on the drug task force and all, don't you have access to that sort of information?"

Oliver rocked on his heels. "You're right, I do. But it doesn't hurt to check with all my sources."

I'm one of your sources? I don't think so.

Vanetta took her husband's arm. "Charlie and I have the flooring all worked out. You're going to love it."

He huffed. "And if I don't?"

She gave him a saccharine smile. "Then one of us will have to be twice as happy."

Charlie made his exit before he got zapped by the static he could feel building.

On his way back to the office, Kyle called. "Guess who got nabbed crossing into Pennsylvania? Mass staties are on their way to pick 'em up."

Charlie whistled. "Really? Both Heidi and the boyfriend?"

"Yeah, but turns out the guy's her brother. His name's Paul like the father in the phone listing you gave us."

"Keepin' it in the family, I see. Got anything else?"

"Won't know much for a day or so, but I'll keep you in the loop."

"Thanks. Do you think we should schedule another meeting at Ted and Binnie's?"

"Probably, but let's wait a week. Donnie and Marie should be singin' by then."

CHAPTER TWENTY-FIVE

A week later, Charlie and his fellow search committee members held their second meeting.

"Before we get settled around the table," Binnie said, "a friend on the Massachusetts drug task force sent me some maps of the drug activity in the eastern half of the state. I thought maybe we could compare that data with that of our town."

Two maps of Plymouth were side by side on the large bulletin board in Ted's study. While the group examined them, Ted and Binnie tacked up the two new state maps.

Binnie looked from the town to the state. "Comparatively, it looks like our town's doing pretty well."

Kyle studied the board. "From what I can see, the overall drug traffic hasn't decreased."

"I beg to differ." Binnie stepped forward. "Look at these two town maps, dated a few months apart. You'll see a definite decrease in drug activity in Plymouth."

"In Plymouth, yes." The colonel pointed to the state task force maps. "There seems to be a direct correlation between the decrease in drug operations in Plymouth and the increase in neighboring towns like Wareham, Carver, Plympton, and Kingston. This is a standard military tactic to push the enemies back. It skews the numbers and offers nothing more than a temporary victory."

"The colonel's right." Kyle ran his finger along the town line. "You can even see the traffic moving across into Duxbury."

Binnie's eyes narrowed. "Are you saying we're pushing drug traffic into other towns?"

The colonel took his glasses off. "I'm not accusing anyone, but according to these maps, that's exactly what's happening."

Kyle crossed his arms and stared at the board. "Colonel, do you think this is a tactic rather than a result?"

"I can't say for sure." He traced the town line with his index finger. "But this sure looks like someone knows what they're doing."

Zach spoke for the first time that evening. "And whoever they are think they're too smart to get caught."

Charlie said, "Like who?"

"Someone who wants to scare away competition," Kyle said.

The colonel eyed Zach. "Someone bent on pointing suspicion over the town line."

"Are you talking about Glenna O'Neil?" Ted said.

Sarah sat up straight. "Let's tread carefully. A person's reputation is at stake."

"I agree," Kyle said, "We treat her no differently than we do anyone else whose name is on our board."

The group adjourned to the dining room and got back to their whiteboard mapping.

Ted asked, "Does anyone have anything new to report?"

Kyle raised his hand. "Heidi Vincent and her brother Paul are in custody. Once the Assistant District Attorney offered them a plea bargain, they didn't stop talking."

"Why would he do that?" Charlie sputtered. "You had 'em dead to right on video, planting drugs in Zach's car."

"What they gave the ADA was worth more. Besides, they're first-time offenders. They admitted they'd had a little side business in Plymouth. Her exact words were, 'We didn't make enough money to write home about.' Then an anonymous person offered to help them relocate. Heidi's words, 'It wasn't an offer we could refuse.' That person's been pulling the strings ever since."

Kyle reported how Heidi confessed to stealing the box of office items from the back of Juliette's Rav4 and to stalling Charlie while Paul broke into his house. She'd claimed they were instructed to make the break-in look like they were after drugs. "According to her, the boss just wanted to make sure Juliette didn't have information that could lead back to him."

Charlie sat forward. "I didn't find anything like that."

"Neither did they," Kyle said. "Heidi said she wasn't even sure what they were looking for."

Zach asked, "Did she give them a name?"

"She claims she has no idea," Kyle said. "Every time the person called, the number was blocked, and they used one of those voice changer apps. Our tech team is on it."

Binnie tried to get as much on the whiteboard as she could.

"Okay, outside of Heidi and her brother, anything else?" Ted said.

Charlie tapped his pencil on his pad. "We discovered a few discrepancies in Glenna's background story."

The colonel swiveled in his chair. "Does it pertain to our case or cases?"

"Not really," Sarah broke in. "It's mostly about her personal life. Besides, it might just be gossip."

Kyle said, "Sarah's right. We need verification before—"

The doorbell rang.

Binnie looked at her husband. "We're not waiting on anyone else. Who could that be?"

"I'll find out." He walked down the hall and opened the door. "Glenna! What a surprise."

"Mind if I come in?"

"Actually, we're in the middle of a meeting right—"

"I'll just say hi. I'm sure they won't mind." She walked down the hall and took a left into the dining room, Ted on her heels.

"Sergeant O'Neil," Binnie said. "I hope your uniform doesn't suggest this is official business."

"Nah, just driving by. I recognized most of the cars, so I thought I'd drop in, you know, with your doors always being open and all." She looked at the faces around the table, then put her hand out to the colonel. "I don't believe we've met, sir."

He stood to shake hands. "Colonel Wickford Annandale, retired."

"Good to meet you, sir, and thank you for your service." She turned to Zach. "Didn't know you attended this church, Jennings."

Zach let his words out slowly. "I didn't until recent events convinced me there are good people here."

Charlie held his tongue.

Glenna grunted then chin-nodded to the whiteboard. "So, what's going on?"

A list of missionaries and the countries they serve were displayed on the whiteboard. Quick-thinking Binnie had flipped the board the instant Ted had spoken Glenna's name at the door.

"The church missions committee has to decide which missionaries to support." Ted crossed his arms loosely. "We can't afford to help them all, but we've narrowed the list down to the families serving in Nigeria, Papua New Guinea, Bolivia, and Cameroon."

He wasn't lying. The whole church knew that's exactly what the missions committee was doing.

"Looks like you could use some rich parishioners," Glenna said. "Charlie, why don't you work on getting Oliver Quinlan to join your church? He's got as much money as he does good ideas."

Binnie put her hands on her hips. "Now, Sergeant, you don't really believe we'd go after members based on their bank accounts, do you?"

"Maybe you should. Besides, isn't that what you people call 'good stewardship'?" Glenna chuckled then motioned to the board again. "Oliver's a problem-solver. His ideas have gone a long way to rid Plymouth of drug trafficking. The numbers don't lie."

Right. Charlie couldn't resist a dig. "Speaking of Oliver, he asked me how the investigation was coming along ... you know, the one where you were fed the false tip about Zach?"

Zach turned to Glenna. "Yeah, I saw on the news they caught the two responsible. Anything you can tell us?"

"Afraid not." She hung her thumbs on her utility belt. "Private police business." She glared at Kyle. "And you'd do well to remember that, Yates."

Sarah looked all innocent. "Private? I thought the Plymouth Police Department was run by the town. Wouldn't that make it public?"

Kyle turned to his wife. "Sarah, you know Sergeant O'Neil can't talk about an ongoing investigation, especially one in which she's directly involved. Not until all the evidence is in and all parties involved are cleared or charged. Right, Sergeant?"

Before she could respond, the colonel spoke up. "Sergeant, they don't consider you a person of interest, do they?"

Glenna's face reddened. "Why would you think that?"

"I've dealt with brass," he said. "They always look for a scapegoat to save their own hindquarters. I'd watch my back if I were you."

With a tight-lipped smile and a lined brow, Glenna bid them goodnight.

All eyes turned to the colonel.

He opened his hands wide. "What? Did I say something wrong?"

CHAPTER TWENTY-SIX

Charlie heard Edy in the yard before he saw her. Apparently, she'd taken on the role of his weekend caretaker, something Charlie neither needed nor wanted. He'd hoped by now she would've gone back to her own busy life.

She'd been at the house the last three consecutive Saturdays pruning trees, seeding bare spots in the lawn, and planting crocus, tulip, and daffodil bulbs. He went outside to join her. "Show me what to do. I'll finish up."

"You?" Edy smirked. "When did you have any interest in gardening?"

"Since now!" He grabbed the spade from her hand. "You need to get a life."

"What are you talking about?"

"I'm talking about you and Matt. September is almost over. How long do you expect him to put up with this kind of long-distance relationship?"

She sighed. "He understands."

"He *says* he understands because he doesn't want to sound like an insensitive schmuck." Charlie dropped a bulb in a hole then threw in some dirt. "He's only human."

"But I'm almost finished …"

"You're finished now! Call Matt, get that dirt out from under your fingernails, and make dinner reservations." He turned her around and shoved her gently toward the front yard. "*Vamoose! Mi dulce dolor en el trasero,* my sweet pain in the butt."

She turned around and planted a kiss on his cheek. "Love you, too, little brother."

Charlie managed to survive September and October by putting one fake smile in front of another—from home to work to church. Five months plus had passed since Juliette's death. Some days, the time seemed longer—others, like her death happened yesterday. Either way, each day felt like she was fading away.

The few authentic belly laughs he'd had since then were short-lived, stabbed to death by a single thought of his wife being gone. Though he'd had plenty of offers to "talk" from Kyle, Hank, and Pastor Ted, he doubted words would make him feel differently anytime soon, if ever. His hope and joy had been snuffed out. No, he'd do what he needed to do as best he could—even if he did it by rote.

If he couldn't help himself, maybe he could help his in-laws. With the tough holidays fast approaching, perhaps he could get them more involved with the interior finishes of their house to keep their minds occupied—his included. When he called them, they agreed to come in that afternoon.

Natalie arrived first. "I came right from Best Foot Forward, so I'm a little early. The colonel will be on time."

Charlie nodded. "I have no doubt." He escorted her into the conference room and pulled out a chair for her.

"Wick's reputation for promptness does precede him." She checked her watch. "Before he gets here, I have something to say."

"Oh?"

"For years, we held off renovating the house because we wanted to wait until you and Juliette started your family. We decided to go ahead with the project in our daughter's memory." She paused and circumvented the lump in her throat. "We wanted your input since you knew Juliette best. The colonel's idea was to create what you two would have liked. Because, when we're gone, the house will be yours."

Charlie leaned forward. "Excuse me?"

"You loved our daughter, you planned your whole lives around each other, and you've been like a son to us. We hope to keep you in the family."

Charlie choked up when he remembered the things he'd said and thought about the colonel. "I don't know what to say."

The colonel entered. "Tell us you accept, Charlie. That'll do."

Bowled over by their love and generosity, he said, "I accept."

His father-in-law took a seat. "What are we waiting for? Let's get this meeting started."

They spent the next hour confirming design details that would work for both their immediate and long-term needs. There'd be two master suites, one downstairs and one up, with two additional guest rooms and an office. The finished basement would be a walkout with steps down to the small private beach. Slide-and-fold doors would open a whole wall to connect the main living area to the large deck. A three-car attached garage was figured in to make room for big boy toys and lawn equipment. Jules would've loved the design.

They were wrapping up when Charlie heard Penny speaking with someone outside in the hall.

"I'm sure he'll see me."

Oliver.

A quick knock, then the conference door half-opened. Oliver stuck his head in. "Excuse me, Dawson, I only need a minute of your time."

Penny fretted behind him. "I'm so sorry, Charlie."

"I'm just finishing up here, Oliver. Be with you in a few minutes."

Quinlan didn't move. "This won't take long."

The colonel stood. "Tell me, Charlie, is this the West Point man you've mentioned?"

"Yes, Colonel, meet Oliver Quinlan. Oliver, this is my father-in-law, Colonel Annandale."

The colonel stuck out his hand, and Oliver took it.

Charlie knew his father-in-law's iron grip well. *You will have my daughter home by 2200 hours, is that understood? What are your intentions toward Juliette? How important is it to you that my daughter completes her college education?* He still trembled at the memories.

The colonel made eye contact as he shook Oliver's hand. "Mr. Quinlan, I don't recall learning manners like that at West Point, do you?"

Oliver half-chuckled. "You're right, uh, sir." He backed out of the room without another word.

"Mr. Quinlan," Penny said, "perhaps you can follow me to Charlie's office." She closed the conference door behind them.

"You're right, son." His father-in-law's jaw tightened. "There's something about this Quinlan character that warrants a second look."

"Both Hank and Artie feel the same way."

"I'll make a few calls and let you know what I find."

Once his in-laws had left, Charlie joined Oliver. "As you can see, my father-in-law is a West Point man through and through."

"Yes, well, I've moved on myself." He grunted. "Can we move on to my project now that your little family reunion is over?"

What a jerk! ... Sorry, Lord.

"Vanetta wants you to vet a few custom floor purveyors and landscape designers." He handed Charlie a list of names and addresses, along with some clippings. "She saw their work in her fancy design magazines and needs you to meet with them ASAP."

Sure, Oliver, I'll drop my life to do that. No problem. "Tell Vanetta I'll do my best."

CHAPTER TWENTY-SEVEN

Charlie second-guessed giving Edy the "get a life" lecture as he stared out his kitchen window to a yard filled with leaves waiting to be raked. He poured his first cup of morning coffee, put his phone on speaker, and placed it on the counter.

His grandmother rattled on. "It'll just be the four of us and maybe Kyle and Sarah and Natalie and Wick. Do you think Edy's Matt would come?"

He cut in. "Grams, I'm not really up to a big Thanksgiving celebration this year."

"None of us are, dear. That's why we'll keep it to family and friends … maybe some lonely souls with no place to go. We could include the Westfalls, too, unless Binnie's planning her own event."

Charlie massaged his forehead. He wanted to stop her but settled for a stall. "We still have a few weeks. Let me think about it."

"Don't think too long, I've got shopping to do."

So, no pressure, huh, Grams?

Pop's filter disappeared years ago, so Charlie was used to not knowing what would come out of his mouth. But Grams was the surprise. The older she got, the more she treated death like any other stage in life. Was it because, other than his parents, she hadn't lost anyone close to her? Not that she was ever overly emotional, but sometimes her sympathy bordered on cursory.

But this was Juliette. Why didn't Grams understand? Did she expect him to resume his life as if his wife hadn't died less than six months ago? He'd barely gotten through Halloween. Knowing he would've been a poor substitute for the girl who always opened the door and acted so surprised or scared by every kid's costume, he did something he and Juliette promised they'd never do. He shut the lights and sat in the dark.

Thanksgiving was a day to give thanks. And he didn't feel thankful.

Sorry, Lord. My head says I should be glad for the time we had, but my heart isn't ready to let go.

The following Sunday, Binnie pulled Charlie aside after church. "Your grandmother approached me about Thanksgiving at your place."

His shoulders slumped. "What a surprise. Grams didn't wait for me to agree."

"She means well, Charlie, but if you're not up to hosting, I have a suggestion. Since our boys aren't coming home, Ted and I could host Thanksgiving. We could focus on the blessings of Juliette."

Visions of long lines of people after an equally long memorial service passed before him. "Um, what exactly would that entail?"

"Instead of you putting up a good front for a crowd, we invite only those who loved your wife best. Everyone comes to the table thankful for something about Juliette."

Not an idea he would've come up with himself, but it was better than having a full church and maudlin music.

Charlie's throat tightened as he accepted her offer. "Thanks. You know I'll cook, but we should probably assign pickles and olives to Edy. Grams will insist on bringing her signature stuffing."

"I wouldn't deny her that." Binnie put her hand on his arm. "And *you* are in charge of the guest list."

"I can give you that right now. Just add Kyle and Sarah to my family, including my in-laws."

She counted on her fingers. "That makes ten. A good round number." Binnie squeezed his hand. "Don't worry about a thing. I'll even call your grandmother to let her know I insisted."

Charlie's mood lightened as he walked to his car. Binnie and Ted were not only good people, they were good friends.

Now, what to say on that day about Juliette without letting on I'm still mad at her?

On Thanksgiving Day, Charlie arrived at the Westfalls' a half hour early. Edy pulled up behind him. They chatted while unloading their cars.

"Hey, little brother, what's this about you not making a green bean casserole? Pop looks forward to that dish every holiday."

"After hearing, taste buds are the first thing to go. And since Binnie charged me with bringing the vegetables, I chose fresh."

"Don't blame me, Mr. Gourmet Chef, when Pop starts whining they're not cooked enough."

"Let me worry about that. So, what's in the bag?"

Edy lifted a small canvas cooler. "Pickles and olives. I probably should've offered to bake a pie."

"Always best to stick with what you know."

She laughed. "Can I carry something for you?"

He handed her the slow cooker then started up the sidewalk.

Russet, orange, and yellow mums lined the front walk. A wreath of autumn leaves, sunflowers, and tiny gourds hung on the front door. Like a little family, a trio of pumpkins greeted him from the porch.

"So, what's Matt doing today? I feel kind of bad about not inviting him."

Edy shrugged. "Matt never had a chance to meet Juliette. Anyway, he has plans with his family."

Now that he knew what being alone felt like, he thought of Edy. She'd been on her own her whole adult life. Successful, yes, but alone.

"Why don't you pick a day after Thanksgiving and let me cook for you two? I'd like to get to know him better."

"That's sweet, but I'm not sure if Matt's a good fit for me."

"What are you talking about—" The door opened before Charlie could finish his question.

"Welcome, you two!" Binnie's greeting echoed the warmth of her home.

"Hope you don't mind us being a little early. I wanted to make sure my vegetables had room in the oven before the pies showed up."

Binnie chuckled. "Those pies can be glory hogs, can't they?"

Edy smiled. "That's the very reason I brought pickles and olives."

Ted greeted them. "Hey, Edy, Charlie. How can I help?"

"If you'll put this in the kitchen," Charlie said, "I'll grab the other dishes from the car."

Ted took the casserole dish by the potholders. "Hmm. What is this? It smells so good."

"Maple-walnut butternut squash. I've got bacon balsamic Brussels sprouts, parmesan mashed potatoes, and slow cooker creamed corn too. As my decorator wife used to say, 'a color for everyone.'"

"Sounds like a meal in itself!" Binnie said.

A half hour later, Pop and Grams arrived with her stuffing and homemade cranberry relish. Natalie and the colonel followed with a stack of pies, and Kyle and Sarah with cranberry bread and apple cider.

"Look at all this!" Binnie surveyed her countertop. "Makes my task of cooking the turkey and making the gravy look easy."

Grams hugged Binnie. "I think you make *everything* look easy."

"Thank you so much for doing this, Binnie." Natalie's eyes glistened. "Juliette would have loved it."

The colonel passed them carrying two half gallons of ice cream. "Hope you have room in your freezer."

While most of the crowd congregated in the kitchen, Pop retrieved a cardboard box from the trunk of his car.

Charlie said, "What's in the box, Pop? Green bean casserole?"

Pop placed the box on the sideboard then whispered, "Just between you and me, son, I hate that concoction. Only eat it to please your grandmother." He called to his wife. "Lana, what do you call these things I made again?"

"Placeholders, dear."

Pop opened the flaps, revealing some small carved wooden figures. Some were Pilgrims and others Wampanoag Indians, a mix of male and female. He handed a Pilgrim to Charlie. "I made you the governor. See. Your name's right there."

Charlie fingered the rough yet detailed figure then peeked in the box. "You did all these?"

"I suspected your grandmother was hinting at something when I got a shipment of aspen all the way from Colorado."

Grams called from the kitchen. "But what you chose to do with it was all your doin', Rollie."

Charlie looked over the one-of-a-kind figures, each hand-painted in shades of harvest. "It's been ages since you've done anything like this. They're wonderful."

"I actually started these a few years back. Uncle Fern helped me finish 'em up." Pop handed a figure to Charlie. "We can set this one in the center of the table."

The carving was of a female Pilgrim, with caramel-colored, sun-streaked hair and bluish-green eyes. "Juliette" was carved into the base. Charlie hugged his grandfather. "Thanks, Pop."

"I couldn't forget our guest of honor."

Before long the table was filled with food enough for five times as many people. Laughter and tears took turns as the stories about Juliette began.

"It was years before I found out Juliette preferred to eat healthy," Grams said. "That sweet girl ate the meals I prepared with nary a word about all those calories."

"Or my bad jokes," Pop said. "She'd laugh at every one."

Grams teased, "Sometimes more than once."

"I admired my daughter's spirit." The colonel cleared his throat. "She wasn't a quitter. I believe she was gearing up to go toe to toe with this problem."

Natalie put one hand over her husband's.

"I believe you're right, Colonel," Ted said. "I remember how Juliette handled our third-grade Sunday school class. She whipped those kids into shape, all the while making Sunday school fun."

"I think she used the same methods on Charlie," Kyle said. "He never knew what hit him."

"Oh, I knew what hit me all right," Charlie came back. "I didn't mind being hit by Jules is all."

Everyone laughed.

Sarah put her fork down. "What I'll always love about Juliette was how she built others up. She could be standing there with a trophy in her hand, yet she'd make the celebration about someone else. I don't know how she did that."

"She allowed me to treat her like the little sister I never had." Edy raised her glass and toasted the memory. "As a bonus, she took over raising my brother."

When the teasing died down, Natalie spoke. "Charlie, I am so thankful my daughter found love. It was a joy being around you two."

Grams spoke, her voice strained. "By the time you get to be my age, you've lost a lot of people this side of heaven. When I think I can't bear another loss, I block the pain out. Sometimes, I come across as uncaring."

Edy reacted quickly. "That's not true, Grams."

"Yes, it is." Plump tears rolled through the deep wrinkles in her cheeks. "Truth is I hold dear every thought of Juliette, the same way I still do of my own daughter and son-in-law."

Pop put his arm around her and pulled her close.

Even through the pain, Charlie could feel the healing. And he was frightened. Somehow, holding onto the anger made his wife feel more real. When the aching stopped, would he forget Juliette?

CHAPTER TWENTY-EIGHT

With only ten days until Christmas, the whole town was dressed in red, green, and gold, Heritage of Faith Church included. Yet every green garland and red-bowed wreath colored Charlie's mood a darker shade of blue. On the drive home from Sunday service, he reaffirmed his decision to skip the tree and decorations this year. He'd survived Thanksgiving without a breakdown. Christmas, Juliette's favorite holiday, would be tougher. Anyway, without his wife here to enjoy the celebration, what was the point?

He would attend Grams and Pop's Christmas Eve dinner, but that was all. Since Dawson-Landau closed the office the week between Christmas and New Year's every year, he'd be off. For the last four years, he and Juliette had had standing reservations at Song Sparrow Lodge on Lake Winnipesaukee in New Hampshire. He planned to keep them. And he wouldn't tell anyone for fear they'd offer to join him.

Edy's car was in the driveway when Charlie got home. She knew he'd be at church, so what was she doing there? His housework or laundry again? This needed to stop.

When he opened the door, she shouted, "Surprise!"

Empty boxes of Christmas decorations lay around the room. Charlie held his tongue, at least most of it. "You shouldn't have."

"No problem, I enjoyed the task."

"I meant you shouldn't have because I wasn't going to decorate this year."

She brushed his comment aside with the back of her hand. "I figured. That's why I decorated for you." She gestured to the tree, resplendent with lights and ornaments, standing in front of the large living room window. "Looks nice, doesn't it?"

He and Jules had splurged on the seven-foot artificial spruce a few years back. "Nice, yeah." There was a snowman on top instead of the angel Jules loved. The crèche they used to display on their deep mantel was still in the box. Instead, Santa in his sleigh with eight reindeer stood in its place. He knew his sister meant well, but her efforts weren't the same. And never would be. Why couldn't Edy get that?

"After I put the candles in the windows, I'll be done."

She looked so proud of herself, how could he be angry? Rather than cause a fuss, he said, "How about I cook dinner while you finish up?"

"Sounds good to me." She lifted the battery-operated candles out of a box.

He changed the subject. "So, what's up with Matt?"

Edy centered a candle on the kitchen window sill. "What do you mean?"

"We didn't get to finish our conversation outside the Westfalls' on Thanksgiving. You said something about him not being 'a good fit for you.'"

"Oh, well, it's not so much that as the timing. We're both so busy."

Charlie stopped what he was doing and looked into her eyes. "If you and Matt want this to work, my advice is *make* the time. You never know when time will run out."

"I know, but it's not that easy."

"No?" He put his hand out. "I'd like my house key back, please."

"Why? How will I be able to get in when you're not home?"

"You won't, that's the point. But you'll have more time to pursue a relationship with the guy who obviously loves you."

Tears flooded her eyes. "I can't, Charlie. You need me now."

"Edy, I'm a thirty-year-old man. I appreciate your help, but I can take care of myself."

She shook her head. "I failed you once, I won't do that again."

"What are you talking about? You've never failed me."

She wiped away her tears with the back of her hand. A sob escaped. "When Mom and Dad died. ... The accident was my fault."

"Why would you say a thing like that? They were killed in a car crash."

She dropped to a chair, her face reflecting anguish. "We had a fight before they left. They might not have died if I hadn't whined about having to babysit you again."

"You've been holding that in for twenty years?" He knelt before her. "The accident was tragic, yes, but an accident nonetheless. The roads were bad that night because of the storm, remember?"

"Even so, after they died, I couldn't get away fast enough and left you with Grams and Pop."

"You didn't leave me anywhere. You went away to college. I had a good life growing up." He tilted her chin up. "And a pretty great sister."

"Then why do I feel so incredibly guilty?"

He smirked. "Well, you always were an overachiever."

"Brat." She hugged him. "Are you sure you don't need me?"

"I'll always need you but as my sister, not as my housekeeper or gardener."

"If you're sure, I think I'll pass on dinner." Her eyes sparkled. "I've got a call to make."

Please, God, let this be Edy's turn to find love.

CHAPTER TWENTY-NINE

After the Christmas Eve service, Charlie shared a simple dinner at his grandparents' house with family and Kyle and Sarah. Gifts were limited, nothing extravagant, and the tone was low-key. Grams and Pop and Edy must have powwowed because no one bugged him about Christmas day or what he planned for his week off.

Needing some peace and quiet to think and to heal, he'd confirmed their—rather *his*—reservation at Song Sparrow Lodge.

The only one who pulled him aside was Pop. "You take a break from this crazy family and spend the time with your heavenly Father. He knows what you need, Bud."

Pop's right, Lord. If I can just get past Christmas and out of Plymouth for a while ...

Christmas morning, Charlie packed his Cherokee for any number of activities. Whether or not he'd actually ski or snowshoe up north remained to be seen. Foremost on his mind was to steep in the memories of his wife and to have a word with God. He had their personal emails and texts to go through, her voice mail messages to hear, and the terrycloth robe that still held her scent.

He stopped at Vine Hills on his way out of town. Placing a mini potted tree on her grave, he nestled her favorite treetop angel on top. "Merry Christmas, Jules." He didn't doubt hers would be merrier than his. "I had no idea grief could be so unrelenting and noisy. Missing you runs in and out of every busy day at work and every lonely hour at home."

His hat in hand, he stood in the cold for a few more minutes. "You left me with some huge unanswered questions. Despite your problem with painkillers, were you still happy with me … with us? Was the life we lived and the future we talked about what you wanted too? Did you really want to have babies with me?"

He couldn't get the answers from Juliette, but maybe he could get them from God. "If you have any influence up there, Jules, I'd appreciate some help."

Charlie drove Route 3 and I-93 North and got through Boston with barely a tap on the brakes. He grinned wryly at the Welcome Bienvenue New Hampshire sign with its proud motto Live Free or Die.

Was it possible to live and die at the same time?

A few exits past the state line, his check engine light came on. *Great.* He doubted the problem was serious. He'd always suspected that bit of added technology was some sort of scam. After considering the odds, he took Exit 3 then turned left toward the town of Hudson. He drove a good eight miles with no sign of an open service station.

As he went through the intersection at Central and Greeley Streets, his engine quit and wouldn't restart. He rolled his Jeep to the side of the road just past a church. His next call was to his travel club. "Being a holiday," he was told, "they'll take at least an hour."

Checking his watch, he sighed. *Good chance I won't get to the lodge today.* He spoke into his phone. "Hotels in Hudson, NH." A bunch of places in Nashua came up. He switched "hotels" to "motels" but got the same results. Hudson must be a small town.

The day was sunny and cold, but the inside of his car felt colder. He lamented not stopping at the Dunkin' Donuts he'd passed a few miles back. Thinking there had to be another one nearby, he walked farther on Rt. 111. *Nope.* He backtracked to an open convenience store but left when the only "fresh brewed coffee" they had was burned at the bottom of a pot.

He jogged back to his Jeep. Before he could climb back in, a black pickup pulled in behind him. He doubted his travel club was that fast.

The driver exited and called over, "Need any help?"

"Thanks. I was told help should be here in about an hour or so."

The guy took a few steps closer. "Charlie? Charlie Dawson?"

He scanned the Good Samaritan's face. "Felix Pinard?" One of his old college roommates. "Of all the strange places to run into you."

"Not so strange seeing as how I live in Hudson. But what are you doing here and on Christmas day no less?"

He kept his answer short. "Headed for some R&R at Lake Winnipesaukee." Since he and Felix had never had much in common when they were at Northeastern, they hadn't kept in touch over the years.

"Good thing you broke down in the town center, or I might have missed you."

Charlie looked around at a church, a small office building, a Grange Hall, an ancient cemetery, and a vacant lot. "This is the town *center?*"

Felix laughed then blew into his cupped hands. "How about we wait in my truck where it's warm?"

"Don't you have someplace to be? I don't want to hold you up."

"My parents can abide my absence a little longer. Besides, what kind of Christian would I be if I left you out in the cold on Christmas day?"

"Christian?" The word popped out of his mouth before Charlie could stop it.

Felix chuckled. "Thought that'd get your attention. I guess all your preachin' finally got to me."

Charlie shook his head. "From what I remember, it must have taken more than my preaching."

"Hey, was I that bad?"

"Not bad, just lost."

"And now I'm found!"

They chatted a bit before Felix asked the question Charlie dreaded.

"So, where's Juliette?" Felix chuckled. "Or is it she who needs the R&R away from you?"

Would he ever get used to this moment? He inhaled deeply. "Juliette died of heart complications this past May." He left out the part about the drugs.

Felix was sincere in his condolences, but as always, the news slowed the flow of conversation.

Charlie changed the subject to smooth the way. "Since you live around here, can you recommend a service station and a hotel?"

Felix referred his own mechanic but doubted he was working that day. "As for a place to stay, are you looking for fancy or function?"

"Function—with heat and plumbing."

"My family owns a small cabin on Robinson Pond not far from here. Too late for swimming and too early for ice fishing, so the place is vacant. Rent's cheap enough. If you're interested, I'll take you over there."

The cabin sounded like what he was looking for but didn't know he wanted. "Thanks."

The tow truck came and took his Jeep to Felix's mechanic's garage.

"I've got the perfect place for you to get a good meal first." Felix took off down Greeley Street. "My parents' home. That's where I'm headed."

Charlie protested. "Instead of me intruding on your family's party, why don't you just drop me off at the cabin?"

"Nope, 'cause we're here." He turned into a long gravel driveway. "And being brothers in Christ makes us family."

Charlie unbuckled his seatbelt. "Are you sure?"

"I'm sure." Felix opened his door. "Anyway, Mom's in charge of rentals, and she's got the key. Besides, I doubt there's any food in the cabin, and you don't have any transportation."

"I feel funny showing up unannounced."

"Well, I can announce you if that's what you're worried about. Besides, of all my roommates, she liked you best."

With no other choice, Charlie trailed behind him into a packed house.

Felix reintroduced him to his mother then explained his situation. "Ma, I told Charlie he could rent the cabin. That okay?"

"Sure thing, but not before he has a good meal." The woman wagged her finger at Charlie. "The cabin may be nice, but I won't have you sittin' there all alone on Christmas."

Felix eyeballed Charlie. "Told you so."

"Well, I appreciate your hospitality. If I hadn't run into your son, I don't know where I'd be."

She patted a chair beside her. "Well, the Lord knew, and that's why you're here."

He surveyed the rooms he could see. "How many in your family, Mrs. Pinard?"

"Thirty-two here today. Of course, we've lost some, and we keep prayin' for others. Sickness kept a couple away today, and there's a few who are just plain stubborn."

He thought of his small family, back down to four now. "Well, by the size of this crowd, you've been blessed."

He jumped when someone slapped him on the back and roared, "Right you are! And we work hard to be grateful!"

Felix grinned. "Did you ever meet my dad, Charlie? He's first in command ... behind Ma."

After the men shook hands, Mr. Pinard was called away to referee a fight between a couple of grandsons.

Charlie was introduced to more people than he could possibly remember, from ages six months to ninety-two, noting none were Felix's wife or kids. "So, I gather you never married?"

"Then you'd be wrong. My wife, Zoe, is in the hospital being treated for bipolar disorder."

His honesty took Charlie aback. "I'm so sorry."

"Thanks. When I ran into you this morning, I'd just dropped our two girls off at her family's place. My in-laws needed some cheering."

"Daughters, huh?" Charlie said. "So what's that like?"

"They're a handful." His smile widened. "My five-year-old is a princess, but her little sister is a mess waitin' to happen around every corner." He sobered. "And as with any disease, mental illness affects the whole family. We're thankful to have a big family nearby to help out."

"How long before your wife is home again?"

"Not sure, but Zoe's got some excellent doctors now. Once they balance her meds, they'll discharge her. And when she's home, we don't waste one minute of her good days."

Did I waste any of my time with Juliette? And did she feel I did?

Around mid-afternoon, Felix said, "We'd better get going so I can show you to the cabin before dark. Once you get your truck back, you'll have to find your way in and out on your own."

Did Felix think he was staying?

Mrs. Pinard packed him containers of leftovers. "Nobody can ever accuse me of allowing my tenants to starve."

In the flurry of food and activity and laughter, Charlie hadn't once felt like an outsider. He accepted her offerings. "Thank you, ma'am. I appreciate your kindness."

"See how polite he is, Felix? I always did like this one."

Felix rolled his eyes. "Yes, Ma."

The cabin wasn't the knotty pine, dark, and drafty shelter he'd imagined. Although rustic, the three-bedroom house was updated and comfortable. He'd slept as well as he ever did away from home. The coffee he found in the cupboard would wake him up. Good thing he drank black.

The morning view from the French doors, overlooking the pond, drew his attention as he sipped the strong brew. The simplicity of the still water and bare trees calmed him.

"Jules, you'd love the back roads and walking trails. The setting is secluded but not scary."

A twinge of self-pity attacked him, but he shook it off. He didn't have far to look to see he wasn't the only one suffering. Felix, his wife, their kids. Would she recover? How would their daughters do with a part-time mother? He thought about others back home. Artie had a sister with cerebral palsy. One of Sarah's coworkers was recovering from a mastectomy. How about Ashlyn Reid, a widow with a baby on the way?

"I know you get this a lot, God, and forgive me for asking, but what is your purpose in all this loss and suffering?"

He quieted himself, hoping for an answer. When he didn't get one, he bundled up and went outside to explore the natural surroundings. He took a less overgrown trail which led to the shore, then stared out over the pond for a good, cold while. When he returned to the cabin, he lit a fire.

Felix called shortly after one o'clock. "Want to swing by the mechanic's shop this afternoon and maybe the grocery store?"

"Are you sure you don't have anything better to do the day after Christmas?"

"Nope. Spent a few hours with Zoe last night, and my girls have 'top secret plans' with their cousins today."

"Then sure."

Felix picked him up a half hour later.

Charlie asked before he forgot again. "You know, I never did ask what you do for work?"

"Electrical engineer. When Zoe was diagnosed three years ago, I transitioned to a smaller firm so I could work from home when necessary." He raised a brow and glanced at Charlie. "If you'd told me you were anything but an architect I'd be shocked. Other than Juliette, that's all you ever talked about."

Charlie shrugged. "Guess I was an easy read, huh?"

"What you were was a good example. You helped me get serious about school. Of course, focusing on studies was probably easier for me since I hadn't met Zoe yet."

Charlie couldn't hold back a chuckle. "If I recall, you had plenty of other female diversions."

Felix smirked as he turned onto the main road. "I did, didn't I?"

When they reached the shop, the mechanic assured Charlie his car would be ready by the day's end.

Felix pulled out onto Rt. 102. "Next stop the grocery store?"

"If you've got the time, I've got the money."

On the way, they took a conversational respite from their heartaches.

"Remember the time you and one of your dates tried to sneak into that meeting room for some privacy and walked in on our Bible study?" Charlie's shoulders shook from laughing.

"Oh, yeah." Felix nodded. "That girl was a devout atheist too. She never did trust me after that."

"She shouldn't have trusted you in the first place."

"What a stinking thing to say about the best roommate you ever had."

"Ha!" Charlie laughed.

"Speaking of stink,"—Felix cringed—"remember how bad our dorm room smelled?"

Charlie almost choked. "Only because you threw your food scraps in the wastebasket."

"No way. It was those ocean-scented, pine-tree fresheners you hung around the room. Made the place smell like low tide."

Charlie shook his head. "To this day, I can't stand the smell of those things." He paused a few moments. "How about those long philosophical talks we'd have about how easy life would be once we got our degrees?"

Felix pulled into the store's parking lot. "Eight years of adult life can change a person's perspective, huh?"

"I wonder how we'll look back on *these* days in another eight years."

"Hold on." Felix pushed a few keys on his phone. "Matthew 6:34 in *The Message* reads, 'Give your entire attention to what God is doing right now, and don't get worked up about what may or may not happen tomorrow. God will help you deal with whatever hard things come up when the time comes.'"

"Never thought I'd see the day you'd be preaching to me." Charlie looked Felix in the eye. "But I'm glad I did."

When Felix dropped him off at the mechanic's, he said, "I'd love to have you meet Zoe and my girls. Maybe we can get together again while you're in town."

"Give me to the end of the week. I promised myself I'd spend some time with the Lord this trip." *And with Juliette.*

"I get it, I do."

I guess I'm staying in Hudson after all.

CHAPTER THIRTY

With a wind chill factor below freezing, Charlie was satisfied to stay inside the next morning. He had another fire going and plenty of food after yesterday's grocery run. He settled on the overstuffed sofa in full view of the shimmering pond.

After his daily Bible reading, he listened to his voicemails from Juliette. The words didn't matter as much as the sound of her voice. Again and again, he immersed himself in her lyrical, often humorous, timbre. Rather than weep, he was comforted.

He pleaded with God for courage as he opened her laptop. He steadied his hands to type her password. She might have kept a messy car, but her computer files were organized by categories in clearly marked folders. "Family & Friends." "Finances." "Fitness." "Heritage of Faith." "Household." "Morris Companies."

When he clicked on "Family and Friends," there were multiple sub-folders—one named "Charlie."

Am I ready for this?

Upon opening "Charlie," he found scanned copies of his birth certificate, their marriage license, his employment records, and medical history. One file name made him smile. "In Case C forgets." That document held a potpourri of PINs and passwords, song titles, memorable events, gifts he'd bought her, when and where he'd purchased household items, and the location of things he'd stored.

Who does this for their spouse?

Charlie skipped to a file named "e-History of Us." The file held copies of emails, instant messages, and texts they'd exchanged since they'd been sophomores in high school. Her last entry, on the first page, was dated the day before she died.

JULIETTE: Hi, Sweetie, Coach Colonel wants me to meet him at Miles Standish tomorrow a.m. to clock me again. I promise to be back in plenty of time for our double date with Kyle and Sarah. Okay by you?

CHARLIE: Jules, at the speed you run, you'll be ready before I am. Okay by me.

Suspecting their earlier communication would be less painful to read, he scrolled to the first page of the 600-plus-page file.

Dear Juliette,

Thank you for offering to tutor me in French. If I can ever help you with math, just ask.

Sincerely,

Charlie Dawson.

Sincerely? He was quite a Casanova back then.

Dear Charlie,

What about half-French, half-math tutoring sessions? They might take twice as long, though. Okay by you?

Juliette.

Sure. I guess that would be okay.

Charlie groaned. What he'd thought about her suggestion back then was not what he'd written. What a doofus. Juliette had teased him for years about his response.

Their sophomore year, they'd stayed after school twice a week to study in the library. One year turned into three. Their mutual tutoring, plus weekly Youth Group meetings, evolved into a steady relationship. Pretty good since, at fifteen, neither of them had permission to formally date.

Awestruck that Juliette had cherished their messages in this way, he wanted to savor every one, from beginning to end.

In an email from her, dated February 14, 2006:

Charlie! Just when I thought you'd forgotten Valentine's Day, the iTunes playlist showed up in my inbox! That you remembered our favorite songs means more to me than flowers or chocolates! I love you.

A few hours later, he'd called her. "I was hoping you'd like the playlist, but just in case …" *Knock, knock.*

Grinning, Charlie had stood outside her dorm room with a bouquet of fuchsia roses and a box of dark chocolate hearts. He'd skipped classes that day and driven over nine hours to Pennsylvania to surprise her at Grove City College. "I couldn't let you spend your first Valentine's Day away from home alone, could I?"

An email from him dated, dated November 8, 2008:

It's hard to focus on exams knowing I'll be seeing you in a few weeks, but I'll do my best. Wouldn't want the colonel to think I wasn't worthy of his little girl.

Juliette had written back:

Coach Colonel might be tough, but my mom and your family are on our side!

The Girl He Knew

He steeped himself in the happy memories.

JULIETTE: I love Sarah! Kyle better be good to her. She could be my best friend.

CHARLIE: Kyle's previous choices were questionable, I agree. But there's hope this time because Sarah chose him.

Reading through the file reminded him how blessed they'd been. But for a few misunderstandings, his life with Juliette had been one good moment after another. At least that's what he'd believed up until she died. He could "if only" and "what if" their time had been longer, but all that bemoaning wouldn't bring her back.

Neither would being mad at her for not confiding in him.

Needing a break, he roamed around her other folders. Sorting by date, the last file Juliette had opened was Rich French Cuisine. The title caught his eye. Juliette didn't cook often, and when she did, it was simple and healthy, never rich and French.

The file was a spreadsheet with names, dates, and addresses. Was it something to do with work? He looked closely at the dozen or so names. Some sounded normal, but many read like descriptions. He couldn't imagine her nicknaming her clients Greasy Blonde, Ivy Leaguer, Gold Tooth, Flat Nose, The Plumber, Jitters, Mother of the Year, or Trench Coat Dude. Two columns of street addresses were titled "Before" and "After."

None of this made sense to him. Then again, none of it mattered now. He closed the file.

He had a lunch of minestrone soup and Italian bread. Feeling a bout of drowsiness coming on, he left the cabin to get some exercise. No nap for him if he wanted to sleep tonight.

The air was cold, crisp, and still, but the sun was shining. He walked along the edge of the pond, stopping to stare at the light bouncing off the intermittent ripples. The soothing sounds of nature were addictive.

"Addictive? Great choice of words, Charlie."

Do you believe all you say you believe?

Where had that come from? He lowered himself to sit on a fallen tree.

Do you trust me?

"Lord, I trust you, but I don't understand how all this could have happened."

Do you believe I love you?

"I want to, but in the midst of all this hurt, I'm not sure what I believe."

A breeze fluttered through the stillness, arousing his senses. Charlie shut his eyes and soaked in the light and warmth of God's presence. A passage from the Gospel of John came to mind. When Jesus had asked his disciples if they wanted to leave him like others had, Peter had replied, "Lord, to whom shall we go? You have the words of eternal life."

Like Peter, Charlie recognized there was nowhere else to go but to God. Though his questions and heartache remained, a measure of peace came with the revelation.

He spent the next few days and nights reading through their e-history, determined to finish by the end of his stay. Some memories evoked smiles, others laughter, many tears. Others, like their talk about having children, were bittersweet.

Their texts back and forth after her surgery felt like a punch to his gut.

JULIETTE: Sorry for being a big grouch this morning. The pain in my ankle seems to be getting worse, not better. Frustrating!

CHARLIE: I know you hate to hear this, but they have pills for that. Tell your doctor.

Why hadn't he kept his mouth shut?

Her last recorded text should have told him something was off.

JULIETTE: We need to talk. Let's make some time soon. Okay by you?

He'd thought she was going to ask him to be more helpful around the house. He'd been so wrong.

Between the muck and mire of emotions, Charlie was assured of two things: God loved him, and he'd be okay one day.

But not today.

Before the weekend arrived, Charlie called the first landscape designer on Vanetta's list.

"Your call is important to us. Leave your name and phone number, and we'll get back to you after the first of the year."

Getting a similar message from the next number on his list, he felt more relieved than disappointed. To appease his conscience, he studied the portfolios on their websites and reviewed their references, so he could have something to report to Vanetta.

On his third try, a live person answered. "Yes, Mr. Dawson, I've spoken with your Mrs. Quinlan."

"You did?" The man's tone told him the call hadn't gone well.

"She was checking to see if you'd called." He grunted. "In the forty-five years I've been in business, I've learned no amount of money is worth dealing with her type."

If only Dawson-Landau had been in the position to have had that choice.

Late morning, he called Felix. "Free for lunch?"

"Lunch out sure beats another PB&J and juice box. And Ma's got my girls today."

"You'll have to choose."

"I've got just the place. North Side Grille. They've got a Whiskey River Burger that'll make you drool."

"And that is appetizing, why?"

Always the architect, Charlie took a good look at the restaurant. He was impressed with the clean, functional layout. Juliette would have approved of the aesthetics too. The fresh pear-green, pale gold, and salmon colors made a perfect backdrop for the framed watercolors and stenciled quotes about family and friends. Just off the dining room, a large collection of vintage prints boasted of the proud heritage of the Granite State.

Felix chose a booth. "Bored with yourself already?"

Charlie shook his head and chuckled at the wise guy he remembered. "Not so much bored as missing human contact. That cabin's pretty isolated."

"Only in the winter."

"Truth is the quiet is what I needed. Thanks again."

"Don't thank me." Felix rested his arms on the table. "This whole thing was orchestrated by a power greater than the two of us."

Charlie put his hands up in surrender. "No argument from me there."

They ordered lunch, then Felix said, "If they discharge Zoe tomorrow, maybe we can have you over for Sunday dinner after church. I like to keep things normal when she's home. But you'll do in a pinch."

"Gee, thanks." He sensed Felix was engaging in some wishful thinking. But, contrary to what the professionals said, Charlie believed small doses of denial were healthy to buffer the pain.

Felix said, "I'm sorry if I've seemed insensitive to your grief. I can't talk to anyone about Zoe's illness without them giving me advice, telling me about their third's cousin's mailman with the same thing, or recounting the latest miracle treatment they heard about online. I'm not looking for their pity or advice, just a listening ear. Maybe some prayer."

"I'm on the same page. I understand. Really."

"I know you do." He paused to stir his coffee. "Romans 5 says, 'We also glory, or rejoice, in our sufferings, because we know that suffering produces perseverance; perseverance, character; and character, hope.' I confess finding hope is easier than finding joy some days."

Over lunch, Charlie opened up to his friend about Juliette's death, his blindness to her addiction, his anger and regrets. They both shared the "why" questions they wished God would answer.

When they left the restaurant, they took a moment to pray in Felix's truck.

Later, in the warmth and comfort of the cabin, he reached for his Bible. A verse in Ecclesiastes came to mind. He found it in Chapter 4. "Two are better than one because they have a good return for their labor. If either of them falls down, one can help the other up. But pity anyone who falls and has no one to help them up."

Is that why he felt better for having opened up to Felix? Did talking to a guy he wasn't as close to make him feel less vulnerable? Or was confessing to someone who was also struggling easier? Why was revealing his innermost thoughts to Kyle or Hank or even Pastor Ted more difficult? Charlie suspected pride was involved.

Saturday morning, Charlie trekked the dirt roads and hiked through the woods around the cabin, his senses taking in all of nature. Chickadees, sparrows, and cardinals called notes of alarm as he passed by. Leaves rustled beneath his feet, cold twigs snapped, giving up their woodsy scent. Though a cutting wind whipped across the open water, the sun found him through the bare oak branches and green and brown needles of the tall pines.

He ended his outing by communing with God atop a hill overlooking the whole pond.

"Thanks, Lord, you knew what I needed—serenity. If you'd left my plan in place, I'd be in the middle of a noisy holiday crowd at the lodge on Lake Winnipesaukee."

Refreshed, he scrambled down the path. Snow, clean and soothing, began to fall before he could reach the cabin. From the picture window, he watched the white, airy flakes cover the ground, bare trees, and frozen inlets to create a greeting card scene.

He inhaled hope then exhaled anxiety. This was the first day in a long time he felt like cooking. Considering his limited supply of ingredients, he managed a decent omelet.

Felix called that afternoon to ask for a rain check on Sunday dinner. "Unfortunately, Zoe had a bad reaction to her latest meds. One of the side effects of anti-depressants is depression. A brand of irony I'll never understand."

He heard the pain in his friend's tone. "That's a tough one. But I'll drive back up whenever you say. I'd love to meet Zoe and your girls."

Charlie had intended to stay through New Year's Day but decided to leave a few days early. Time at home before he returned to work sounded good. He straightened up the cabin and packed most of his things for an early morning departure.

The idea of preparing New Year's Day brunch for his family lifted his spirits. He'd invite Kyle and Sarah, too, and tell Edy to bring Matt. Before he got carried away with menu planning, he thought to give them some notice.

"Sounds wonderful," Grams said. "I'm not even going to offer to bake anything."

Charlie tried his best to sound pathetic. "Not even your cranberry walnut bread?" He knew his grandmother well enough to see the pleasure on her face.

"Okay, but that's all."

Edy sighed. "I'm not sure about Matt. We're going to a New Year's Eve party in Plymouth. He might not feel like driving back down from Boston the next morning."

"He can always stay at my place."

"You're not a bad brother, you know that?"

Sarah answered, "What can I bring … besides Kyle's appetite?"

"That'll do."

As he put Juliette's laptop cord into a side pocket of her case, the plug got caught on a folded sheet of paper. He took it out for a closer look. The paper was a photocopy of a handwritten list. The names and addresses matched the spreadsheet he'd found on Juliette's laptop in the file named Rich French Cuisine.

What were you up to, Jules?

CHAPTER THIRTY-ONE

The two-hour drive back to Plymouth went by in a blur as he created one bizarre scenario after another involving the odd names on the mysterious list.

Minutes after he arrived home, he called Kyle. "Our search committee needs to meet ASAP."

"You back already?"

"Yeah. I found a list in Juliette's things. Not exactly sure how the names and places fit, but I'm pretty sure they're important. And I'm wondering if Heidi Vincent would think so too."

"My interest is officially piqued. Perfect timing too. Theo called me last night with his findings."

"DEA Theo?"

"One and the same."

"How much time before you have to hand the DEA findings over to the chief?"

"Maybe a day or two," Kyle said. "I don't want to add withholding evidence to the charge of not following procedure."

"Then let's see if we can meet tonight. I'll call Zach and the colonel. You see if Ted and Binnie are free."

That evening, Charlie opened the meeting around the Westfalls' table with an apology. "When I joined this group, my main purpose was to find someone to blame for my wife's death. Once I was able to accept that my wife had a problem, well then, my focus changed." Charlie passed out copies of the spreadsheet titled Rich French Cuisine. "I found this file on Juliette's computer. Do these names look familiar to any of you?"

Moments passed as they studied the list.

Kyle spoke first. "Hey, we've picked up some of these guys on suspicion of dealing." His index finger ran down the names again. "Others, like Jitters, Wally Holden, The Plumber, and Iggy Luciano have all done time. I'm pretty sure I know the identity of Trench Coat Dude and Ivy Leaguer too. We haven't seen them in months though."

Binnie adjusted her eyeglasses. "Chief Eason and Sergeant O'Neil reported the same in recent task force meetings. I remember because the sergeant gave credit to Oliver Quinlan's 'tough stance solutions.'"

Zach asked, "Where'd you say Juliette got this?"

Charlie filled them in about the copy of the handwritten list. "And the handwriting isn't Juliette's."

Kyle cracked a smile and a few knuckles. "I bet *this* is why the Vincents broke into your house. And I'm thinking anyone privy to this information might hold rank in the organization."

Charlie's face turned into one big question mark. "But the Assistant District Attorney offered them a deal, so why would they hold out on him?"

"Greed. Fear. Insurance." Kyle pointed to the columns on the right. "But my top guess is stupidity. See these addresses under Before? They're the dealers' known business locations, more like corners and alleys. At least, they used to be." He chuckled. "Looks like she left us their forwarding addresses in the After column. There goes the plea bargain!"

Ted leaned forward. "Can the ADA do that once it's signed?"

Kyle smirked. "You bet. A plea deal is predicated on those charged telling the truth—the whole truth."

Zach choked on a swig of water. "Well, that's gonna smart."

Charlie chin-nodded to Kyle. "Okay, now it's your turn. Tell us what Theo had to say."

"The DEA found the same chemical makeup and mold marks in other illegal drugs being sold in Washington, Wyoming, Texas, Illinois, and Pennsylvania. Theo thinks they're hop-skipping over states to avoid leaving a trail."

The colonel's eyes narrowed. "Cartel?"

"They don't think so." Kyle skimmed his crew cut with his palm. "Not as widespread and no discernible gang, Mexican, or Columbian connections. DEA's checking with their Canadian counterparts now."

Binnie commented that the DEA's theory seemed to fit with what she'd heard at the last task force meeting. "Nothing points to the major player being your typical drug lord. No known violence to speak of. He appears to be running his drug business like any other corporation."

Sarah's eyes ping-ponged from Binnie to Kyle and back again. "You mean his business is a cover?"

"That's their assumption," Binnie said. "The belief is he's too smart to live his preferred lifestyle with no discernible or legitimate income source."

Zach twirled his pencil between his fingers. "Did your guy say if the drug operations were still active in the states he mentioned? If not, do they think this cell is a simple relocation or a traveling show?"

"Interesting." The colonel tapped his upper lip with his index finger. "It would be harder to hit a moving target."

"What about a franchise?" Charlie asked. "Maybe they're opening new branches in each state."

"Even more difficult to track, which would be in their favor." Kyle sighed. "Coordinating a multi-layered investigation among federal, state, and local law enforcement organizations is complicated, time-consuming, and fraught with battling egos."

The colonel grumbled, "Sounds like the military."

Ted put his pencil to his pad. "Would it help if we knew which cities or regions in the states were involved?"

"Theo didn't give me that info, but I'll see what I can get." After Kyle texted the agent, he said, "I also asked him if he knew if the other operations were still up and running."

While they waited on a response, they set to deciphering the old and the new clues. Drug traffic in Plymouth seemed to have left town—but not too far away. Same brand drugs and similar operations in multiple states. Most likely a lone operator with business savvy. Too smart to be a user. Probably lives the good life with an equally good cover.

"There's still the matter of Sergeant O'Neil," the colonel reminded them. "She lied repeatedly—about where she was raised, why she followed Charlie, and why she's still holding a grudge against Zach. Speaking of which, Kyle, did you ever find out who called in the anonymous tip which got Zach arrested?"

"No, but now that we know Heidi withheld the whole truth, she's my likely suspect." A minute later, Kyle read Theo's answer. "'So far we know these locations: Bellingham, WA; Gillette, WY; Waco, TX; Moline, IL; Allentown, PA, and Plymouth.'"

"Other than Plymouth," Ted said, "what do any of us know about these cities?"

Most of them shrugged.

"I've only heard mention of one," Binnie said. "When Oliver Quinlan told us about his drug cleanup efforts in Waco."

Charlie rolled his eyes. "He doesn't miss a chance to mention that, does he?"

Binnie wagged a finger at Charlie. "Now, now. Whatever you think of Oliver personally, his efforts to help seem sincere."

He felt convicted. *Lord, help me to see past the gloat on that man's face.*

The colonel jotted notes down. "We can divide and conquer if we each research a city or town and report back in a few weeks."

"What are we looking for?" Sarah asked."

"Give me forty-eight hours to come up with a list." The colonel clicked his pen. "The data we gather will be the constant, the states the variable. That'll make it easier to find common denominators."

Ted's face betrayed his doubt. "What chance do we have of discovering something the professionals haven't?"

Charlie couldn't resist, "'O, ye of little faith.'"

The colonel quipped, "Sometimes it takes a grunt to see the obvious." He smirked. "Then the top brass take credit for the solution."

As a group, they agreed Charlie and Kyle should get Heidi's list and the DEA results to Chief Eason soon.

When the subject turned to Sergeant O'Neil, Charlie tried his best to understand. "Maybe her bitterness is all part of grief over losing her brother, a grief she never processed?" No sense bringing up rumors of Garrett being her son until he knew for sure.

Kyle shook his head. "If that's the case, she's long overdue for counseling."

"How did the young man die?" the colonel asked.

"Glenna suspected drugs." Kyle glanced at Zach. "I think that's where you come in."

"Garrett on drugs is a foreign concept to me. He was the one who begged me to quit until the day I left for boot camp. The guy I knew never drank *or* did drugs. That would have shown up in the autopsy, right?"

Kyle cocked his head. "Kind of hard to do an autopsy without a body."

"What do you mean?" Zach pulled back. "Then how did Glenna find out he'd died?"

"Garrett left a note," Kyle said. "I don't know exactly what it said. Something about her not ever having to see him again."

Charlie shrugged. "I guess eight years without a word or a sighting has finally convinced her."

Zach's eyes widened. "Eight years? That can't be right. Garrett emailed me about six months before my discharge, which would be about four years ago. Told me stuff was going on between him and his sister after his parents died."

"Four years?" Kyle sat forward. "Are you sure?"

"Yeah, I'm sure. When we lost touch, I assumed he'd finally moved out West."

"Out West?" Ted said. "Why would you assume that?"

"When we were kids, Garrett loved hanging around the horse stables in Carver. He used to go on and on about going out West to work on a ranch one day."

"Did he ever go?" Charlie asked.

"Not sure, but I remember something about a ranch for underprivileged boys in one of his emails." He held up a hand. "Before you ask, I don't have the emails *or* the computers. I was too busy hitting bottom to care about those things."

They looked around the table at each other, the news sinking in.

Kyle whistled. "Are we saying Garrett O'Neil was alive when Glenna had him legally declared dead?"

Ted prayed, "Lord, help us. What on earth do we do now?"

Sarah tapped a finger on the table. "Let's tread carefully. We're dealing with a sister's heart here."

Or was it a mother's?

CHAPTER THIRTY-TWO

Not wanting to disturb the pre-dawn stillness, Charlie lay quiet. An old hymn played in his head:

When peace like a river, attendeth my way,
When sorrows like sea billows roll
Whatever my lot, thou hast taught me to say
It is well, it is well, with my soul
It is well
With my soul
It is well, it is well with my soul.

He took a deep breath then exhaled. "It *is* well with my soul, Lord."

When daylight filled the room, he climbed out of bed and into the shower. An hour later, he stood at Juliette's grave. He stooped to brush the leaves and debris away with a gloved hand. Sweet memories of their life together permeated his being. Never knowing when tears would show up again, he took time to see the joy in each remembrance.

"We had a good life, didn't we, Jules?"

Alone at the cemetery, he thought about the silly gift he'd left for Ashlyn weeks ago. What had he been thinking? Like a cheap bamboo back scratcher could replace her husband. *Idiot.*

Curious, he walked the line to Mrs. Shouting-man's site and read the inscription on her gravestone:

The Girl He Knew

Peaches Papadopoulas
1930-2012
Nobody will ever make baklava like you.

Shouting-man's familiar noisy truck pulled to the side of the narrow road. *Busted.* Too late to move away, he turned his coat collar up against the wind and waited.

The old man shuffled over and stuck out his hand. "Howdy!"

He shook it. "Thought I'd pay my respects. Hope you don't mind, sir."

"I'm sure Peaches was pleased you came by."

At a loss for something tactful to say, he blurted, "So, Peaches was your wife's real name?"

"*Peaches* was easier for Americans to pronounce. In Greek, it's *Rodákina.*" His smile was broad, his eyes bright. "I knew she was the one for me the first time I heard her name."

"Why's that?"

"My first name's *Pershing.* Know what it means?"

"Afraid not."

"One who deals with peaches!" He burst out laughing.

Charlie grinned then read the inscription out loud. "'Nobody will ever make baklava like you.' Is that true?"

"Sure is." Pershing winked. "She made me bury the recipe with her." He backed a few feet away and motioned for Charlie to follow.

He did.

"Shh." With mischief in his eyes, he whispered, "But I made a photocopy." His Carhartt jacket open, he pulled at his suspenders.

Charlie raised his right hand. "I swear I'll never tell her." Somehow, he managed to control his urge to laugh. "Well, I'll leave you to your visit."

Pershing slapped Charlie on the back. "Stop by anytime, whether I'm here or not. My Peaches loves having company."

With eight joining him for brunch the next day, Charlie had shopping to do. He'd made sure his menu included friends' and family's favorites: maple bacon sweet potato hash for Grams and Sarah, savory crepes for Pop and Edy, fruit compote with lemon curd for his in-laws, and mushroom, spinach, and cheese "scrambled egg pie" for Kyle who still believed the adage "real men don't eat quiche."

He checked his list in the grocery store. While pushing his cart toward dairy, he rear-ended a shopper who'd stopped short.

"Ouch!"

Ouch is right. Glenna O'Neil.

"So sorry, Sergeant."

She glared at him. "You sure about that?"

"Yes, I'm sure." Determined not to take offense, he held up his list. "I got distracted."

She looked at his cart. "So big New Year's Eve bash, huh?"

He shook his head. "No, brunch tomorrow with family. How about you? Any New Year's plans?" Making small talk with Glenna O'Neil—not one of his best moves.

"Yeah, plans. Working a double, trying to keep drunks and druggies from killing themselves or others."

"Tough job." His eyes passed over her cart. A half a gallon of milk, a box of granola bars, and three Lean Cuisine frozen meals. He almost filled the awkward moment with an invitation to brunch.

She frowned. "If I were you, I'd stay off the roads."

Why did everything she say sound like a threat? "Never was one to go out New Year's Eve."

She grumbled some sort of valediction before she continued down the aisle.

Glenna didn't make it easy for people to like her. Not that *he* liked her either. But now that he knew what losing someone you loved was like, he had more empathy for her.

Maybe I'll reach out to her after the holidays.

Up ahead, Glenna shoved an elderly man's cart to the side so she could pass.

Or maybe not.

Charlie spent the evening prepping food. At ten p.m., he turned on the annual New Year's Rockin' Eve show. At 10:05, he turned off the TV, left a light on for Edy's Matt, then went to bed.

Though brunch was scheduled for eleven, Charlie's grandparents arrived at ten. Thankfully, the house was clean. Edy had seen to that as soon as she'd discovered where he kept his spare key. She'd even taken down the Christmas decorations.

Serves her right for putting them up in the first place.

While Grams occasionally yielded to his "fancy" cooking, she was always in charge of holiday table settings and serving pieces. That suited him just fine. He reached and fetched for her while Pop and Matt made small talk over coffee.

Edy showed up a half hour early, probably hoping to save Matt from a family inquisition. Per usual, his in-laws arrived at the stroke of the appointed hour, without a second to spare. Of course, Kyle and Sarah called to say they were running late.

The Tournament of Roses parade marched in the background while guests moved about and chatted. When all were present and seated around the dining table, Charlie asked Pop to say the blessing.

As was his style, the prayer was simple and to the point. "Thank you, Lord, for the blessings of food, friends, and family, especially our Juliette. We know you're taking good care of her. Help us to follow you closer this coming year. Amen."

A round of thick-voiced amens followed. Once the conversation started up again, no amount of protection from Edy could stop Charlie, Pop, and Kyle from teasing Matt. The colonel stayed out of it, but Grams, Natalie, and Sarah asked a few pointed questions.

The final shot came from Grams. "Someone isn't getting any younger."

"Tell me someone who *is*." Edy apologized to Matt. "Please ignore them."

"Are you kidding?" He laughed. "I'm flattered to be treated like family."

Charlie caught the blush on his sister's face and was glad.

When he and Kyle were alone in the kitchen, Charlie asked when he planned to speak with his police chief.

"Don't dare wait. He's back tomorrow." Kyle leaned against the refrigerator. "Can you come by to talk about the list and Heidi?"

"Tell me what time, and I'll be there."

The colonel wandered in and spoke in a low voice. "Charlie, I sent you a spreadsheet of items to compare in each of those cities."

"Wow, Colonel," Kyle said, "that was fast."

"Couldn't sleep." He refilled his glass. "Mind looking my topics over before I send it to the others?"

"Sure thing." Charlie could count the times his father-in-law had asked his opinion on one finger, maybe two. "We'll do that this evening."

Natalie and Grams shooed them out of the kitchen so they could clean up. Another few hours of Pop's back-in-my-day tall tales, the colonel's military accounts, and Kyle's stupid criminal anecdotes brought the afternoon to a close.

Kyle and Sarah stuck around after the others left.

Charlie opened the colonel's file on his laptop. The column titles included population, average age, median income, airport(s), land transportation, colleges, crime rate, drug task force, drug use, top news stories, and big businesses. A note at the bottom read: "Didn't include climate and geography because we already know they vary in the cities in question."

Kyle looked over his shoulder. "The only thing I'd add is results of an online search. Never know what'll come up."

"How about social media posts?" Sarah asked.

"Good thinking." Charlie added the additional columns and sent the file back to his father-in-law.

Sarah rapped her fingers on the arms of her chair. "Now can we talk about Glenna O'Neil? I can't get the idea out of my head that her brother … or son … might still be out there."

Charlie shivered at the thought of outright asking Glenna if Garrett was her son. "Aren't birth certificates public records?"

"No, they're not," she said. "Let's leave Glenna out of our conversation for now. I think we need to focus on Garrett."

Kyle sighed. "The police *did* look for him. When the case went cold, I think Glenna even hired a private investigator. Garrett's room looked like he hadn't taken much of anything with him. They had the note, then found his car, but never his body."

Sarah protested. "Did the police know about his dream to work on a ranch out West? Did Glenna know?"

Charlie bit his lower lip. "What do you suggest?"

"I've been thinking." Sarah sat up straight. "Kyle, could you work this as a cold case without Glenna's knowledge?"

"Maybe. I'd have to get the okay from the chief."

She continued to outline her plan. "First, Kyle checks Garrett's missing person's file for his DOB, height, weight, coloring, and any photos he can find. Maybe we could use aging software to see how he'd look now.

"Second, Charlie rattles Zach's brain about the emails again. Get as much background info about Garrett from him as you can. Hobbies, favorite foods, habits, anything he can recall, even if it doesn't seem important.

"Third, if his goal was to start a new life away from Glenna, he wouldn't use his real name. I'll gather names connected to him. Mother's maiden name, father's middle name, towns, favorite pet, etc. I'll check his parents' obits first.

"Finally, once we have that information and the proper permissions from the chief, we start contacting ranches that deal with troubled boys."

Kyle looked at Sarah then Charlie. "Here I am waiting to make detective when I'm living with a real live one."

Sarah narrowed her eyes. "Are you poking fun at me, Kyle?"

His hands went up. "I am not. Those are great ideas. I'll talk to the chief tomorrow."

The thought of keeping Glenna out of the loop suited Charlie just fine. "One more thing. I think you should take the lead on this, Sarah."

Kyle agreed, kissed his wife, then yawned. "Now it's time to go home."

They stood to leave. Charlie got their coats.

Sarah buttoned up. "We have our assignments. Now, if either of you find anything, shoot me a text."

As they walked to the door, Kyle saluted her ... behind her back.

She looked over her shoulder "I saw that, Kyle."

Charlie laughed. "Whoa. She is good."

CHAPTER THIRTY-THREE

The minute Charlie walked through Dawson-Landau's door, the serenity he'd found on Robinson's Pond was drowned out in the racket of ringing phones, beeping extensions, and collating copiers.

The shock of Penny's black and white Cruella de Vil hairdo didn't help. Of course, he'd never tell her that. "Wow! I see your daughters have been practicing again."

She smiled as if he'd paid her a compliment, then handed him a stack of messages. "You've got three callbacks to make. Staff meeting is set for one today, so I need your input by noon for the agenda. And Quinlan's on his way." She took a breath. "Hope you enjoyed your vacation."

Vacation? What vacation?

In her pressed navy suit, starched blouse, and polished pumps, Dee joined him at the coffee counter. "Let's hope this is a start to a happier year, Charlie."

"Thanks, Dee." He knew what she meant, but how could he be happier without Juliette?

As he and Dee got their coffee, calls poured in, and Penny handled them with ease. "I'll be sure to give Mr. Landau the message when he comes in, ma'am. May I repeat it to be sure I have it right?" … "Hey, Artie. Hank said to expect the lumber delivery around nine-thirty." … "Yes, Mrs. Quinlan, I will give your husband the message the second he arrives. He's to turn his cell phone on, correct?"

A minute later, Quinlan made his usual grand entrance. "Dawson! Hope your crew will be back up to speed now that the holidays are over."

Before Charlie could respond, Penny relayed the message from Vanetta.

Quinlan looked at his cell phone. "Darn thing's dead." He placed the phone on Penny's desk blotter. "Can you charge this before I leave?" Turning on his heel without waiting for an answer, he brushed past Charlie on the way to his office.

Penny snarled after him like he was one of the 101 Dalmatians, then she picked up his phone with her thumb and forefinger and moved it aside.

Charlie stifled a chuckle before he caught up with Quinlan.

Before he could get to his desk, Quinlan pounced. "What's next in the interior?"

He took his seat before he answered. "Again, Oliver, I'm the *design* in our design-build firm. Hank's the *build*. I'll have him call you after our staff meeting today."

"When will that be?"

Doesn't this guy have anything better to do?

Charlie folded his hands behind his head. "Mid-afternoon. Anything else I can do for you?"

"Yes, Vanetta's still waiting for your report on the landscape people."

Still? He'd only been at work fifteen minutes. "Two were away, and the third one isn't interested in the job."

Oliver grunted. "Must be nice."

"I've worked with some excellent landscape designers. I'll send Vanetta their names and a list of references. When she's ready, we can all meet."

"Make it quick," Oliver said. "We'll be out of town next week."

Figuring Oliver might respond better if he was the main topic of conversation, Charlie said, "Tell me, could a guy like me benefit from your wealth management services?"

"Probably, but I'm not taking on any new clients right now."

Charlie's turn to grunt. "Must be nice." When Oliver didn't react to the barb, he added, "I didn't know Plymouth was such a hotbed of wealth."

Quinlan snorted. "With clients all over the country, I hardly depend on this town."

Penny knocked, then slid the glass door open. "I don't mean to interrupt, Mr. Quinlan, but your wife is on line one."

"Please. Take the call in here." Charlie walked around him and out the slider.

Oliver wheedled, "Sorry, Van, my phone's dead ... I know, I know ... Could you please confirm our flight to Washington?"

Penny whispered to Charlie on their way to reception, "So do you think Mr. and Mrs. Big Shot are meeting with the President?"

He raised an eyebrow. "Do we really want to know?"

Penny scrunched up her face. "Good point."

Once Oliver left, the morning flew by. Charlie returned calls, dealt with design changes, and gathered notes for the staff meeting. When the work crews returned to the warehouse around noon, he sought out Zach. "Mind if I pick your brain about Garrett?"

Zach grabbed his lunch. "What d'ya wanna know?" He sat on a makeshift bench near a heater and took a bite of his sandwich.

"Anything you can recall, whether it seems pertinent or not."

He washed down the bite with a swig of water. "We used to rib each other about music. I was into Pearl Jam and Red Hot Chili Peppers. Garrett was more Brooks & Dunn and Blackhawk."

"Do you still like classic rock?"

"I may be a bit more particular about lyrics now, but, yeah, I still like that style of music. Why?"

Charlie brightened. "Then there's a good chance Garrett still likes country too."

He cocked his head. "He also loved reading Westerns. Louis L'Amour and Zane Grey kind of stuff."

Charlie remembered Sarah's instruction to collect names Garrett might have used as an alias. "Can you think of any other authors?"

He took a minute. "Yeah, his favorite was a guy named Max Brand. That might be a pseudonym though."

"Was he serious about going out West?"

Zach shrugged. "As serious as any kid with a dream. He even traded his bike for a secondhand pair of black and red cowboy boots—two sizes too big." He chuckled "Claimed they were one-of-a-kind, custom tooled leather." He hung his head. "I should have been a better friend to him, but those were my sorry days. I don't remember a lot, and what I do remember, I'm not proud of."

"You're not alone." Charlie put a hand on Zach's shoulder. "We'll let you know if we come up with anything."

When texting his findings to Sarah, he included the names Brooks, Dunn, Blackhawk, Louis L'Amour, Zane Grey, and Max Brand. Long shots at best.

When he checked his email, he found one from the colonel with his assignment to research Moline, Illinois.

That'll have to wait until the weekend.

After their week off, Charlie knew they'd all feel pressed to catch up. He doubted the staff meeting would run long.

Artie reported on his jobs. "The Clark garage addition is complete, and the big ol' colonial you plan to flip is scheduled to be gutted this week. How soon before we get the floor plans, Charlie?"

Charlie starred an item on his agenda. "Give me until the end of the week."

Hank added, "The plumbing and electrical are completed at the Annandale house. Sheetrock is going in tomorrow." He sucked in a breath then blew it out. "And we have our usual stack of change orders for the Quinlan interior finishes."

They groaned as a chorus but then agreed a week's reprieve from Quinlan's surprise inspections would be nice.

"There's still the phone," Penny grumbled. "When he can't reach Hank or Charlie, he calls me … over and over."

Charlie made nice. "No one can handle him like you, Penny. Not even me."

She fussed with her hair and adjusted her Dalmatian-print framed glasses. "Flattery is a poor consolation prize, but I'll take it."

Dee ran her pen down her list of accounts. "Speaking of Quinlan, he's late paying again. I emailed a second notice. A phone call is next. Unless you or Hank want to handle it?"

Hank shook his head. "Not me."

Charlie did the same. "We trust you, Dee. Besides, you know better what's going on with his account."

Dee tapped her steepled fingers together. "And when Oliver gets behind in his payments, I make one call to Vanetta. That woman wants what she wants when she wants it. She won't abide his tardiness or anything else that will pull the crew off her job."

Kyle had scheduled a meeting with Chief Eason at four-thirty that afternoon. Charlie promised he'd be there.

He pulled into the police station at 4:15. As he was about to get out of his car, Glenna O'Neil exited a side door and walked in his direction. He slid down in his seat until she passed by, then waited until her black Impala disappeared down Long Pond Road.

Phew.

He told the desk sergeant he was there to see Chief Eason.

Kyle came out to meet him. "I paved the way for us. Sorta. The chief isn't happy about the mini undercover DEA investigation, but he was well aware of Glenna's accusations and understood my reason for doing it." He knocked on the chief's door.

"Come in!"

They entered.

Charlie shook hands with the chief. "Thanks for seeing me, sir."

"Kyle tells me you found something that might change the ADA's plea deal with the Vincents?"

"I believe so, sir." Charlie handed him the photocopy of the handwritten list and a print-out of Juliette's matching spreadsheet. "We believe the handwriting will match Heidi Vincent's." He explained Heidi's connection with Juliette.

Kyle added details about the list from his perspective.

Chief Eason said, "First, Mr. Dawson, I'm sorry for your loss."

Charlie responded with a brief nod.

After Eason examined the spreadsheet, he said, "Yates, you're right about these characters. The drug task force has long assumed they're making inroads, but the drop in drug traffic was unrealistic—despite what some of our members prefer to believe."

"Oliver Quinlan is my client," Charlie said. "I've heard his claims."

Since Kyle didn't mention their search committee, Charlie didn't either.

"Some of our task force members are convinced Quinlan's the best thing Plymouth's seen since William Bradford or Massasoit, depending on who's talking. Problem is those same members worry more about politics than rehabilitation—but you didn't hear that from me."

Charlie liked this guy.

Eason rested his fists on his desk. "Once I call the district attorney's office, they'll want to speak with you. Some things may come out."

Charlie swallowed hard. "I understand, sir."

He turned to Kyle. "I'll handle Sergeant O'Neil. Got that, Officer Yates?"

Kyle shifted in his seat. "Got it, sir."

The chief looked up. "Anything else?"

"Yes, sir, about Sergeant O'Neil's brother." Kyle told him what they'd discovered from Zach. "Now we know for sure Garrett was alive for much of the time Glenna thought he was dead. Any chance I could work this as a cold case without O'Neil finding out about it, sir?"

"Under the auspices of the Plymouth PD?" He thought for a moment. "That might work. My personal assistant can see to your needs." He stood as if to dismiss them. "Tread carefully, Yates, and keep me informed."

As they left the chief's office, Charlie said, "Speaking of keeping people informed, Sarah's gonna want to know what we found out. Do you have time to look at Garrett's missing person's file now?"

"I already did. Found a couple of photos too. Our tech officer gave me a few aging apps to try."

"I got some more background from Zach, but I'm not sure how valuable it is."

Kyle's phone beeped. He read the message. "Sarah says to come for supper, so we can go over our findings."

Charlie laughed. "No slack, huh?"

"Not only that, we've gotta bring supper."s

While Sarah enjoyed her Greek salad, Charlie and Kyle made a quick end to a large meat-lovers pizza.

Sarah opened with news about Glenna's parents. "Her father's name was Everett Robert. Her mother's, Maeve Neala Kagen. Garrett's middle name is Kagen too. Let's put the female names aside for now."

Charlie recapped his conversation with Zach. "He'll let us know if he thinks of anything else."

They found Max Brand's biography online then added his real name, Frederic Schiller Faust, and three more of his pseudonyms to their growing list.

Sarah flipped a page on her legal pad. "No names of pets to consider since Mrs. O'Neil was allergic. And most of the stables in Carver had catchy phrases for names like Happy Trails or Horseshoe Haven. I found a few names we could add. Kilkenny and Troy. Let's add Carver too."

The final tally was two dozen separate names with umpteen possible combinations and no clue if any would match. They sorted them alphabetically.

Kyle briefed them on Garrett's missing person case and showed them the pictures he'd found in the file. One, a candid shot—the other, a senior class photo.

Sarah put her readers on. "There's a keen resemblance to Glenna."

Kyle opened the app and uploaded the class photo. Seconds after inputting dates and data, eight years appeared on Garrett's face. Not a dramatic change but some.

"Anything else we need to add to our notes?" Sarah clicked her pen.

Kyle straightened his shoulders. "Isn't this enough?"

She set her jaw. "Won't be enough until we find him."

Charlie's phone interrupted. "What's up, Zach? Were your ears burning?"

"I just remembered something from my emails with Garrett."

"Let me put you on speaker. I'm with Sarah and Kyle." He held the phone up.

"When I was stationed on Guam, I complained to Garrett about the tropical climate. He wrote back saying I should try winters in the Dakotas."

The three of them fist-bumped each other.

Spurred by Zach's information, they spent the next few hours collecting contact information for troubled teen ranches in North and South Dakota. They compared Garrett's aged photo with candid shots they found on the websites. The faces were blurred, probably to protect the teens' anonymity.

They agreed a well-thought-out certified letter on police stationary—signed by Kyle yet composed by Sarah—would be the best way to present their case to the ranches. That way they'd have less chance of sounding like debt collectors or spammers. If they didn't hear back, they'd follow up with a phone call.

Early the next day, Charlie received the final draft of Sarah's letter. Impressed with the progress they'd made, Charlie rapped on his desk and sang the words he could remember to "Celebration" by Kool and the Gang.

Any chance you're jumping to conclusions like the members of the drug task force?

Bam! His exultation imploded.

The idea that Garrett O'Neil had been in hiding for over eight years seemed more and more farfetched. Still, he liked to imagine what it would be like to tell Glenna. How would she react?

Much like you'd react if someone told you Juliette was still alive.

He blinked back tears.

Any chance of God sending you back, Jules? … No? … Have you at least asked?

CHAPTER THIRTY-FOUR

Dressed in high heels and gold satin jodhpurs, Vanetta Quinlan shouted, "Ready, set, go!" then fired a pistol in the air.

A jockey on a spotted pony bolted toward Charlie. Red and black cowboy boots slapped against the horse's flanks. A runner's bib flapped against the rider's chest.

Charlie strained to read the number on the bib, but the dust billowed and blinded him. If it were Juliette's favorite, 316, everything would be new again! He jumped into Glenna O'Neil's black Impala and chased them down the track.

Charlie shot up in bed, his thoughts battling reality. He lay back down, trying to reenter the dream from this side of the veil. *Let the rider be you, Juliette, let it be you.*
Gone.
Fully awake, loneliness weighed like a ton of stone. Gathering his strength and wits, he threw his legs over the side of the bed and scrubbed his face, hard.
"Lord, I thought the real bad days were behind me. Help, please."
He shaved, then showered with hot water, ending with cold, which helped. A cup of strong coffee helped more. Spending time with the Lord and in his Word helped most. Psalm 73 revealed his heart and revived his faith.

When my heart was grieved and my spirit embittered, I was senseless and ignorant; I was a brute beast before you. Yet I am always with you; you hold me by my right hand. You guide me with your counsel, and afterward you will take me into glory. Whom have I in heaven but you? And earth has nothing I desire besides you. My flesh and my heart may fail, but God is the strength of my heart and my portion forever.

He prayed, "Juliette's spirit is with you, Lord. For that, I'm grateful. But I'm still here. Maybe I could help those like her, who are stuck in dangerous places. Or their loved ones, like Natalie and the colonel. Please give our search committee the wisdom and facts we need to make a difference. And may the news about Garrett O'Neil be good for Glenna's sake."

His softening toward Glenna surprised him. Hope welled up, giving him a sense of purpose.

With clarity and vigor, he opened the colonel's spreadsheet and began his online search on his assigned city, Moline, Illinois. By eleven-thirty, he'd filled in most of the columns: location, heart of the Midwest, within 300 miles of six metropolitan areas; population about 43,300; median income, $52,000; median age, thirty-eight; median price of homes, $100,000; major businesses include Deere & Company world headquarters, United Healthcare, and McLaughlin Body Company. The city boasted Greyhound and Trailways stations, MetroLink, and Quad City International Airport, serving four major airlines.

Past news stories reported the influx of illegal drugs had grown exponentially in Moline over a ten-year period. However, more recent articles revealed the flow had slowed dramatically soon after a drug task force had been formed two years ago. A random article highlighted an increased shortage of beds for recovering addicts.

Fewer drugs equaled less usage but resulted in a shortage of beds? Didn't make sense to him. He noted the contradiction in his email to the colonel.

After a few hours of reading newspaper stories, journals, posts, and public task force reports, one thing stood out: Moline's drug trafficking seemed to have taken a detour much like that in Plymouth.

He needed a break.

A light snow fell on Plymouth proper as Charlie made his way to Vine Hills. Enough white to lace bare branches and blanket dead lawns but not enough to stick to the roads. A crowded graveside service was going on nearby Juliette's site when he drove in. Since he'd come to believe every grief was private—no strangers allowed—he circled back to the exit. As he passed the mourning party, he got a glimpse of a Carhartt-brown jacket in a sea of black wool. Shouting-man stood among the family, head bowed, petting the coonskin hat in his hand.

He pulled off to the side of Samoset Street to text Sarah.

CHARLIE: Need any help with those letters to the teen ranches?
SARAH: Want to stuff envelopes? Meet me at BFF.
CHARLIE: C u in 5.

To keep the investigation on the QT, they did as much as possible outside of the police station, away from Glenna.

Sarah was out by her car when he arrived. She handed him a box of letters and another of envelopes. "They're addressed and all in order. All you have to do is fold and insert." She dug in her purse. "Here're the stamps."

"Kyle must have been up late getting these together." He managed to keep a straight face.

She gave him a look. "Yeah, right. But he did scribble his signature."

Charlie put the boxes in his Jeep then looked over at the shop. "Open late this afternoon for another one of those private client fittings?"

"Not exactly. Ashlyn's boss, Jillian McGee, dropped by to invite us to her baby shower."

That news cleared his head. "Ashlyn had her baby?"

"Not yet, but she's due in about three weeks. Jillian wanted to be sure the pregnancy was going well before she planned anything. The situation is sensitive, as you know, but the girl needs all the support we can muster."

Not sure about cemetery relationship protocol, Charlie asked, "Should I get the baby a gift too?"

Sarah was gentle. "I don't think that's necessary."

"Right."

Hank carried a large box of pastries into the office Monday morning. "Morning, ladies, Charlie. I've got good news and bad news. Which do you want first?"

Dee tugged at the hem of her suit jacket. "Today is only Monday, how bad can it be?"

Penny moaned. Her black and white spotted hair looked like she'd spent the night curled up in a dog bed.

Hank said, "Okay, good news first! We're all invited to the Clarks for their new garage open house."

Dee wrinkled her nose. "An open house for a garage?"

Hank shrugged. "It's a three-car."

Penny narrowed her eyes. "If that's the good news, I can wait to hear the bad."

Hank opened the pastry box. "Have one, ladies. They're from that bakery down on Court Street."

Penny peeked inside the box to make her choice. Dee cut a muffin in half while Charlie stirred his coffee.

"Although one of the Quinlans will be away for the week,"—Hank cleared his throat—"the other has decided to hang back."

Penny glared over the top her glasses. "Would that one be Oliver? If so, I need another Danish."

Charlie's cell rang. He read the ID and rolled his eyes. "Good morning, Oliver."

Hank leaned against a file cabinet, grinned, then took a bite of a Boston cream donut.

As Quinlan babbled on, Charlie stabbed a finger at Hank's phone.

Hank held it up then mouthed, "Turned off."

So wisdom does come with age. Charlie took a sip of coffee. "Yes, Oliver."

"I want to see a lot more progress before my wife returns."

"Speaking of Vanetta, she still has some finish choices to make. When will she be back?" Charlie'd almost said, 'from DC', but remembered he'd been eavesdropping.

"I'll be handling all construction details from this end."

"Then you're in luck. Hank's right here. I'll let you speak with him." He smirked as he handed the phone to his partner.

Hank swallowed his last bite of donut. "What can I do for you? … Let me reassure you, the painters are priming today, and the tile installers will finish the bathrooms by Wednesday … Good, good. Here's Charlie." Hank played hot potato with the phone.

Charlie caught it. "I'm sorry you felt you had to forego your business trip."

"Vanetta's business trip. She's not just another pretty face, you know."

What was he supposed to say to that? "I'm sure you're very proud of her."

"Of course, I am. She runs circles around most in her field."

What field? He couldn't recall. Did he dare ask? All he could think to say was, "I don't doubt that."

Dee waved an invoice at him and whispered, "Let me speak with him."

Charlie excused himself and passed the call off again.

"Dee Jennings, Mr. Quinlan. Would you like to handle the payment on your invoice … or would you prefer I contact Mrs. Quinlan?"

She wasn't on the phone long. When she attempted to hand the phone back to Charlie, Penny intercepted.

"It's Penny, Mr. Quinlan." She held up a wool scarf. "I think you may have left a scarf behind the last time you were here. It's one of those Burberry lookalikes, tan with black and red stripes? I bought one like it on sale at Sears as a Christmas gift for my husband." She pulled the phone away from her ear and grimaced. "No? Oh, well, just thought I'd check."

Charlie took the phone back. "I'll let you go, Oliver. Remember, anytime you have a question about construction, Hank's the one to contact." Would the man ever get that?

Quinlan responded, "Maybe, but I know where to find you."

Ah, the truth comes out.

Charlie clicked off and eyed Penny. "Really? A scarf from Sears?"

She put on a face of innocence. "Well, everyone else had a turn at him, I wanted mine."

Before Charlie could get to work, his father-in-law walked in.

"Have a minute, son? I was in the area, thought I'd stop by."

He couldn't read his father-in-law's face. "Sure." Charlie led him into the conference room and closed the door. "What can I do for you, sir?"

The colonel took a seat. "Remember my old West Point buddy … the one I inquired about your client, Oliver Quinlan? He called me today with an odd bit of news."

Charlie tilted his head. "News?"

The colonel swiveled in his chair. "Oliver died of a massive stroke last week."

"What?" Charlie put his cup down. "But I just spoke with him minutes ago."

"Yes, well, we did some digging. Turns out *your* Oliver Quinlan and his are not the same person. The man who died spelled his name Q-u-i-n-l-*i*-n."

"West Point had two students with that name?"

"No, just the one. Yours is a fraud."

Charlie's mouth dropped open. "Why on earth would he lie about that?"

"Good question." He grunted. "I'd love to hear his answer."

"And I'd love to see his face."

CHARLIE: Oliver, are you at your jobsite?

QUINLAN: Yes, and I need you here now.

CHARLIE: On my way.

Mischief on his mind, Charlie said, "Ready, Colonel? This should be good."

The colonel rubbed his hands together. "The element of surprise. One of my favorite tactics."

Since Quinlan would most likely try to evade confrontation, Charlie parked across the driveway, blocking his Mercedes.

In the doorway at the top of the temporary steps, Quinlan checked his watch. He took no notice of the colonel but pointed to a pallet and growled at Charlie. "Vanetta's going to explode when she sees this. That's not the tile she ordered for the kitchen!"

Deadpan, he answered, "You're right. She ordered that tile for the guest baths."

"Oh." Oliver paused. "Well, with all the delays and errors, I needed to be certain."

Charlie bristled at his false accusations but said nothing.

The colonel stepped forward but didn't extend his hand. "Do you remember me, Mr. Quinlan? I'm Charlie's father-in-law … and fellow West Point man."

"Uh, yes, I think we met at the office." He turned his attention back to Charlie. "So, when will the kitchen tile be in?"

"When Italy ships your wife's special order." Charlie motioned to his father-in-law. "Colonel, why don't you tell Oliver about the interesting phone call you got today from West Point about the rumors of his death."

Oliver tried to step around Charlie. "Sorry. No time to chat. I have an appointment with a client in—"

Charlie put a hand up. "This will only take a second. Why did you lie about going to West Point?"

Oliver mumbled and stuttered. "I didn't … I wasn't … you might have misunderstood me."

"No, I distinctly recall you telling the group of us at the Westfalls', then again in my office."

"Look, West Point was my first choice, but it didn't work out." He combed his Julius Caesar hairstyle with his manicured nails. "When Vanetta came across an article about the other Oliver Quinlin there … spelled similarly … she thought it would be fun to tell people it was me. We were only joking."

The colonel's shoulders stretched taut. "Assuming someone's identity, especially that of a decorated veteran, isn't a joke, Mr. Whatever-Your-Name."

"Things got out of hand, that's all." Oliver groveled, "And I'd appreciate you not mentioning this to Vanetta right now. Let me handle that, okay?"

The colonel stepped aside and let Oliver pass. "We'll consider your request, Mr. Quinlan."

Charlie chuckled as they headed back to the office. "Thanks to you, Colonel, I have a hunch he'll be much less of a thorn in my flesh from now on."

"I'd watch him if I were you." The colonel shifted in his seat. "By the way, I've asked Ted and Binnie if we can meet soon to discuss our findings on those six cities. I'm still waiting on results from a few in the group, but there does seem to be a similar traffic pattern. And your Quinlan's connected to two of the states."

"If the results reveal he's involved in an unlawful way," Charlie said, "what would our next step be?"

"We'd present our findings to Chief Eason. He'll get them to the appropriate law enforcement."

Charlie nodded. "Kyle trusts the Chief. Says he's a man of integrity."

"Let's hope so."

CHAPTER THIRTY-FIVE

"Heads up, Charlie." Kyle sounded out of breath on the phone. "A one-woman SWAT is on her way. O'Neil found out I checked her brother's case file."

"How?"

"Not sure, but she tortured the file clerk until he broke. I was able to sneak out the back door to my cruiser, but you're a sitting duck."

"Why would she come after me?" Charlie swiveled in his chair to look out the window to the street.

"Because she's smart enough to put two and two and you and me together. Sarah thinks we should stonewall her until we exhaust all possible leads to Garrett."

"Better than getting her hopes up, I guess." Charlie pinched the bridge of his nose. "Has Sarah heard back from any of the ranches yet?"

"Ranches?" Glenna O'Neil stood three feet from his desk. "You plan on becoming a cowboy *and* a detective, Dawson?"

How'd she get by Penny?

Covering the phone's mouthpiece, Charlie managed a smile at Glenna. "I'll be with you in a second, Sergeant. Let me finish up here." He leaned back in his chair, legs uncrossed, arms loose—as much body language training as he could muster under the circumstances.

Kyle whispered, "I knew it! Call me later."

Charlie continued talking. "I'll get back to you with that information, sir." … "Probably later this afternoon." He clicked off then turned to Glenna. "Now, what can I do for you, Sergeant?"

"You and Yates can stay out of my business."

Charlie figured lying would only infuriate her. "Look, Glenna, you've been haunting me ever since my wife died as if I had some fault in it. I asked Kyle if the circumstances surrounding your brother's disappearance might have something to do with your feelings toward me. He reviewed the missing person's file. That's all."

She jabbed her finger at him. "Fact that he warned you is proof you two are up to something, and I'll find out what it is."

Charlie stood. "I know what it's like to lose someone you love. Despite what you think of me, I would never intentionally cause you any further pain. I'm sorry if I have."

Without a word, she stared him down then walked out of his office. But not before Charlie saw the hurt in her eyes.

Still, she sure didn't make helping her easy.

After work, Charlie picked up Thai food on his way over to Kyle's.

Sarah arrived home just as he and Kyle opened the cartons. "Hey, you two! Save some for me."

"Thought you had to work late." Kyle walked over and kissed her.

"I thought so too."

Kyle's phone pinged as he reached for a plate. "Another email from one of the ranches."

Charlie asked, "How many does that make now?"

"Four," he said. "The first three said they didn't have anyone who looked like the sketch." He began reading out loud. "We received your inquiry regarding Garrett O'Neil. The photo doesn't resemble anyone we have working at our main office. I will forward the picture to our other locations. Until then, I've attached our employee roaster for your review. Please let us know if any of the names sound familiar." Kyle fell silent.

Sarah stared at him. "So? What are the names?"

"Shush. I'm reading them now. There're dozens."

"*Out loud*, Kyle." She took a sheet of paper off the kitchen bulletin board. "And slowly, so I can check them against the names we collected."

"Good idea." His fingers flicked back up. "Here goes. Andres, Walter … Auber, Burt … Binder, Hugh … Capen, Lance … Doane, Daniel … Grant, Timothy … Jackson, Butch … Any matches?"

"Not even close," she said. "Keep going."

He read to the end. "That's all."

Sarah slumped in her chair. "Unless the enhanced photo looks familiar to someone at one of their other locations, this lead is dead too."

"How about we run the names by Zach?" Charlie bit into a spring roll.

Kyle shrugged. "Can't hurt."

Charlie texted Zach to see if he could stop by Kyle and Sarah's house that night.

A few minutes later, there was a knock at the back door.

Kyle answered it. "That was fast."

Zach laughed. "I'd just passed your house on my way to get supper. What's up?"

"We got a list of employees from one of the ranches," Sarah said. "Garrett's not on it, but we wondered if any names might ring a bell with you."

Sarah took Kyle's phone and began reading the roster.

Name after name, Zach shook his head. "Walter, Burt, Hugh? Nope. Not anything Garrett would pick."

She continued, "Manners, Jason … O'Bannon, Roy … Paris, Mitchell—"

"Wait!" Zach's eyes narrowed. "Back up. What was the name before Mitchell?"

Sarah scrolled back. "O'Bannon, Roy."

Zach's smile widened. "Owen Wilson played Roy O'Bannon in *Shanghai Noon*,"—he paused, making eye contact with all three of them—"which was one of Garrett's all-time favorite movies."

Sarah bit her thumbnail. "You think Roy could be Garrett?"

"Either that or it's one glaring coincidence, which I thought Christians didn't believe in." Zach crossed his arms and smirked.

Kyle slapped him on the back. "You've just earned yourself a plate of Thai food!"

Sarah's phone rang as Kyle microwaved their now cold takeout.

"Hi, Natalie, what's up? … "She did? … Everything okay? … Is she still in the hospital?"

At the word *hospital*, Charlie raised his head. "Who? What?"

She held a finger up. "How long will they keep her? … Sure. … Okay, tell Ashlyn I'll see her later."

Charlie's fork dropped to his plate. "Ashlyn Reid's in the hospital?"

She smiled. "Yes, but only because she had her baby. James Luke weighed in at eight pounds, three ounces. Mother and son are doing fine."

Charlie exhaled. "That's great."

"Who's Ashlyn?" Kyle took a steaming bowl out of the microwave.

Zach picked up a plate. "Does this woman have something to do with Garrett?"

"No," Sarah said. "She's Charlie's cemetery friend and a BFF client."

Kyle's forehead creased. "Huh?"

Charlie got a queasy feeling in the pit of his stomach. "So, everything's okay?"

"Yes, according to Jillian who called Natalie."

"Who's Jillian?" Kyle asked.

"Just eat, dear."

Well, that's it. From widow to mother in one day … or was it nine months? He was happy for Ashlyn. She had a son. He shuddered as he imagined her going through the delivery alone. Without warning, panic seized his senses. His hands sweat, his heart pounded, and his mind went fuzzy.

I should have been there for her and the baby. What kind of man am I? What if something had happened? How could I ever forgive myself? I've got to get to them now!

Except Ashlynn's face was not the one he was seeing—it was Juliette's.

What's happening to you, Dawson? Get a grip! He downed a full glass of water.

"Charlie? Did you hear me?" Zach said.

He cleared his head and his throat to compose himself. "Sorry. What did you say?"

"Just wondering if Hank or Artie mentioned what jobsite I'd be on tomorrow?"

Charlie mumbled an answer.

Still rattled by his odd response to a virtual stranger giving birth, Charlie called Edy when he got home, "Hey, Dr. Sister, did I wake you?"

"No. I'm unwinding with a cup of chamomile. What's on your mind little brother?"

263

"Actually, I'm looking for a psych evaluation, but a pediatric one will do since you're free." He hoped joking would lessen his anxiety.

"*Zo, mein herr,* what ist dein problem?"

He explained his reaction to Ashlyn and her baby, and how he'd pictured her being Juliette. "I've seen this woman less than half a dozen times, mostly at the cemetery. Why would I feel guilty for not being there for her? Doesn't make any sense at all."

Edy's tone turned serious. "Well, I assume she's visiting a loved one's grave. You've probably related to each other because of your mutual loss. Then, this woman goes through something you'd hoped to experience with Juliette one day. Freud and Jung probably would've called it *transference*. But most mainstream psychologists today would say your feelings in this situation are all part of the mixed-up emotions of grief."

"So, I'm not going nuts?"

"As a physician, I say no. As your sister, I cannot give a definitive answer."

He smiled. "Thanks."

"Now get off the couch, it's my turn to be analyzed."

She had his attention. "You?"

"Yes, me. What do you say to a thirty-seven-year-old woman who keeps refusing a marriage proposal from a man she loves?"

"Matt asked you to marry him? That's great!"

"Yes, great." Edy sighed. "Yet every time he brings the subject up, I panic. What's wrong with me?"

Charlie remembered one of their earlier conversations. "Fear. You've alluded to it in the past. I think you're afraid if you get too close to someone you might lose them. Like we did Mom and Dad." He paused. "And like I did Juliette."

"Maybe. But how would I handle a medical practice *and* a husband? Would Matt resent me if he had to commute to

Boston? How would I fit him and his stuff in my one-bedroom condo when there's barely enough room for me?"

Charlie let her catch her breath before he spoke. "First of all, you don't *handle* a husband. You love him. Second, Matt's a genius with a following. If he doesn't like commuting, I'm sure MIT would let him telecommute. Third, Juliette and I had eight years in Mom and Dad's house. Maybe it's time for you to have a turn. I'd be happy to switch places with you."

She answered quickly. "You don't mean that, Charlie."

"I wouldn't say it if I didn't. Besides, without Juliette, the house seems more like Mom and Dad's again. You're here a lot anyway, cleaning, gardening, bossing me around."

"I am not!"

"Are too. Anyway, think how it would bless our parents to know we'd each had a turn to enjoy the old homestead." He waited out her silence.

"When did you get so smart?" she said.

"I had kale and anchovies for lunch."

She laughed. "Very funny, Sigmund."

CHAPTER THIRTY-SIX

Over the next few days, everything seemed to happen at once, but in slow motion, if that was possible.

The manager of the ranch called Sarah to say Roy O'Bannon was a match for the enhanced photo they'd sent of Garrett O'Neil. He'd been hired on to care for the horses, not the teens, making it easier for him to fly under their radar. When they questioned him, he told them his whole story.

Once Zach spoke with Garrett, he was able to convince him to come home and make amends. "The best thing you can do for yourself and your sister is make peace."

Before Garrett could change his mind, Sarah booked a flight for him the following evening. They called Glenna but got her voice mail. Charlie even drove down her street a few times. Her house was dark, and there was no car in the driveway.

Kyle called Charlie from the station the next morning when he learned Glenna had taken a leave of absence. "I told the other patrols to keep a lookout for her Impala, but nothing so far."

"Keep me posted," Charlie said. "If you don't reach her in time to meet his flight, Zach and I will have to go. We can't leave the guy stranded."

With only a few hours remaining before Garrett's plane landed in Boston, Charlie picked Zach up at his apartment. Traffic was heavy, but they reached baggage claim ahead of the horde of weary-looking passengers.

"There he is!" Zach shouted. "The tall, scraggly-haired guy with the black cowboy hat."

Charlie craned to see where Zach pointed. "Are you sure? It's been a while since you've seen him."

"I'm sure. He looks the same. So do those black and red boots of his." Zach wrapped his old friend in a hug. "Good to see you in the flesh—even if you do smell like a barn!"

"You, too, man." Garrett's eyes teared-up. "Dang! Your fancy cologne's making my eyes water." He stepped back and took a closer look at Zach. "I kind of expected you to greet me with some kind of screwball martial arts move."

"Nah, I left my Jackie Chan days behind me. I'm a reputable carpenter now. This is one of my bosses, Charlie Dawson."

Charlie stuck out his hand. "So glad we found you, Garrett … or is it Roy?"

"Legally, Roy, but I kept Garrett as my middle name." He scanned the area. His face fell. "So I guess Glenna didn't wanna come?"

"The thing is," Zach said, "Glenna doesn't know about you yet. Since she had you declared dead and all, we wanted to be sure you were alive before we said anything."

Garrett blinked. "You didn't mention that. She really had me declared dead?"

"After years without a word," Zach said, "what d'ya expect?"

"All I wanted to do was change my name and start a new life." Garrett's shoulders dropped. "I never meant for that to happen."

"Unfortunately, right about the time we found you," Charlie said, "your sister took some time off, and we haven't been able to track her down."

Garrett's face scrunched up. "So, if Glenna doesn't know, then who's been searching for me … and why?"

Charlie answered. "That would be me, Zach, and Kyle Yates—one of Glenna's fellow cops—and Kyle's wife Sarah."

"As for why," Zach huffed, "you know Glenna. She hasn't stopped blaming me for your disappearance. Says you got involved with drugs because of me."

Garrett shook his head. "Sheesh. I got high *once,* accidentally, on fudge, I think, made with pot. Even though it happened *after* you joined the Army, she wouldn't let up about your bad influence. Went crazy over it." He shook his head. "Anyway, that's only one of the reasons I left."

"Well, according to her fellow officers, including Kyle," Charlie said, "she's been a mess ever since. When we realized you and Zach had been in touch, we started our own investigation, uh, sort of behind her back."

Zach slapped Garrett on the back. "And we're pretty sure you showing your goofy face again will put a smile on hers."

When the three of them reached Plymouth, Charlie checked in with Kyle one last time.

"Still no word on Glenna's whereabouts," Kyle said.

Until she appeared, Garrett agreed to stay out of sight at Zach's.

Five days later, Kyle called Charlie when Glenna returned to work. "Sarah thinks we should try to lessen the shock and have Glenna and Garrett reunite in private."

"What did you have in mind?" Charlie wondered, though, if a public place might be *safer.*

"Well, an invitation from Sarah and me might seem suspicious to her, but I bet she'd accept one from Binnie."

Charlie had a random thought. "Maybe we can get Glenna over there when she's *not* in uniform."

Kyle chuckled. "You mean when she's not carrying her weapon?"

"That's exactly what I mean."

"I think she wears it to bed."

In the end, Binnie, who never took "no" for an answer, invited Glenna to Sunday dinner, and she accepted.

When Glenna arrived at the Westfalls', Binnie ushered her into the living room where Charlie, Kyle, and Sarah were waiting. Zach and Garrett had been sequestered in Ted's office.

Binnie smiled. "I believe you know everyone, Glenna."

Charlie could almost feel the tension fill the room.

Nodding to the threesome, Glenna muttered, "Yeah, I know them." She crossed her arms. "What's this all about?"

Charlie was convinced she'd make a good detective someday.

Sarah sat then patted the sofa cushion next to her. "Why don't you join me, Glenna."

Glenna sat at the opposite end of the sofa. "This isn't about dinner, is it?"

"Not exactly," Charlie sat, rubbing the top of his thighs with the palm of his hands. "Recently, you accused Kyle and me of snooping into your business. You were right, but we had good reason."

Glenna spat out, "My personal life is off-limits!"

Kyle held his hand up. "Please, Glenna, hear us out." He took a deep breath. "One night, Zach Jennings said something to Charlie and me about his last email exchange with Garrett. The time period he mentioned seemed off. We checked and found out Zach and Garrett had emailed each other years after everyone had presumed Garrett was dead."

Glenna's face turned red, and her hands balled into fists. "Why are you doing this to me?"

Sarah scooted over and covered Glenna's fist with her hand. "We saw you suffering and wanted to help, so we started digging."

Glenna shot up out of her seat. "Without my knowledge?"

"Yes." Sarah stood beside her. "In case we were wrong, we didn't want to get your hopes up."

Glenna's eyes filled. "And what do you think you're doing now?"

Sarah put her arm around Glenna. "Restoring your faith, we hope." She nodded at Binnie and Ted.

Ted opened the door to his office. Zach walked out with Garrett close behind him.

Glenna's knees gave out, and she dropped to the couch and froze.

Garrett walked over then knelt at her feet. He held her eyes with his. "Glenna?"

She shook her head and pushed him away. "No, no, get away from me. You can't be—"

Charlie said, "Listen to him, Glenna."

Garrett sat next to her and brushed a tear from her cheek. "It's me, really."

She covered her mouth with her hands. "Garrett, oh, Garrett. How? Why?"

"After Mom died, I discovered the truth about our family. All I wanted to do was get as far away from home as I could—and I did."

"The truth?" She looked intently into his eyes. "You mean—"

He nodded. "I was confused and angry and hurt. I was also immature and stupid. Later, I wanted to come back, but I thought I'd ruined my chances. Can you ever forgive me?"

She held his face in her hands. "You're alive, and you're here. Of course! But I'm the one who needs forgiveness."

Binnie interrupted, "Glenna, would you and your brother like to retreat to Ted's office for some privacy?"

Glenna studied the faces around the room. "I spent years retreating, so to speak. No more secrets. I want the world to know Garrett is not my brother. He is my son."

So, they had guessed right.

Garrett said, "I didn't handle the news well, didn't even tell Glenna I knew."

Glenna shook her head. "We should have told you earlier. There just never seemed to be a good time. I'd like to explain."

Sarah said, "Please don't feel you owe us any explanation."

"Maybe not, but I owe one to my son." She took a moment to compose herself. "I was fourteen, unpopular, and naïve. When some high school kids invited me to a party, I snuck out and went. The only thing I remember about that night is one of the boys offering me a soda. When my parents found me the next morning, about a half mile from our house, I was groggy, bruised, and my clothes were torn. The doctor suspected I'd been drugged and confirmed I'd been raped. I had no idea by whom—and still don't. Probably explains my attitude toward drugs and everyone associated with them."

Garrett put his arm around his mother's shoulders.

"When I discovered I was pregnant, your grandparents and I discussed the options: Raising the child myself, having my parents raise the baby as one of their own, or adoption. We agreed on what we all thought was best—for my child. That decision meant a move out of town and a change of jobs for my dad." She looked at her son, her eyes filling again. "They sacrificed so much for us both."

Garrett handed her a tissue. "When Glenna tried to move into the role of mother after Mom died, I resented her and rebelled. I assumed she'd been ashamed of me all those years."

"Never!" Glenna hugged him.

He held her tight.

"If you all hadn't persisted—" Glenna choked up. "Let's just say, I don't know how to thank you."

Zach said, "Just be happy."

Glenna raised her right hand. "I swear, I will—and no more secrets! And, Garrett, if you ever want to find out about your biological father, I'll do whatever I can to help."

"I'm pretty sure I have all the parents I need for now." He chuckled. "Besides, I hear you're a handful."

Charlie tried to look innocent. "He didn't hear that from me, Sergeant O'Neil."

"Or me," Zach said.

Glenna smiled, "I suspect he could have heard that from any number of my fellow officers, right, Yates?"

Kyle zipped his lip. "I have the right to remain silent …"

CHAPTER THIRTY-SEVEN

Ted Westfall emailed the other committee members: "After reviewing our accumulated findings, suspicions, and assumptions, Binnie and I feel that, as a group, we have reached the limit of our combined resources. We're convinced we need to bring in Chief Eason."

Charlie wasn't a cop or private investigator, so he had no problem agreeing. Besides, the side snooping he, Kyle, and Sarah had done to find Garrett had been challenging enough for him.

Ted briefed the chief in an email, and a meeting was set for Friday at the usual hour. However, the location was changed from the Westfalls' home to the Annandales' to avoid Glenna O'Neil popping by. Things were going smoothly since she and Garrett had reunited. They didn't want to stir her up again.

That effort was undone when Chief Eason showed up with O'Neil by his side. "I believe you all know Sergeant O'Neil."

An understatement, to be sure.

Despite Natalie's offer of iced tea and cookies, the awkwardness was palpable.

His jaw set tight, the chief was the first to speak. "I was not aware the Town of Plymouth had a private committee investigating so-called curious incidents. Not sure how I feel about it either." He crossed his beefy arms. "And what did you all hope to accomplish on your own?"

Kyle took a swig of his tea. "We didn't start out as a committee, per se, Chief. We were just a bunch of people affected by illegal drugs, commiserating with one another." Kyle motioned to the others. "Charlie and the colonel needed answers about Juliette. Pastor Westfall was concerned about the drug addiction problem in his congregation. Zach wanted to know who framed him and why."

Zach crossed his legs, his ankle resting on his knee. "And with my history of drug abuse and recovery, I was able to speak from both perspectives."

Binnie clasped her hands in her lap. "One confusing question led to another, then to even more confusing answers. What we found made us even more curious."

"When rabbit trails and people started to connect, and not in a good way," Sarah added, "we figured we'd hit on something."

The chief grunted. "And coming to the police wasn't an option?"

Kyle sat forward then looked from Glenna to the chief. "With Sergeant O'Neil's accusations and well, uh, loyalties, we didn't know who we could trust." He turned to Glenna. "Sorry, Sergeant."

The chief scowled. "*Loyalties?* Yates, I hope you're not questioning the Sergeant's loyalty to the department."

"Not at all, sir." Kyle looked Binnie's way. "Perhaps Binnie could expound—"

Binnie jumped in. "As a fellow member of the drug task force, I'm sure you've noticed the way certain members garnered favor from others, in particular, Oliver Quinlan."

The chief grunted but said nothing to dispute Binnie's observation.

"They're not wrong, sir," Glenna addressed the chief in a firm and steady voice. "In their defense, early on, I gave them plenty of reason to mistrust us—me, in particular. I believed Charlie had some responsibility in his wife's addiction, and I thought the break-in at his house was in search of drugs. I also blamed

Zach for Garrett's disappearance. I was wrong on both counts, and I apologize."

All eyes were drawn to Glenna. Getting her son back seemed to have softened her ... or maybe strengthened her.

Kyle interjected, "Sir, if you recall, the DEA found the same markings on the drugs sold here as those sold in six other cities. The MO of the distributors in all seven locations seems to be the same. First, they infiltrate some manner of a civic committee or task force. Then, the drug traffic goes down in that area. Now we're not saying it *is* Quinlan, but we can't eliminate him either."

Charlie added, "As you already suspect, the decrease in sales is all smoke and mirrors. The traffic is only pushed over the town line and brought under *new* management. According to Heidi Vincent, those forcing independent dealers to join their home-grown cartel keep a low profile. She said her contact even disguised his voice.

"Chief, the fact is Oliver Quinlan either lived in and or traveled to those cities in the past five years. He's served on drug task forces in three of those cities. He lied about his name and affiliations and most likely about his business operations. And there's no end to his money source."

Chief Eason looked across the room at Charlie. "A money source Dawson-Landau has benefitted from." He sighed. "The fact is, nothing you've told me *proves* anything you suspect him of doing."

"We know that," Charlie said. "But check the timing of events. Everything seems to have happened when Quinlan was around."

Ted handed Eason a thick packet. "Chief, we didn't think we had enough to bother you with—until now. You'll find all our notes and research in there."

The colonel added, "I'm a military man, not a trained police investigator, but I know bad fish when I smell it. Rather than give you our opinions, we figured letting you do your job would be best. Our only suggestion is to take special note of the timing of the events."

"I'll review your findings." The chief stood. "Lest you good citizens of Plymouth think the department is blind or slow, I'll let you in on this much. Sergeant O'Neil's recent leave of absence was to follow up on a connection she discovered between a certain board member and several of the other states on your list. Please keep that bit of information to yourself." He turned before he walked out the door. "And I strongly recommend you leave police business to us."

Glenna, head down, followed him out the door.

A few weeks later at Charlie's house, he and Kyle talked between periods of the hockey game—the Boston Bruins versus their nemesis, the Montreal Canadiens.

"Heard anything back from the chief?" Charlie scooped homemade buffalo chicken dip with an oversized taco chip.

Kyle shook his head as he finished chewing. "Personally, I think he's keeping me in the dark as punishment."

"Can you blame him? You may be a cop, but I'm sure he doesn't want us amateur sleuths interfering in the case."

"Nah, it's more than that. I hear nothing, and I mean nothing, about the investigation, even in the office grapevine. Something's afoot, I tell you. I just wish I knew what."

"I thought you said you trusted him?"

"I do, but does he trust me?"

The Bruins lost, and Charlie bid Kyle good night.

The hockey score had nothing to do with Charlie's despondency, but he couldn't point to a specific reason. He choked down his frustration. Thirty-nine weeks to the day had passed since he'd lost Juliette—he'd counted that morning. He was certain he'd gone through all five stages of grief, including depression. Yet here he was again, feeling empty. Now, instead of hot and painful, the grief was cold and numbing, like a lesser form of death.

Would his heart always feel barren and frozen like the rock-hard February ground? His mind answered aloud, "You're not the first person to lose someone they loved. You'll reach the end of grief someday."

His heart countered, "But do you want to?"

He trudged through his days, offering phony smiles to family and friends and burying himself in his work. Every day he prayed, "Lord, when will your peace replace my pain?"

CHAPTER THIRTY-EIGHT

With one arm in his jacket sleeve, Charlie answered his phone. "I'm leaving the office now, Vanetta. Be there in five." He shook his coat into place then snatched the Quinlan job folder from his desk.

Two weeks had passed since the committee had given Chief Eason their findings. Was no news good news? Maybe Oliver wasn't involved after all. With winter ending, slipping into spring without any more drama sure would be nice.

Dawson-Landau had been working on the Quinlan house—a monument to expendable cash—for almost a year now. Charlie had started the plans last March. Due to the number of design changes, finishing the final construction drawings had taken him over three months. The original completion date had been pushed back by Vanetta's numerous special orders. Now, seven months after they'd broken ground, the traditional home, its façade a combination of brick and hewn stone, was in the final stages.

Oh, for the days when people wanted a simple Cape with a white picket fence.

He pulled up in front of the imposing house. Both Quinlans' cars were there. Before he climbed out, he fortified himself with a whispered plea, "Lord, please give me patience."

Angry shouts greeted him as he reached the door. He hesitated, not knowing whether to knock or to walk in as he usually did on jobsites.

Oliver didn't sound happy. "We'd already be living here if it weren't for all your outlandish purchases!"

"Just so you know, *dear*, what you think really doesn't matter to me."

Ouch. So much for marital bliss.

"Well, you should think twice about that since I'm paying for all this!"

"You silly little man. If *I* didn't handle our finances, we'd be in one big mess."

Charlie was backing down the steps when he noticed the oversized, ornate doorbell which had been installed since his last visit. After a few seconds of silence passed, he pushed the button. The sound of old-fashioned harmony bells rang out. He didn't miss the irony.

Oliver yanked the door open. "What is it?"

"Hey, Oliver. Vanetta wants me to approve the hardwood flooring."

Oliver brushed passed him. "You'll find the queen in her kitchen." He snarled, then turned back to Charlie. "Tell me, Dawson, why would a woman who only eats celery sticks, tofu, and bok choy need a six-burner Lacanche designer stove which costs over $10,000?"

Charlie shrugged.

"Mark my word, that fancy oversized refrigerator-freezer combo will be empty most of the time!" He stomped down the steps, climbed into his car, and tore out of the driveway.

All righty, then. Charlie took a deep breath before he entered.

Vanetta greeted him. "Ignore Oliver's foul mood. He's insulted because someone's been asking his clients questions about his business practices."

He wasn't sure how to reply. "Oh?"

Her laugh turned to a scoff. "My husband may be a lot of things, but a cheat is not one of them."

He wondered if she really believed that.

"Now, Charlie, before the installers get here, you need to make sure we have the right flooring."

He looked at the packing slip, then stooped to pull back the wrapping. "Just what we ordered. American walnut." He ran his hand over one of the planks. "The tung oil gives the wood a deep, rich tone."

"But is it rich enough?"

"You've got excellent taste, Vanetta. Don't second-guess it."

She murmured, "Good taste in finishes, at least."

He pretended not to hear her.

On his way back to the office, Charlie called Kyle. "Do you think Oliver Quinlan could've gotten wind of the investigation?"

"Why do you ask?"

"Well, his wife just told me he's upset because someone's been questioning his clients."

"The chief's been tight-lipped … even after the FBI and DEA agents both showed up at the precinct yesterday. Let me run this bit of news by him and see what he says."

Charlie wasn't sure how he was supposed to feel about this whole scenario. Proud that he might be part of an investigation to bring down a drug cartel? Weird that the leader might be one of his clients? Worried that his company had been paid from illegal proceeds? Disappointed that Vanetta might lose the house of her dreams, the one he'd been helping her create?

Since these were the drugs that had taken Juliette from him, mostly, he felt sadness and anger.

After Christmas and Easter, Valentine's Day had been one of Juliette's favorite holidays. Though Charlie'd never needed a special day to remind him how much he loved her, he'd been smart enough not to tell her that.

So, there he was, standing at her gravesite at seven a.m., the temperature below freezing, with a fuchsia silk rose heart. Not exactly sure what to do with the floral arrangement, he lay it flat on the ground. Then, changing his mind, he stood it up against the headstone. The heart wobbled and fell facedown.

It's the thought that counts, right, Jules?

But this particular thought seemed silly to him. Juliette loved *fresh* flowers, not fake ones. And even if they were real, she couldn't smell them, so what was the point?

I'm freezing my butt off to express love to my Valentine who's no longer here.

Claiming self-pity as his anthem for another holiday alone, he felt righteous in doing so.

He got in his car to circle around to the exit. He caught a glimpse of Ashlyn Reid, huddling with her bundled-up infant son at the foot of her husband's grave.

In addition to self-pity, he added envy.

Lord, help me. I'm jealous of a dead man, because he still has a wife and now, a new baby boy.

Charlie checked his phone before he answered. "Hey, Edy."

"I said yes." She practically choked on her words.

"You said yes to what?"

"Matt's latest marriage proposal."

"Congratulations! I'm proud of you!"

"Now I'm freaking out. All I know is I want Pop to give me away and you to stand by my side. Other than that, I don't know anything about planning a wedding."

"And you think Grams won't help?"

"That's what scares me. I want a simple ceremony with a few close friends and family. She'll get carried away."

"Then wo-*man* up and tell her."

No sooner had he reached his desk than his grandmother called. "Charlie, we need to reserve your house for June 6."

"For what?"

"Edy and Matt's wedding, of course."

He looked at his watch. Only forty-five minutes had passed since Edy called him with her announcement.

Grams continued, "She insists on an intimate ceremony with a limited guest list. You're the only one with room for a tent in the backyard. We can handle the food—she prefers a lighter fare—maybe appetizers and desserts. As usual, Edy will make sure the gardens are beautiful. And Natalie gave me the name of a business in town that does event décor."

He tried to get a word in when she took a breath, but he wasn't quick enough.

"Do you know Don Douglas?" she asked.

"Of course. He's my insurance agent and an elder at church."

"He's also a justice of the peace, and he's available on June 6. I gave Edy his number before she got just any old person to marry them."

"It's only February. Why the hurry?"

"June is only four months away. No time to dilly-dally. I'm off to Partyscapes for my appointment with the owner."

Partyscapes? Why does that name sound familiar?

With Edy's wedding officially on the calendar, Charlie revisited his idea to move out of the house and into her condo. Had he meant it? Or had he made a spontaneous offer he'd later regret?

When he and Juliette first took over the house, Grams and Pop had been at the root of that idea. As newlyweds, they'd been grateful to live anywhere as long as they were together. Had they planned on making this their forever home? Without Juliette here, he couldn't answer for sure.

Even though he designed houses for a living, Charlie knew a true home was built by the people who lived there. When he reminded himself that Juliette didn't live there anymore, the idea of moving became simple.

He called Edy. "I meant what I said about you and Matt taking over the house. Just say the word."

"Truth is, Charlie, I wanted to refuse your offer. Then I thought how perfect the setup will be when Grams and Pop are too old to live on their own."

He laughed. "I wouldn't mention that idea to Grams yet."

"I'm not insane. So, do you still want my 929-square foot condo?"

"Howland Street is way closer to my office. The location is walkable to the harbor and restaurants. And I won't have a yard to deal with—or you in it—which suits me just fine." Charlie suggested they move *before* the wedding so the honeymooners could settle in when they returned.

Just like Juliette and I did.

A week later, Grams called. "Charlie, Edy and I have an early afternoon appointment today at the house with Jillian McGee— she's the party décor girl. Will you be home?"

Charlie wondered if she was hinting at something. "Do you want me to be home?"

"Well, your presence might be helpful in case she has questions. But, mostly, we just need you to stay out of the way."

Coy was not a word he'd use to describe his grandmother.

Before Edy and Grams arrived, a car pulled into his driveway. *Great. The party girl's early.* Trying to recall the woman's name, he opened the door and settled for, "Welcome!"

Open-mouthed, Ashlyn Reid stood on his front stoop. "Charlie?"

"Ashlyn?" His did a doubletake. "I wasn't expecting to find you here."

"Um, I guess I could say the same. I'm supposed to meet my boss. We're doing the décor for a wedding." She opened the calendar app on her phone. "Am I at the wrong house?"

"No, this is the right place. Come in, come in. My grandmother told me to expect you. Well, not *you* exactly, but someone from your company."

Ashlyn stepped inside. "So, a wedding, huh?"

"Yes, but I know nothing. The bride's in charge. She should be here soon." Charlie led the way to the living room. "I believe congratulations are in order since the last time I saw you. How's James Luke doing?"

"Very well, thank you." She smiled. "You remembered his name."

"Because you chose a good solid one."

She scrolled to a picture on her phone. "Here's my boy. Four weeks old today."

All babies usually looked alike to Charlie, but not this little guy. "He's a male version of you. Even has your nose and eyes. And what little hair he has looks auburn."

"Think so?" She gazed a few seconds longer at the photo.

The sound of a car caught their attention.

Ashlyn looked out the window. "Here's Jillian now. I should see if she needs help."

He followed her out. "And pulling in right behind her is the bride-to-be and my grandmother."

As instructed, Charlie stayed out of the way while the four women walked the property, inside and out. He caught snippets of their discussions on theme, colors, and mood.

They'd had no questions for him until Ashlyn asked, "So, Charlie, is there anything you'd like to add?"

"Me? Nope. All I have to do is make sure I'm standing in the right place at the right time."

Edy smirked. "I put Grams in charge of directing you. I'm sure you'll do just fine."

Jillian stuffed her notebook in her tote bag. "Looks like we have everything we need for the Dawson wedding. If you think of anything else, please call."

Charlie followed the chatting women out to the driveway.

"Oh, I almost forgot." Edy turned to Charlie. "I've got a bunch of things in my trunk. Where should I put them?"

Charlie shrugged. "Anywhere you want. The house will be yours soon enough."

Ashlyn walked by him and whispered, "Smart man."

Smart? Me? Why?

"Uh, thanks." At least he was smart enough to accept a compliment.

Grams sidled up alongside him and whispered. "Changing homes was a brilliant idea! Edy will be too busy to fret or second-guess marrying Matt. We don't want her messing this up."

Yeah. Coy. Nope.

CHAPTER THIRTY-NINE

Thirteen months after his initial meeting with the Quinlans, Charlie scheduled the final walk-thru. According to Hank, he should expect a nonevent since, the day before, Artie had checked off the punch list items to both clients' satisfaction.

Charlie knew Vanetta's internal interior decorator was dying to be released, which was why he was hopeful they'd sign off today. He decided to bring Artie and his tools on the off chance (or was it *on* chance?) Oliver and Vanetta had come up with something in the past twenty-four hours.

Artie yelled over from the warehouse. "Charlie, you wanna ride over with me?"

Everyone knew Artie's truck served as his office-slash-restaurant-slash-fast food wrapper receptacle. "I'll follow you over just in case."

Thankfully, Artie didn't ask, *Just in case of what?*

Charlie pulled up the crushed shell driveway of the waterfront property to the breathtaking views of the ocean. He'd designed the two-story dwelling to conform to the natural lay of the land. The custom-stacked stone walls and lush mature shrubbery filled in the expansive lot. Unlike most gardeners who buried their bulbs in the fall, Vanetta had demanded that blooming bulbs of crocuses, tulips, and daffodils be planted. Seeing the project dressed in spring colors made him believe working with them had been worth the aggravation.

Almost.

The four of them went over every custom square inch of the 6,800-square-foot home. Other than two or three minor fixes, which Artie took care of before he left, Vanetta had nothing but praise. Even Oliver, who acted like a jerk most of the time, was full of charm. Without Charlie having to ask, they transferred funds for the final invoice electronically. He was actually enjoying the morning.

Vanetta checked her phone. "Perfect timing. The movers are on their way with the contents of our rental home. Our new furnishings will be delivered early next week."

"My wife will do a fantastic job decorating this place. With any luck, we can stay put for a while."

"Luck will not be a factor." Every angle of Vanetta's face seemed to sharpen. "We're not moving again."

"You're right." Oliver laughed. "And as soon as you give me the go-ahead, we'll have a dinner party to celebrate. And, Charlie, your friends the Westfalls will be eating their hearts out in their sad little house."

Okay, so he was still a jerk.

Vanetta looked out the window. "Here's the first moving van now." She strode to the front door. "Oliver, come."

Charlie took the van's arrival as his cue to leave before Vanetta put him to work unloading. He followed them outside.

Two black SUVs and a navy pickup truck pulled in behind the Mayflower moving van. Two Town of Plymouth police vehicles followed.

Three cars full of movers and a police escort? How much did they pay for this?

The SUV and truck occupants, all dressed in dark jackets with big yellow letters, exited the vehicles quickly. Chief Eason climbed out of the lead police car, Glenna O'Neil and Kyle, the second. All three approached the Mayflower driver.

Huh?

Oliver stepped forward.

Four men approached the front step and flashed badges.

"Sir, I'm Oliver Quinlan, the property owner here. Are these movers in some sort of trouble?"

The agent motioned to Vanetta. "Is this your wife, Mr. Quinlan?"

"Yes." Oliver seemed confused. "Vanetta may have hired them, but I assure you she wasn't aware of any illegal alien status."

The agent addressed Vanetta. "Vanetta Joyce Quinlan, we have a warrant for your arrest on the charges of interstate drug trafficking."

"Interstate drug trafficking?" Oliver put his arms up to protect his wife. "This is crazy! She's never even met these movers."

Vanetta mumbled, "Stop talking, Oliver."

"No! I'm not going to stand here and let these people falsely accuse you!"

"Sir, step aside unless you want to be arrested too."

"You're making a huge mistake!" Oliver's voice grew louder. "The only *interstate* operation my wife runs is her consulting business. This past month alone she's been in Waco, Moline, Allentown." He turned to Vanetta for help. "What's that city in Washington?"

Vanetta spoke through clenched teeth. "I told you to shut up!"

The lead agent Mirandized Vanetta, handcuffed her, then led her to his SUV.

"Let her go!" Oliver shouted. "Do you know who I am?"

Vanetta turned and glared at him "You're a fool! That's who you are."

Oliver looked like he'd been struck in the face.

Once Vanetta was seated behind tinted windows, the lead officer addressed Oliver. "Mr. Quinlan, you're not under arrest at this time, but we would like to take your statement at police headquarters. Chief Eason is here to escort you."

"Do I need a lawyer? I don't understand."

"Why don't you make that call on the way, Oliver?" The chief took him by the arm and walked him to the cruiser.

Charlie hadn't said a word the whole time. He glanced over at Kyle and raised his hands. "What just happened?"

"A lot. I'll fill you in when I can. Hope your clients didn't owe you any money."

The cavalcade of law enforcement vehicles motored down the driveway, leaving a single DEA agent behind.

The driver of the moving van leaned out the window to speak with the agent. "¿Qué *vamos a hacer ahora?* What are we to do now?"

"The contents of the van are being seized as evidence. You'll have to empty the truck and leave."

"*¿Y nuestro dinero?* And our money?"

The agent shrugged. "I hope you have good liability insurance."

Vanetta Quinlan was smart. Just not *that* smart. She'd married Oliver, who insisted on defending her in the press, doing more harm than good.

He was quoted as saying: "Vanetta is the most civic-minded person I know! Even getting me seated on all those drug tasks forces was *her* idea. She was always interested in every detail of our progress."

Upon a search of their rental home in Plymouth, the DEA discovered a stash of burner phones, all equipped with a voice changer app. The feds froze all their personal and business assets, including numerous off-shore banks accounts and other property.

If found guilty, everything would be seized for violation of federal law—including their house built on a volcano of special orders.

Amid the revelations, Charlie came to an odd conclusion. He and Oliver had something in common after all. Neither of them had known what their wives had been up to.

As the weeks progressed, more information came out about Vanetta's drug operations. She had small franchises in more cities than they'd originally suspected. By manufacturing her own brand, she was able to stay under the radar of the DEA *and* the big cartels. In every city, each of her chief operating officers was educated, discreet, and clean. She ensured their loyalty with corporate perks and hefty bonuses, not threats, which helped grow her business. However, their silence only lasted as long as their benefits and the time it took to secure a deal.

The Quinlan case provided fodder for the local press and national news sources. The publicity, which included multiple stories about the Quinlan house, brought an unexpected boost to Dawson-Landau's business. The phone hadn't stopped ringing since Vanetta had been charged.

CHAPTER FORTY

Charlie and Edy's house swap had taken a total of three weekends to complete. Though not planned, the first anniversary of Juliette's death landed on the first day he awoke in his new home.

He groaned out from under a blanket of bittersweet memories, "Lord! Is this move some sort of clichéd metaphor for a new life? If so, what on earth am I supposed to do with the old one? And what am I supposed to do with today?"

Without waiting for an answer, he shook the questions off, got dressed, and left for Vine Hills. His phone pinged multiple times in the five minutes it took him to get there—Grams, Sarah, Kyle, Pop—prompting him to shut it off.

Yes, I know they mean well, Lord, but I need some alone time right now.

He set his chair graveside. A warm, breeze brought back memories of sweeter spring times. A fresh flower arrangement signified Natalie and the colonel had been there the day before as they'd mentioned.

"So, Jules, a year has passed since you've been gone. Am I supposed to do something different? Cake and a candle? Balloons? Stop wearing black?" He scrubbed his face with both hands. "Sorry. If there's some sort of system to this whole grief thing, I've missed it. People say I'm strong, but I'm weak."

A verse came to mind. *I can do all things through Christ, who gives strengthens me.*

He bowed his head but didn't even have the strength to pray. *Oh, God, please ...*

A tap on his shoulder startled him. He looked up into the homely face of Pershing Papadopoulos.

"Hey, Mr. Papadopoulas, I didn't know you were here."

"Name's *Pershing.*" The man winked. "And I can be pretty quiet when I'm not talking to Peaches." He cleared his throat. "How're you doing today being the first anniversary and all?"

Charlie felt a twinge of guilt for not having a clue when Pershing's wife died. Was he supposed to? "Uh, as well as one could expect, I guess."

"Your young friend was here yesterday. Had that sweet baby boy with her."

"Did she?"

"Roman—he was her husband—had his first anniversary yesterday, a day before your Juliette."

What was this guy? The graveyard historian?

"Have you seen that little one?" Pershing asked.

"Only a picture."

"Looks just like his mama, I think."

Charlie smiled. "I thought so too."

"Mind if I pray for you, Charlie?"

Pershing? Pray? What left field had that come from?

He shrugged. "If you want."

The man put one hand on Charlie's shoulder. "It's me, Lord, Pershing. Your word says, 'I can do all things through Christ, who strengthens me.'"

Charlie's nerve ends tingled.

Pershing continued. "I'm here askin' you to strengthen this man as he marks this milestone. I'm standin' in the gap because he may be too hurt to pray. Thank you and amen." He patted Charlie a few more times then walked away without another word.

Charlie bowed his head and let his tears flow.

When he returned to the condo, he took a fresh look at his new home. He'd left his parents' mid-century modern furnishings behind as part of the family estate and traded his oversized sectional for Edy's sofa, a better fit for the condo. The big pieces of furniture were in place, but everything else was still in cardboard boxes.

I'll empty them soon. Just not today.

He entered the bedroom. The placement of the handcrafted furniture he and Juliette had splurged on wasn't quite right. When he adjusted her nightstand, the secret bottom drawer slid open. He retrieved their ribbon-tied packet of love letters and breathed in their lavender scent. Another hit to his heart. He sank to the floor and untied the ribbon. What better way to commemorate the day?

Handwriting letters to each other had begun their first semester at college. Juliette's idea, of course. He'd rolled his eyes at her suggestion—but not so she could see him. After reading her first letter, he'd changed his mind.

September 15, 2007

Dear Charlie,

I thought today would be a good day to write since it's the third anniversary of our first French-Math tutoring session. Though we didn't qualify our session as a date-date, without my need for your help in math and yours in French, "we" never would've happened. For me, that makes it a date to commemorate!

Mixed feelings are a big part of my days here at school. I'm sure the next four years will be exciting, interesting, and fun. I'm also sure they won't be *as* exciting, interesting, or fun without you!

We're less than ten hours apart, but it seems like we're living light years away. Do you get what I mean? I feel like I'm on hiatus from real life, a life of being with you. Again, the experience is not totally unpleasant, but certainly no place I want to live forever.

All this melodrama to say I miss you!

Though they'd talked on the phone and emailed daily during those first weeks away, her letter seemed more intimate. He'd written back that same night.

Dear Jules,

Confession: I thought your letter-writing idea was corny. Then you wrote me. Now I think corny is kind of romantic. But you knew that already, didn't you?

Tenth grade seems like eons ago. I was such a doofus. Although happy about it, I was shocked when you continued to meet with me week after week. By the time I realized you didn't need my help in math as much as I needed yours in French, I wasn't willing to let go of that extra hour. *C'est votre faute d'être si joli!* It's your fault for being so pretty!

Now, being so far away from you, every so often anxiety causes me to imagine a line of less goofy guys standing at your door, hoping for a chance with you. Then I remember all the effort you put into straightening me out. You'd never let that go to waste, would you?

Reading their letters, he felt like he was seeing their relationship in time lapse. Their June wedding anniversary had eventually become their semi-official letter-writing day. They didn't harp at each other if one of them missed occasionally or wrote too-short a note. The "one of them" always being Charlie.

He remembered protesting. "Isn't writing more about love than legalism?" Or, "It's the meaning behind the words, not the length of the note, right?" And his favorite, "But the depth of my love is too great for words."

Jules, you ignored my lame excuses and kept on writing.

He put the letters down and stared beyond the wall. "Lord, what am I supposed to do with my regrets?"

Let them go.

"How?"

Let them go.

Charlie closed tear-filled eyes and held out open hands. "Take them, Lord, please. Take all of me."

He began where he'd left off, about two-thirds of the way through the pack, in the middle of their life together. He laughed and smiled more this time.

He reached for the next envelope. Having exchanged their last yearly the previous June, he didn't remember the envelope being that thick. He read the first page of the one from Juliette ... with hindsight this time. Instead of the sincerity he'd previously seen, he detected sadness, fear, and sorrow in her tone. *What did I do to deserve a guy like you?... Getting pregnant may take longer than we hoped ... Sometimes things don't work out the way we think they should.*

Why hadn't he suspected something was off? His short note, scrawled in a big hand to fill up the paper, read:

Jules,

If I've told you once, I've told you a million times, meeting you was the best thing that ever happened to me! I look forward to every day with you. I love you.

Seriously? I couldn't have come up with something more original?

He opened the last folded sheet. The date on this letter read May 10. His hands trembled as he realized Juliette had written to him the day before she died. He hopped up off the floor and sat on the edge of the bed.

Dear Charlie,

If you're reading this letter, it means I've checked myself into rehab before I changed my mind. I planned to tell you everything, but in case that didn't happen, or I was too emotional, I'm putting my words down on paper.

I'm so sorry for all the grief I've caused and am still causing us. If I had a life verse, I think it would be Proverbs 16:18, "Pride goes before destruction, a haughty spirit before a fall." I needed help handling the pain from my ankle injury but wouldn't admit it. My competitive nature got in the way again.

I thought taking additional health supplements would relieve my need for medication. Wrong, so wrong. When I finally accepted the prescription from the doctor, I thought if I doubled the dosage I'd get better faster. Then, believing my craving was only temporary, I rationalized. Such pride!

He took a breath to slow his pace then continued.

I lied to you and to others: about my leave of absence from work, about where I was going half the time, about how I was feeling. I'm ashamed to confess I even took Edy's prescription pad to get more painkillers. I promise to apologize to her in person. She didn't deserve what I did. None of you did.

My biggest shame is in lying to you about trying to get pregnant. Not being in control, I went back on the pill. I may've been able to do harmful things to myself, but I could never endanger a child.

Even though I was taking precautions against pregnancy, please know everything we planned for and talked about for our family was real to me, still is—the baby names, the ideas for the nursery, our parenting principles. In my irrational mind, having a baby was just on hold. I look forward to the day it will be safe to try again.

He buried his face in his hands and sobbed—harder than he had since the day she died. The grief was so heavy he felt like he'd join her. Part of him wanted to. Eventually, exhausted and tears spent, he found enough strength to finish reading.

I finally became desperate enough to attend an addiction recovery meeting. The people I met there seemed to understand more about me than I did myself. After attending a few more, someone told me about a long-term, faith-based recovery program. I need and want the help they can give me. (I chickened out on telling my parents. Will you please make sure they get the note I wrote to them?)

As your last anniversary letter said so succinctly, "If I've told you once, I've told you a million times, meeting you was the best thing that ever happened to me. I look forward to every day with you."

I love you, Charlie. Please forgive me, pray for me, and wait for me. Okay by you?

Juliette

Charlie still didn't know why Juliette had to die, but he knew one thing. She'd loved him the whole time she'd been here.
"Okay by me, Jules."
He found a postscript on the back.

PS: One more thing. Heidi Vincent, my coworker and latest supplier, suspected I'd snapped a photo of a handwritten list of dealers I saw on her desk. I haven't seen her since my leave of absence, but I'm pretty sure she stole my box of office stuff out of my car looking for it. For safekeeping, I entered the names in a spreadsheet then dropped my Mac off at the Apple Store. I pray the info does some good in the right hands.

Later that day, Charlie drove to his in-laws'. Juliette's letter would bring them comfort.

In the privacy of his in-laws' home, he shared most of her last letter with them before he handed them a sealed envelope. "This one's for you."

Natalie settled under her husband's arm as they read their daughter's words.

The colonel's eyes filled, his voice broke. "I knew that daughter of mine would find the right way out."

"She did, didn't she?" Natalie patted her husband's back. "But God had other plans."

CHAPTER FORTY-ONE

Charlie got a frantic call from his sister the day before her wedding.

"Edy, calm down!"

"Calm down? I've got a full schedule of patients to see today. Pop was supposed to be at the house by eight this morning to oversee the crew putting up the tent. Then he remembers he has a yearly physical scheduled this morning. Seriously? He couldn't have postponed it?"

Charlie laughed. "You of all people should know how people revere doctors, especially the elderly. Nothing as mundane as a wedding can trump a prostate exam. What time should I be there?"

"Is now too soon?"

"What kind of a maid of honor would I be if I said no? I'm walking out the door now."

He arrived a few minutes ahead of the party rental truck. Since the area in the backyard had already been staked out, the crew erected the tent and set up the tables and chairs in a little over an hour. Before he could lock up the house, a Partyscapes van pulled in. He went out to greet them.

Ashlyn got out the passenger side. "Hey, Charlie."

Jillian came around to open the van's sliding door. "We didn't know you'd be here. Your grandmother gave us a key."

Charlie shrugged. "Wedding emergency. I imagine you know all about those."

"We do hear stories." Jillian laughed. "No cold feet, I hope?"

Charlie raised his hands to ward off the thought. "Don't even think it!" He stepped up to the van. "As long as I'm here, let me give you ladies a hand."

"We'll take you up on that." Jillian pointed to a heavy box of dishes.

Ashlyn followed him into the house with a thick stack of table lines. "Gee, the house looks different than before."

"Yes, Edy's a minimalist. Leans way more toward modern than I do."

"I see." Ashlyn placed the linens on the dining room table.

By her tone, Charlie suspected the design wasn't to her taste. "You don't like modern?"

She shrugged. "Every couple has their preferences. What I like doesn't matter."

"What I like doesn't matter either."

"But—" She stopped short then fell silent.

"No, tell me."

"Your business, not mine."

Charlie pushed. "But I've asked for your opinion,"

She bit her lower lip. "Well, I believe a home should reflect the tastes of the wife *and* the husband."

Charlie did a one-eighty to survey the room. "I agree, but I have no idea what taste Matt has."

"Who's Matt?" Ashlyn looked up from smoothing a tablecloth.

"Matt? He's, uh, the groom."

She straightened. "Then who are you?"

"Me?" He pointed to himself. "I'm Edy's brother."

Her mouth dropped open, her eyes widened. "How did I not catch that?"

"Sleep deprivation, maybe? Is sweet baby James keeping you up at night?"

She smiled. "That's what I call him sometimes too."

Charlie smiled back. "Well, I'll leave you ladies to your partyscaping." He sang a few lines of James Taylor's "Sweet Baby James" tune on his way out.

Edy and Matt's wedding was due to begin in an hour.

Charlie called out from the far end of the tent. "Edy, is this where I'm supposed to stand? I've never been a man of honor before."

She raised her arms and shrugged. "Who knows? I've never been a bride before."

Charlie thought back to weddings he'd attended. "I think they usually walk in after the bridesmaids. Maybe I should do that."

Edy sighed. "I don't have any other bridesmaids. You're it."

Grams stepped in. "Chill, Charlie. The JP stands in the middle. You walk down ahead of Edy, then stand to his right. Matt and his best man stand on the other side. Edy, after Pop walks you down the aisle,"—her voice cracked—"then you and Matt come together and face the JP."

Edy hugged her grandmother. "Don't start, Grams, or you'll get me going, and I'll never get my makeup repaired in time."

Pop walked over and put his arm around his wife's shoulders. "Lana, we talked about this, remember? Get a hold of yourself for the girl's sake."

Grams dabbed the corners of her eyes. "This day's been such a long time coming."

Edy rolled her eyes.

"Um, speaking of time,"—Charlie tapped his watch—"plan on getting dressed soon, Dr. Dawson."

She blinked at him then looked down at her jeans and tee shirt. "Eek!"

Later, in the presence of family and friends, Pop walked a radiant Edy, now dressed in ivory silk and lace, down the aisle. Big fat tears rolled through the crevices in Pop's cheeks as he gave her away to a beaming Matt.

When the justice of the peace pronounced them husband and wife, math-geek Matt let out a shout, "Gadzooks! We're finally one squared!"

As guests mingled, Charlie stopped at Edy's Steinway baby grand—her one concession to traditional furnishings. The piano was draped with a white satin cloth. Displayed in the folds of the fabric were generations of wedding portraits from both the bride's and groom's families. Charlie and Juliette's wedding photo sat among them.

Natalie slipped to Charlie's side. "Our girl sure looked beautiful, didn't she?"

He took her arm. "And every day from that day forward."

CHAPTER FORTY-TWO

On their ninth wedding anniversary, Charlie wrote one last letter to Juliette.

Dear Jules,

Maybe you know this, maybe you don't. I spent most of last year alternately aching for you and being angry with you. I wondered what had happened to the girl I'd married.

It never occurred to me there were parts of you I'd yet to discover, secrets you hadn't revealed. You hadn't changed after all. I found the girl I knew again, with all your vulnerabilities, in your final letter.

Loving you was a privilege and a blessing. I'm beyond grateful for those years. Now, as I bumble my way about earth without you, I pray God guides me to a new beginning. Okay by you?

Love,

Charlie

He put the letter in an envelope, sealed it, and added it to the pack.

The thing Charlie liked best about his new home was the location. Whether he went right or left out of his parking lot, he was within walking distance to the ocean, historic sites, museums, and restaurants. Even his Dawson-Landau office was less than a mile away.

Saturday was clear and sunny when he stepped outside his door. He filled his lungs with sweet and salty air. A bit more hope blew in on a breeze, peace flowed within him. He took a left toward Court Street on the way to his new favorite café.

Before he could round the corner onto Court, Ashlyn Reid passed by, pushing a stroller.

He called out, "Ashlyn! Do I finally get a real live look at sweet baby James?"

"Charlie! This is a surprise." She stopped then adjusted the pacifier in her fussy son's mouth. "He hasn't been real sweet lately. Pretty sure he's teething."

"All part of being a baby, I suppose." *What a dumb thing to say.* He peeked under the canopy. "But at least he still looks like his mother."

Light shined on her face. She looked a bit tired but happy. Pretty, too.

She raised her chin and cocked her head. "If you like, I'll let you have him for the day."

Charlie chortled at her straight-faced delivery. "I see sleep deprivation has set in. Afraid I don't have much experience with babies."

She cracked back, "Neither did I before I had this one."

He laughed louder and took hold of the stroller. "Then the sooner we get started with my training the better, don't you think?"

"Okay, but training doesn't come cheap, you know."

He countered, "How about we discuss the terms over coffee at the Pilgrim Bakery & Café? My treat."

"Throw in one of their Mayflower Maple Muffins, and we have a deal."

Standing in front of the baker's case, an item caught Charlie's attention. He nudged Ashlyn. "Hey! Look at the tray to the right of the William Bradford Butterscotch Bars."

She read the handwritten card. "Peaches Papadopoulos Baklava." Her hand flew to her mouth. "I can't believe he sold her out!"

"You knew about the recipe?"

"Yes." She put her hand over her heart. "And I thought his burying that secret with his wife was such a romantic gesture."

"Perhaps Pershing considers sharing his wife's recipe a gift to the world."

She raised a single brow at him. "Or perhaps he's looking to buy himself a new bowling shirt with this unsanctioned income."

They shared another laugh then found a corner table.

She peeked in on James. "Sleeping soundly. You just aced your first childcare lesson, Mr. Dawson. Now, I hope you remember what you did so you can do the same thing the next time."

Charlie searched her verdant green eyes and measured his words. "The … next … time?"

Ashlyn's face turned a shy shade of pink. "That is, if you don't mind having a next time."

He took in her tentative smile and vulnerable eyes. "I rather like the sound that idea."

Okay by you, Jules?

ABOUT THE AUTHOR

Clarice G. James writes smart, fun, relatable contemporary women's fiction, woven together with threads of humor, romance, faith, and mystery. To date, her novels published by Elk Lake Publishing, Inc. include Party of One, Doubleheader, Manhattan Grace, and The Girl He Knew.

Clarice grew up on Cape Cod. She also raised her three children there. Eight years after she was widowed in 1998, she was blessed to remarry (Ralph) David James. She and David now live in Hudson, New Hampshire. Counting their five married children, ten grandchildren, and extended family, they have relatives in eight different states. Clarice says, "So, you can just imagine what our 'vacations' are like."

David, a short story writer, and Clarice both enjoy the writing process and host a critique group in their home. When she's not writing, Clarice is reading, encouraging fellow writers, or giving author talks around New England.

Connect with Clarice:

Email: cjames@claricejames.com
Facebook: https://www.facebook.com/clarice.g.james
Twitter: https://twitter.com/ClariceGJames
Website: http://www.claricejames.com

A Special Request from Clarice: If you enjoy reading my books, I would be so pleased if you would write a review on www.amazon.com or www. goodreads.com. Thank you!

OTHER BOOKS BY CLARICE G. JAMES

Party of One (Elk Lake Publishing, Inc., 2017): Risking her privacy, widow Annie McGee founds Party of One, a communal table for single diners, where she meets an electric mix of colorful characters who cause her to confront her fears, question her beliefs, doubt her self-assurance, and take another chance on love.

Manhattan Grace (Elk Lake Publishing, Inc., 2018): When a door opens for Gracie Camden to leave Cape Cod and move to Manhattan as a nanny for a Juilliard drama instructor, she fully expects God to use her acting talent and launch her to stardom. It's been six months. What's taking him so long?

Doubleheader (Elk Lake Publishing, Inc., 2019): Casey Gallagher credits a carefully crafted game plan for her wins: her solid marriage, her lucrative marketing career in Boston, and her popular sports column, Doubleheader. When Casey discovers that her late father, the one man she idolized, had an affair which produced a son he never knew about, she's determined to identify this so-called brother before he sullies her father's reputation.

Ask for *Party of One, Manhattan Grace,* and *Doubleheader* at your local bookstore or go online to www.amazon.com or www.barnesandnoble.com. If you enjoy the books, please write a review on www.amazon.com and www.goodreads.com. Thank you.

DISCUSSION QUESTIONS

(Spoiler Alert!)

1. Why was Charlie so shocked when his wife Juliette died unexpectedly? Had there been any warning signs? If so, why or how had he missed them?

2. Do you know anyone personally who developed an addiction to prescription drugs? Do you know how long it would take for that to happen? What would you do if that person was you?

3. Juliette's father (Col. Wick Annandale) was tough on Charlie. Did he dislike his son-in-law? Did he blame him, indirectly, for his daughter's death? What softened him?

4. Not long after Juliette's death, her mother (Natalie Annandale) volunteers at Best Foot Forward, the shop Juliette's best friend (Sarah Yates) ran for women starting over. How do you think this helps Natalie? Why do you think she takes such an interest in Ashlyn Reid?

5. How did Charlie's grandparents (Rollie and Lana Somers) handle the news of Juliette's death? What is their solution to avoid getting involved with drugs in the first place? What do they learn through this experience?

6. Ashlyn Reid is in a tough situation—newly widowed and pregnant with her first child. Who are the people who rally around her? In what way could you help a person like her?

7. After years of his mother (Dee Jennings) enabling him, Zach Jennings gets clean and sober. How do his past sins follow him around? Once steadfast in recovery, how does he give back?

8. Pastor Ted Westfall and his wife Binnie often share their dinner table with people from all walks of life and different stages of belief and/or unbelief. Do you think every minister is called to do that? Or, do you think it's a gift given to a select few?

9. When Charlie takes off for some time alone, he ends up breaking down in a town where he reconnects with an old college roommate (Felix Pinard). What's happened to Felix since college? How does connecting with him help Charlie?

10. When Charlie and the "search committee" do some police work on their own, what comes of their efforts? Are they a help or a hindrance? How does the local police chief respond?

11. At the end of the story, how do you envision Charlie's and Ashlyn's future relationship? How should they proceed?

12. The theme running through this book is pride. Juliette's pride prevents her from seeking help. Oliver and Vanetta Quinlan's pride is in their wealth and position. Charlie's sister Edy's pride is in her medical degree. Col. Annandale's pride is in his country. Rollie and Lana Somers' pride shows up in self-righteousness. Sergeant Glenna O'Neil's pride is bent on blaming Zach Jennings for her brother's death. How did Charlie's pride affect him?

AUTHOR EVENTS

Meeting my readers and aspiring writers at my various events is such a pleasure. Check my website at https://claricejames.com/ to see where I'll be next.

If you or your group would like to host an author event, these types of venues are an ideal fit:

- Book Clubs: If you're in my area of the country and your book club selects one of my books, I can join you to discuss it—either on video chat or in person.
- Bookstores: I love to support small, locally-owned bookstores by doing author talks.
- Cafés & Coffee Houses: Chatting about books is always better over coffee.
- Family-style Restaurants: I'd be happy to set up a table in a private room, a corner, or the foyer.
- Ladies Church Groups: My books, Party of One, Doubleheader, Manhattan Grace, and The Girl He Knew are written with women readers in mind. Themes include forgiveness, grief, loneliness, pride, surrender, and discerning God's purpose for your life. I'd be pleased to speak on those topics.
- Over 55 Communities or Senior Activity Centers: Invite me, and I will come.
- Private Author-in-the-House Parties: Author-in-the-House home parties (local to me) are fun and more personal. This venue gives readers and authors the chance to get to know one another better.

Call or text me at 603-689-8945 if you live in the New England area and want to hear more about the interactive Lessons Learned on the Way to Publication Writers Workshops for new or pre-published writers. Attendees are encouraged to come armed with curiosity and questions. Here are just some of the topics covered:

- How to know if you're a "real" writer
- Being professional before you're published
- Step by step guide through the writing and publishing processes
- Editing your own work
- Finding the right kind of agent, editor, and publisher
- Things to do before you submit a manuscript to an agent or publisher
- What to include in a book proposal
- Reasons why your submission may have been rejected
- Pros of both self-publishing and traditional publishing

Call or text me at 603-689-8945. If you prefer, email me at cjames@claricejames.com. Thank you.

REFERENCES & RESOURCES

(By genre, in order of appearance)

Bible
Scripture from New International Version (NIV) Holy Bible, New International Version®, NIV® Copyright ©1973, 1978, 1984, 2011 by Biblica, Inc.® Used by permission. All rights reserved worldwide.

Ch 5: Psalm 46:10 (NIV)
Ch 30: John 6:68 (NIV)
Ch 30: Romans 5:3-4 (NIV)
Ch 30: Ecclesiastes 4:9 (NIV)
Ch 34: Psalm 73:21-26 (NIV)
Ch 40: Philippians 4:13 (NIV)
Ch 40: Proverbs 16:18 (NIV)

King James Version (Public Domain)
Ch 31: Matthew 6:30 (KJV)

The Message. copyright ©1993, 2002, 2018 by Eugene H. Peterson. Used by permission of NavPress. All rights reserved. Represented by Tyndale House Publishers, Inc.

Ch 29: Matthew 6:34 (MSG)

Movies
Ch 35: Shanghai Noon. Director, Tom Day, produced by Touchstone Pictures, Spyglass Entertainment, and Roger Birnbaum Productions, 2000, Mount Cautley, Banff National Park, British Columbia, Canada

Songs

Ch 32: "It Is Well with My Soul." Hymnist, Horatio Spafford. Composer, Philip Paul Bliss, 1876.

Ch 33: "Celebration." Songwriters Ronald Nathan Bell, Claydes Charles Smith, George Melvin Brown, James "J.T." Taylor, Robert Spike Mickens, Earl, Eugene Toon Jr., Dennis Ronald Thomas, Robert Earl Bell, and Eumir Deodato. Performed by Kool and the Gang. Producer Eumir Deodato, 1980

Ch 41: "Sweet Baby James." Lyrics and music by James Taylor, 1970

Television Shows

Ch 9: CSI New York. Alliance Atlantis Productions, CBS at CBS Studio Center, 4024 Radford Avenue, Studio City, Los Angeles, California, USA 2004-2013

Ch 10: Dr. Phil. Harpo Productions, King World Productions, Paramount Domestic Television, Stage 29, Paramount Studios, 5555 Melrose Avenue, Hollywood, Los Angeles, California, USA, 2002 to present

Ch 20: Days of Our Lives. A television series created by Irna Phillips, Allan Chase, and Ted Corday, NBC Studios, 3000 W. Alameda Avenue, Burbank, California, USA, 1965 to present

www.ingramcontent.com/pod-product-compliance
Lightning Source LLC
Chambersburg PA
CBHW072204030726
47501CB00015B/595